B.T. CLEARWATER

A PERMUTED PRESS BOOK

ISBN: 978-1-68261-308-5

Cover art by Christian Bentulan

Permuted Press, LLC
New York • Nashville
permutedpress.com

Published in the United States of America

This is for my kids, without whom my life
wouldn't have meaning:
Sarah, Andrew, Kolby, and Kaycee.
You four make me who I am, and I love you all.

Chapter One

Annie Brown stood, hands on hips, supervising the movers as they carried a large, framed painting up the front steps and across the porch. Beside her, Jason looked at the old place, wrinkled his nose, and clucked like an old woman seeing a tattoo.

She had to agree with his sentiment—she hadn't exactly inherited a peach.

The old Victorian didn't just sit on the street. It didn't hunch, stand, rest, or exist. Instead, it loomed, seeming to lean out over the front sidewalk to intimidate passersby. The porch's white rail gleamed like a sadistic grin, slashing through the pallor of the gray shingle siding, while dark windows stared like half-lidded eyes, their smoke-stained shades still in the half-drawn position they'd been in the last time human life had occupied the house nearly a year before.

The houses around it sported fresh coats of paint, most in bright, almost garish colors popular when they were built over a century ago. All had lush, green lawns and flower boxes bursting with color, not drab gray-green weed forests with wilted, long-dead skeletons of flowers. The house also lacked the bright Memorial Day banners, flags, and window trimmings of its neighbors, making it the only unpatriotic house on the block.

The sun baked Annie's exposed skin, slicing through the thin Colorado atmosphere like a laser through tissue, turning the sidewalk into a skillet and her shoulders into broiling meat. Only her red horn-rimmed glasses bounced the sun's rays back to the sky.

"That goes in the smallest bedroom," she shouted. "That'll be my studio."

Jason gripped her forearm with his manicured hand and tugged her into the shade of a towering, ancient oak. His gold-colored eyes shone in the sunlight, while his mocha skin gleamed.

"You'll look awful if your skin turns tomato-red."

She smiled up at him, thankful he'd come along for his practicality and common sense, as well as the emotional support he provided. She'd fought for this day—fought hard and fought dirty at times, making more than a few enemies in the process. But now that the day was here, she dreaded it.

The movers seemed to feel a malevolence in the house. They whispered in Spanish, all the while glancing sidelong at her, eyebrows raised as doubt danced macabre in the deep brown of their eyes.

"Do they all think I'm crazy?" she asked Jason. "The crazy woman moving into her dead mother's rotting old home to live alone with her cats."

"I'm sure they don't think any such thing," Jason replied, patting her on the shoulder. "They know you don't have any cats."

She elbowed him in the ribs, but couldn't stop the smile from spreading across her face. Jason always knew her better than she knew herself, and always knew how to make her smile.

The sound of heels clacking on the sidewalk made them both turn as a tall, white-haired woman in a calf-length navy skirt, cream blouse, and black high-heels strode down the sidewalk. One of the movers started to cat call her, but a single down-the-nose glare from the frozen blue of her eyes stopped him cold, his mouth half-open. If he'd had a tail, it would have tucked between his legs.

Annie groaned and fought the urge to walk away. She'd dreaded this part of the day the most.

The woman came to a halt two or three yards short of their position, still exposed to the brutal sun, seeming not to notice its heat. Annie wondered if the woman's cold demeanor kept her cool even on a hot summer day like this.

"Ms. Brown," the woman said, contempt dripping from her words like blood from fangs, "I see you're moving in, right on schedule."

"Nice to see you too, Mrs. Mudge." Annie put on her sweetest tone, disguising the contempt she felt for the woman. "Yes, move-in is going as planned. Thanks for your concern."

Mudge didn't seem to notice Annie's sarcasm, or didn't understand it. "Be sure the moving truck is off the street by eight o'clock tonight, whether move-in is done or not. If you don't finish on time, have your ... employees come back in the morning. If Immigration hasn't scooped them up."

At the word "immigration," the foreman looked up, then turned back to his crew and spoke in Spanish.

"Don't worry," Jason told her, "they'll be done long before then. Will you be coming to the housewarming rave tomorrow? We have the most chiseled male dancers coming to perform on the front porch, followed by our own personal gay pride parade right down this very street."

His smile oozed sarcasm and Annie fought back a snicker.

"He's just kidding, Mrs. Mudge," she said. "I'm not having any parties. They're not my style."

Mudge wrinkled her nose and looked at Jason over the frame of her bifocals. Annie couldn't tell if she resented his blackness or his gayness. Probably both. Either way, Mudge didn't grant him the pleasure of a response, turning instead back to Annie. Reaching in her ultra-conservative handbag, she produced a thick packet of papers wrapped in a tasteful red jacket.

"Here are the Historical Society covenants," she said. "They're only eighty-nine pages long, so you should have no trouble reading them in a week. Maybe ten days. If you have any questions, anyone from the Society can help you. Just email the address on the cover."

Taking the packet, Annie rolled her eyes. "I'm sure I read much more complicated texts during my graduate studies. What's your degree in again, Mrs. Mudge?"

If the remark fazed her, Mudge didn't let it show. She adjusted her spectacles and looked down her nose again.

"Your late mother—God rest her soul—agreed to these covenants, but over the last two years failed to maintain their minimum standards, as you can see." Again she wrinkled her nose, as if offended.

"Yes, I'm aware of the lien your society so kindly placed on my mother's home right before her death. I like to think of it as helping her to her grave."

Mudge flinched, as if Annie had slapped her.

"We only did what our attorneys advised us," she said, pulling her glasses off and using a handkerchief to dab at the tiniest droplet of perspiration on her forehead. "In the best interests of the neighborhood."

Annie drew herself up. "I suppose it was in the best interest of the neighborhood to team up with my brother and sue for the house? To leave the house empty for over a year while we battled in court?"

"Your brother's interest—"

"My brother was only interested in money! He wanted to profit from the house, while you just wanted to control it."

"As I recall," Mrs. Mudge said, "you testified that you didn't really want the house. It holds bad memories for you. Remember?"

Annie winced, but she also recalled their early, happier days in the house, before her mother turned to vodka for companionship. Memories of pipe smoke and aftershave, crackling hardwood fires and laughter.

"I also testified that it held the only memories I have of my father. And this is all irrelevant anyway. The judge found the will legally binding and awarded the house to me. You lost."

Mrs. Mudge squared her shoulders, straightened her backbone, and sniffed.

"As you know, under the agreement reached in court, you have ninety days to get the house back in acceptable order on the exterior before we take further action."

"Don't worry, Mrs. Mudge," Annie assured her, "I'll make sure it gets done."

The Historical Society matriarch turned on her heel and strode off the way she came.

"Remember quiet hours, Ms. Brown," she tossed back over her shoulder. "This isn't the downtown bar scene."

As soon as she disappeared around the corner, Annie stomped and let out a shriek of frustration.

"First she fought me in court," she fumed, "and now she comes to terrorize me on move-in day. Lovely!"

"Don't let her get to you," Jason said. "You won in court. You beat her, the Society, your brother, and their lawyers. You can handle Mudge herself."

Jason was right. He always was. Annie had persevered, and would do so again. The happy memories were blurry, ending when she was six, but they were all she had and she intended to hold them tight like she should've done her dad.

"You know," she told Jason, "even after he left he kept paying the mortgage from wherever he was. Right up until my mother owned the place outright."

"Is that why you decided to fight for this pile of scrap wood?"

"I suppose," she replied. "Fighting for the house was like fighting for the last part of him I ever had."

They returned to supervising the movers as they carried another painting off the truck and into the house.

"I can't wait to start painting again," she told Jason.

"Do you even remember how?"

"It's only been a year," she answered. "And it's not like I stopped because I wanted to. I just didn't have the time or energy while the court fight was going on."

Jason patted her on the shoulder. "I know. But your creativity might have slipped away from you."

She smiled up at him, dazzled by his golden eyes. "I got a year's worth of creativity bottled up inside me. I'll be fine."

An older couple, dressed in long pants and cardigans despite the heat, strolled by on the sidewalk, offering only obligatory smiles as they passed. They put their heads together and whispered as soon as they were out of earshot.

"Oh, honey, you most certainly need to have a housewarming party," Jason exclaimed, watching the old couple trail off down the street. "It might be the only way you meet a guy your own age in this old neighborhood. It ought to be renamed 'Geriatric Street!'"

Annie laughed and hugged her friend tight. He really could make her laugh at just about anything.

"A man is the last thing I need," she said. "You know how my last attempt at a relationship ended."

"Yes, but Frank violated your first rule of dating: No coworkers. You don't violate a rule like that without something going to hell in a handbasket."

Annie nodded. "I know, but I fell for his act. You have to admit—he looked good."

"Sure, if you like bald weightlifters with fuzzy-butthole-looking goatees. Personally, I found him repugnant." He shook his head for emphasis.

"I guess he just overwhelmed me. I mean, he did it all. Mountain climbing. Extreme skiing. Crossfit. If it was manly, Frank did it. That kind of charisma is hard to ignore."

"He captivated you enough to overlook dating rule number two: Don't date guys shorter than you."

Once again, Jason was right, and the smug look on his face said he knew it. Frank had all the red flags. So it shouldn't have surprised her when things went south. They'd been out at a concert, and when they got back to his place, Frank invited himself in for a drink.

Of course he really wanted more than a drink, so when she finally said good night, he became insistent, then pushy. Then forceful. Annie had cracked him on the noggin with a tumbler, slicing his scalp—and her hand—deep enough to send them both to the emergency room. The E.R. staff called the cops, and by two a.m., Frank had been taken into custody for attempted rape.

"Ground control to Annie Brown," Jason said. "You in there, sweetie?"

Annie shook herself out of her memories, aware of the movers staring at her.

"I'm all right," she said. "Just remembering *why* I don't need another man in my life. I don't pick them well."

Jason laughed, his brilliant white teeth glittering like a toothpaste commercial in the hot summer sun. Annie wished, for an instant, that he liked girls, realizing right away that it wouldn't work. He was her best friend, but far too manicured and preened for her tastes. The son of a white man and a black woman, Jason had inherited the best of both races, as if he were the poster child for racial harmony. His cocoa-colored skin was immaculate, so smooth she'd have put it up against the finest silk. He stood five inches taller than her at five-foot-ten, and his frame was lithe and cat-like from years of gymnastics. And those eyes! They shone like golden suns in a milk chocolate sky.

He might not be her type, but had he not been gay, he'd have made some girl mighty happy.

The movers brought out the largest framed painting yet, a canvas-draped monstrosity the size of a wall that took two of them to carry. Annie knew which one it was, and was thankful for the tarp covering it.

Almost on cue, a gust of wind whipped down the street, swiping the tarp off the frame and blowing it a few feet away, just out of reach of the flustered movers. They looked first at the crawling tarp, then at Annie.

For her part, Annie stood, transfixed on the painting of her late mother. Jet-black hair seemed to wave in the wind, and her mother's deep blue dress looked three-dimensional, real enough that Annie could almost feel its soft, velvet pile. The eyes, though, stood out the most, their pale blue slicing like blades of ice through the hot summer air, locking with Annie's gaze as the painting moved from truck to sidewalk to porch. Only when it entered the house did she feel like her mother's gaze no longer bore into her soul.

She shook herself, a tingle running down her spine.

"That was creepy," Jason said.

"You saw it too? It was like she was watching me!"

Jason laughed his musical trill of a laugh. "No, honey. That dress she wore for the portrait. Navy blue velvet? I mean even ten years ago no one wore velvet."

Annie started to laugh with him, then paused. "How did you know it was velvet? I painted a blue dress, but it's all oils."

Jason shrugged. "You must be that good! Your paintings are just that realistic."

Annie nodded, but didn't buy it.

"Anyway," Jason went on, "as I was saying, you do need a man in your life. Someone to convince you you're worth being loved."

She shook her head. He was nothing if not persistent. And he did have a point. Her self-confidence was at an all-time low, partly as a result of Frank's actions, and partly because the system had blamed her. She'd consented before. She'd been drinking. She'd dressed too sexy. They had a long-standing sexual relationship.

As if any of those things made it okay to demand sex, to try to force her legs apart, leaving fingerprints on her thighs. It was one thing to be assaulted by someone you trusted, but even worse to be victimized again by a judicial system that pre-determined your guilt based on your clothing and personal sexual history. Her most intimate secrets had been dragged before a jury of strangers, hung out like laundry on a line for the world to see.

Her cheeks burned just thinking about it.

Jason squeezed her arm and smiled at her.

"This is your new beginning," he said, gesturing to the house. "Even if all your potential suitors wear dentures, adult diapers, and bifocals."

Again she couldn't help but laugh.

Her mirth didn't last, though, as a moment later, someone yelled in Spanish inside the house. The movers spilled out the front door, across the porch, and onto the front yard. They stood, chattering like teenage girls during a scary campfire story, mopping at brows or pacing like cats. Then one—an older man with salt-and-pepper hair and skin ruddy from years in the sun—gasped and pointed at the upper window, the one in the master bedroom.

Annie looked in time to see the right-hand drape slide closed.

"Someone must have farted in there," Jason murmured. She elbowed him in the ribs. "Ow! Come on, now. You saw how many beans they had for lunch."

This time, Annie didn't laugh. The foreman had joined them now, jabbering in Spanish, just like his men. Annie set her shoulders and marched toward them.

"Oh no," Jason said, following on her heels, "I know that look!"

The foreman saw Annie coming and peeled himself from his men. Hat in hand, he approached Annie, his hands scrunching his painter's cap into a ball.

"I'm sorry," he said. Annie stopped, feeling guilty for expecting a heavy Mexican accent instead of flawless English. "The men are frightened. Something happened in the master bedroom."

"I said no one was to go in the master bedroom!"

He turned and asked the men something in Spanish. Annie wished she'd taken their language in college instead of German. The men gibbered back, shaking their heads and holding their hands up in front of them.

"They did not go in the room," said the foreman, returning the rumpled cap to his grizzled head. Sweat soaked the armpits of his tee-shirt. "They saw someone else in there. A woman, dressed in blue."

He wrung his hands, his face twisting in a knot of conflict, like one side of his face warred with the other. He glanced over his shoulder at his men, looking like he might say more, but held his tongue instead.

"It's okay, you can tell me." She dropped her hands to her sides to appear less threatening.

Beside her, Jason nodded. "You'd better tell her. You don't want to see her angry. Trust me."

"Hush," she snapped at him. Then she smiled at the foreman. "It's all right. I'm not angry. Tell me what they said."

The foreman shifted his stance from one foot to the other and back again. He glanced at the window, then studied Annie's face for a moment before nodding.

"They say they saw the woman from your painting," he said, still wringing his hands. "'Madre Muerta.' I'm sorry. They are simple men, from farms. They believe such things."

Annie suppressed her urge to chuckle. The portrait had freaked her out, so she could imagine what it did to strangers in a house that looked like the names Poe, Hitchcock, and King should be on the door. She smiled again and patted the man on the shoulder. To her surprise, he seemed to relax at the gesture. He must have thought their paychecks were in jeopardy.

"I will go inside and talk to my mother," she said. "I will tell her to leave your men alone. She will listen to me."

The foreman smiled, his face relaxing to symmetrical proportions again.

"Thank you," he said. "I will tell the men."

Annie nodded and turned toward the front porch. Jason followed close behind, while the sounds of the movers' whispers followed like puppies at their heels.

As they mounted the stairs, Jason whispered, "I hope you know what you're doing."

"Me too," she said. "I'm in no shape to move furniture myself."

Chapter Two

Annie fought back a sneeze as the smells of mildew, dust, and alcohol assaulted her nose. She shouldn't have been surprised, since her mom had been an accomplished drinker, and the house had sat empty for a year since her death. Sunlight sliced through the curtained windows in dusty blades of gold, lighting up the sitting room to their left, but leaving the hallway ahead of them shadowed and dark. Stairs rose to the left, carpeted with a red-patterned runner, leading up to the second floor. Annie led Jason down the corridor, peeking in the dining room, living room, den, and kitchen before stopping at the end of the hall.

Despite the smell, the interior was cool, as Annie had convinced her mother to install a central air conditioner during her last year. It had made her mother's final, bed-ridden days less painful, she thought, though her mother had never admitted it.

"No one home," she said. "Just furniture covered in sheets, some moving boxes, and dust."

Jason moved around her, his nose wrinkled. "And mice. I think I just stepped in their poop."

"You're such a girl," she told him, walking back the way they'd come.

"You should try it sometime," he said. "You might hold onto a guy."

She was about to wheel on him when the front door opened and the foreman peeked in. He looked like a child peeking into his parents' bedroom, wide-eyed and nervous. Apparently, he was a simple man from a farm, too.

"The men said you must go upstairs," he said, pointing. "Madre Muerta was there."

Then he disappeared like a mouse from the kitty's lair.

Annie sighed and put her foot on the steps. She paused, turned to Jason, and laughed. "We could run out like they did and scare them."

"Then who's going to carry all your furniture upstairs?" her friend quipped. "I know you sure won't do it. And that leaves me, so get up there and talk to your mom's ghost or whatever you need to do. Those sweaty men need to finish their job."

Annie chuckled and climbed the stairs, their wood complaining with every step. The house had been built in 1913, so some creaks were to be expected. Still, Annie knew each step's whiny voice, having grown up listening to them whenever her mother stumbled up to bed. They'd grown quieter, as if afraid now that her mother had died, or perhaps no longer protesting as much.

The upstairs hallway had four doors. On the left stood doors to the second and third bedrooms, with the second bathroom in between. On the right, the door to the master bedroom suite sat open, dusty light spilling out into the hallway from the tall window on the street-facing wall. Closing her eyes—a habit she'd acquired as a little girl who wasn't supposed to see inside that room—Annie tugged the door closed, letting out a breath she'd been unaware of holding.

Jason looked at her like she'd gone crazy, but she ignored him. He didn't understand. Couldn't.

"I closed that before the movers showed up," she told Jason. "One of them must have opened it after I told them not to. Remind me to yell at them."

"Oh, leave the poor men alone," Jason chided. "What harm is there in looking?"

No, he definitely didn't understand.

She peeked in the first bedroom on her left, the one where the movers had been stacking her things. The patterned wallpaper her brother had favored as a boy would have to go, sunlight having faded its hues, its corners peeling. Annie had managed to talk herself into taking the room, as it was a little bigger than her old space. She told herself that if she couldn't quite make herself take over her mother's old room, she at least deserved more than she'd had growing up. She was a successful marketing specialist now, not a frightened, bashful little girl, and Daniel had no claim on the house—Annie did.

Other than boxes and furniture, the room was empty, as was the second bathroom, with its outdated green toilet, matching sink, and shower. She liked the old, cracked subway tiles in that bathroom, and made a mental note to keep them when having the bathroom renovated. The room smelled of mold and had no heater vent, making it cold during the rough Denver winters, but she still couldn't make herself use the more modern master bath.

The third bedroom, at the end of the hall, held her paintings and boxes of art supplies, all stacked and piled like puppies dumped at the pound. The portrait of her mother had been covered again, but Annie had to shrug off the feeling that even through the thick, rough canvas, her mother somehow watched her, those cold eyes piercing material and flesh to see inside her heart.

Satisfied those three rooms held no supernatural threats, Annie took a deep breath, screwing up her courage, and faced the door to the master bedroom. Its cool, mahogany surface gleamed in the dim light of the hallway, showing a faint, twisted reflection of her face. She wondered how the door had remained so polished and shiny during the year since her mother died, but had not even completed the thought when something clattered on the hardwood floor inside. She jumped, grabbing Jason's shoulder for support. Her friend raised an eyebrow, but said nothing.

Annie gripped the chilly metal of the brass doorknob and eased the door open, peering through the growing opening. She felt like a little girl again, peeking inside the mysterious room, forbidden to both her and Daniel, fearing she might find her mother glaring back at her, ready to deal a slap or at least a sharp reprimand.

Something rushed at her on the floor, darting for the opening with a skittering sound. She jumped back, feeling stupid the instant she recognized the mouse. It dashed into the hallway and down the steps, leaving Annie panting like she'd run a marathon.

Jason laughed. "We probably shouldn't tell the men they were scared of a tiny mouse. Their machismo might cause some hurt feelings."

"Probably not," she said. "I'm hoping they'll finish this job just to avoid looking more frightened than a woman. "

"You're a devious one," Jason said with a wink.

Annie hesitated at the door, her heart pounding, breath quickened. It had been a year since she'd gone inside, since her mother lay dying in the large, king bed. It seemed like an invisible force field blocked the door, pushing against her ever so gently, growing stronger the closer she came to entering, coalescing into an almost solid barrier that she couldn't force herself to step across.

"She's gone, Annie," Jason said, touching her shoulder. "It's all right."

She sighed, patted his hand, and steeled herself. Then she stepped inside.

It remained as she remembered it, a cavernous room with a vaulted ceiling, gleaming-if-dusty hardwood floors, and walls papered with an elegant floral pattern that gave the room an old-fashioned rich-person look. An oak dresser and matching vanity stood against the right wall, bracketing the tall, curtained window that looked out over the street.

To the left, doors led to a walk-in closet and the renovated master bathroom, with its travertine tiles, heated floor, and claw-foot tub.

But it was the massive, four-poster king-sized bed that dominated the room. Against the far wall, its dark, cherry wood posts rose almost to the ceiling, gossamer curtains falling like snow to the floor so the bed itself appeared hidden behind mist. A huge print of an old Wyeth painting over the headboard showed a giant striding away through a landscape while little people watched in hiding. The painting had always made her sad.

Annie stood by the left side of the bed where she'd sat the day her mother passed, and ran her fingers across the satin sheets. Their cool, smooth surface sent a shiver up her arm and down her spine, as if they'd been charged with electricity. She stepped back, snatching her finger away.

"You okay?" Jason asked.

She hesitated, then nodded. "Yeah. Let's go."

She turned to go, but Jason stopped her with a hand on her wrist. "You're forgetting something. You promised them you'd talk to her."

She rolled her eyes, longing to exit the room. "All right, fine. Mom, leave the movers alone. They won't come in here, I promise. And they're not going to hurt me."

She looked around, receiving just the reply she'd expected: silence. Shooting her friend an exasperated look, she left the room. When Jason followed her out, she pulled the door closed behind him.

Back outside, she tracked down the foreman and ignored her urge to chew him out for his men entering her mother's room. Instead she chose the more comforting approach.

"Tell your men I spoke to my mother. She will not bother them further, as long as they do not open the master bedroom door."

He looked dubious, but translated for the movers. They whispered among themselves, arguing under their breaths.

"I will throw in an extra twenty for each of them," she promised. "Call it a tip, but only if they finish the job."

That proved to be the urging they needed, and a moment later, they returned to work, all fear of ghosts forgotten. Amazing the power of Andrew Jackson.

Annie and Jason wound up in the shade of the front porch, drinking bottled water as they lounged in her mother's old outdoor furniture, watching the men carry box after box into the house. They sat and watched a few cars zip by on the street, apparently not caring if they ran over an undocumented worker or two. Some drivers even shot Annie dirty looks from behind the safety of their windshields.

She wasn't even moved in and her neighbors hated her already. How had she managed that?

One car—an older Monte Carlo with peeling red paint—went slower than the rest, cruising down the street well under the posted twenty-five-mile-per-hour limit. At first she didn't recognize it, but when it neared, her stomach twisted. Beside her, Jason tensed.

"What is *he* doing here?" she muttered. "It's been months."

"He won't try anything," her friend insisted. "Not with all these witnesses around."

He gestured at the movers. Annie hoped he was right as she watched the driver out of the corner of her eye, hoping he wouldn't notice.

Frank didn't even look away, instead glaring at her with his own oily smirk. He drove around the front of the moving truck, then mashed the gas, squeaked the tires, and flew off down the street.

Annie looked at Jason, surprised to see him holding his cellphone, recording the drive-by.

"That was creepy as hell," he said. Annie flinched, not used to hearing him swear.

"Should I call the cops?"

"For what?" Jason asked. "Driving by once isn't a crime. If he does it again..."

"If he does it again, I'll move to Alaska."

*

Mary watched from the upstairs window, the one in the off-limits room, while her daughter talked with the black man on the lawn below. She'd only remembered Annie's name when the black man spoke it in the room, clearing the fog that had suffocated Mary's memory for so long. Annie. Her daughter. The one she had lost, who'd fled for so long, but had finally come home.

Just like she'd planned.

It felt like she'd waited a lifetime for her daughter, an eternity of floating formless and impotent through the empty house. She'd had no direction, forgetting early on why she'd stayed behind instead of crossing like she should have. She'd ignored the light when it beckoned her, feeling a stronger pull, like a freight train hauling a heavy load, dragging her away from the light.

That lifetime had been lonely, almost unbearably so. At first, the brother had lived in the house, unwanted and intrusive, sleeping in her bed and bathing in her tub. She'd tried time and time again to make him leave, but he didn't see her, couldn't hear her. The brown men had seen her and run, scattering like mice before a mighty cat, foolish and frightened and weak. But the brother had only left when he was ready, leaving her alone for a long, long time.

Now Annie had returned, ending her mother's isolation and renewing her sense of purpose. Mary felt again the pull of that train, the push of its meaning and reason. But she couldn't remember what that purpose was, could not dredge up from the depths of her being why she needed to be there. Only that she did, that she could not leave. Could not lose Annie again.

She looked again upon her daughter, seeing her smile at the black man, the man who was her defense, her lie. She spent time with him to avoid real men, men who might have hurt her. It was a coward's excuse, but one Mary understood. Men were hurtful, scornful beings, set upon causing pain and suffering to all around them. Mary knew this first-hand, had experienced it, though she remembered only the pain, not the faces nor the voices nor the touch. She knew one thing: Men caused pain and tears and heartache. Nothing more.

Mary had failed to protect herself from this pain, and failed to protect her daughter as well. She knew Annie had suffered, had been damaged by a man. She remembered her daughter's tears, the powerful pain of her broken heart as she wept, but everything else had blurred. She'd failed, though. She knew that much and knew it well.

She would not make that same mistake again.

Annie and her black man disappeared onto the porch, out of her sight, and she turned away from the window. But a car drove past then, slow and deliberate, as if the driver was looking at her, studying her through the window. She turned back and saw his face: cruel eyes, sculpted beard, shining bald head.

She knew she should recognize him, should know his name and how she knew him, but she recognized only the feelings inside her of fear, sadness, and rage.

The man stared at Annie, glaring at her with malice and hatred, the will to hurt her burning through the air like a pillar of black fire. Mary saw the spite in his cold, blue eyes, and could feel her daughter's own fear.

As the car rounded the corner and disappeared down a side street, Mary's purpose became clear as day: protect Annie.

Her daughter made bad decisions. She always had and likely always would. It was a mother's job to help her children make good decisions, to guide them, urge them, even compel them to do the right thing, and by doing so, to protect them from those who would hurt them.

Yes, that was it. She was there to help Annie, to show her right from wrong, and to protect her from people like the man in the car. From men.

And by doing so, Mary would not lose her again, would never face loneliness like she had, loneliness that descended into despair.

She stepped back from the window, crossing her arms over her chest. She would not lose Annie again, and would not allow her to be hurt.

She knew now. She had purpose again.

She just needed to make Annie understand.

Chapter Three

Mike swerved around a Prius that pulled out of a 7-Eleven on his right. Apparently the driver didn't care about right-of-way, choosing to place his tiny hybrid in front of Mike's five-thousand-pound Ford pickup just to make Mike swerve. As Mike cruised past him, a hipster with a scruffy beard and a frown flipped him off and shouted something about Mike's gas guzzler.

Typical Prius owner, Mike thought. *More interested in making a political statement than learning how to drive.*

It wasn't like Mike drove a pickup by choice. It was simply the vehicle best suited for a handyman's job. The truck was clearly marked, too, so the jerk had to have known it was a work vehicle. Some people protested just to have a cause.

Traffic on East Colfax had thickened more than Mike expected on a holiday, making his drive to his next job site slow-going. He hated working on Memorial Day, but he needed the money, and his customer—an older woman whose husband had just passed—needed help. This day he normally reserved for remembering his fallen comrades, the men he'd lost in that God-forsaken, overheated litter box called Iraq. Men—boys in some cases—who'd died in gruesome, horrible ways, usually screaming or frightened out of their minds.

Guys Mike would never forget.

Guys like Kyle.

They'd been on patrol in a suburb of Fallujah, a squad of Marines working to keep looters at bay and insurgents hunkered down. Corporal Kyle McElroy had point, with Mike following about ten yards behind. The sun turned their Kevlar into slow cookers, boiling their bodies and simmering their minds. They were professionals, but even pros struggled in that kind of heat.

Mike was looking up at a rooftop when the car bomb detonated, slamming him to the ground. His ears rang, and his vision blurred. He struggled to his feet to find Kyle on his back beside him, blown backward from the blast. Where Kyle's right leg had been only a bloody stump with a jagged spear of bone remained, the rest gone from just above the knee. Blood oozed from Kyle's nose and ears, and his left arm was bent underneath him, twisted almost beyond recognition.

Mike knew what would come next. The staccato firing of AK-47s erupted all around them, bullets whizzing past, ricocheting off the street, surrounding buildings, and vehicles. Mike managed to drag Kyle's limp body into an alley, while the rest of the squad ducked for cover. Mike applied a tourniquet to Kyle's leg, stopping the loss of blood, but they needed help fast. Kyle was alive, but not for long.

He heard Sergeant Ortiz on the radio, calling for air support to suppress enemy fire. Mike raised his M-4 carbine, peeked around the corner, and found himself staring down the barrel of an AK. A lone insurgent, scarf covering his mouth and nose, aimed at Mike's head.

Mike dove right, the AK firing next to his ear. He came up deaf, stunned from the percussion, but squeezed off a three-round burst, killing the insurgent. Mike ran back to Kyle, but it was too late. The AK round that missed Mike had hit Kyle in the top of the head. All that was left was a bloody mess.

A car horn snapped him back to reality in the middle of an intersection. The light had turned red, but Mike, lost in his thoughts, hadn't seen. He swerved around another pickup, dodged a white compact, and managed to stop at the next light. Traffic flowed in front of him on Columbine, as Mike trembled behind the wheel. The other pickup pulled up beside him and a gruff-looking man shot him a glare. As he saw Mike, though, his expression softened and he rolled down his window.

"Hey, buddy," he called. "You okay?"

Mike nodded, thanked him, and eased through the intersection as the light went green. Less than a block later, he pulled into a Sun Mart gas station, parked, and killed the engine. His hands shook on the wheel, and sweat dripped into his eyes. He wiped his forehead against his shoulder, then leaned back in his seat, eyes closed.

He'd done it again. Too often lately he'd had near-debilitating memories of that day, flashbacks that shut his system down. He'd jump at loud noises, take cover for car backfires, or just get lost inside himself until something like this happened. But the worst part was the quagmire of depression that often grabbed him, sucking him down like quicksand, until he felt surrounded by darkness. It was as if he'd fallen down a deep well and couldn't even see a circle of light at the top.

The Veterans Administration's counseling services were targeted at this kind of thing, and Mike's counselor—Larry Collins—knew what Post-Traumatic Stress Disorder did to a person. He was very good at dealing with it. So good, in fact, that Mike had stopped the counseling sessions and declared himself cured about a year and a half ago.

Then his life fell apart and his symptoms returned. He'd known for a month now that he needed help again, but he needed money right now, and every hour he spent at the VA Hospital meant an hour he wasn't earning money.

He thought about turning his truck around. The hospital was a few blocks back the way he'd come. Then he remembered it was Memorial Day. They'd be closed. He'd make it back when he could.

He took a deep breath, wiped his forehead with a greasy rag, and was reaching for the key when his cellphone rang. He knew from the ring tone—the theme of the Wicked Witch of the West's appearances in The Wizard of Oz—that it was Michelle.

He considered sending it to voice mail, but that would piss her off. The last thing he needed was his ex-wife pissed at him. She'd take him back to court in a heartbeat, and since he could barely pay alimony and child support as it was, a trip back to family court made his stomach tie itself in knots.

Sighing, he answered. "Hi, Michelle. What's up?"

"I'm calling to remind you about Maria's birthday this week." Her voice carried irritation and mistrust over the airwaves as well as it did in person. "She's really looking forward to seeing you, so don't forget."

"I'll be there," he said. "She's turning six, right?"

Dead silence on her end told him she didn't appreciate his humor. "Nine," she said after the pause.

"I know, I'm kidding."

"I can never tell anymore. It's like you're a stranger to me."

Mike fought back another sigh, knowing it would set her off. "I'm sorry," was all he could manage.

"So am I." Something softened in her voice, as if she remembered for a moment that they hadn't always been enemies. "I'll see you at the party. You know how to find Pitt's place?"

Mike's left hand tightened on the wheel. Paul "Pitt" Emerson had been Michelle's divorce lawyer, and now that they were dating, she split time between her ratty apartment and his high-end two-story in Highlands Ranch. Mike wanted to spend an afternoon at Pitt's house about as much as he wanted to hammer his thumb flat. But for Maria, he'd do either and smile about it.

"I remember," he told her. "I'll see you there, but I have to go now."

She hesitated again, sending an almost palpable tension through the phone. When she spoke, that tension vibrated in her voice. "Sure, Mike, get going. You have more important things to do than talk about our daughter."

Mike bit his tongue, literally drawing blood to keep from snapping at her. Her passive aggressive bullshit drove him nuts sometimes. "Nothing's more important to me than

Maria, and you of all people know that. But right now, I'm trying to make it to a client's home so I can pay my bills."

"I don't even want to hear it!" she fired back. "I barely get enough from you to feed Maria, much less get her clothes, shoes, school supplies, and so on. You think you're the only one trying to scrape by?"

Mike rolled his eyes. He'd walked right into her trap. By now he should have seen it coming, should have figured out her tricks. Yet he walked into setup after setup. Time and time again he gave her exactly what she wanted out of him. It was almost like they were still married.

He thought about retorting, about reminding her that Pitt, with his lawyer's income, paid her rent for her, how her lawyer stocked her fridge, bought Maria endless supplies of new clothes, even made Michelle's car payment a time or two. But he didn't need the argument. He didn't need to go back to court, either. So he sucked it up and put a fake smile into his words.

"I pay what the court ordered," he said. "All of it, every time."

"Would it hurt you to pay a little more?" she asked. "Would it kill you to be on time consistently?"

That straw broke the camel's back. His anger rushed to the surface in a torrent. "I'm a handyman, Michelle. I pay when I get the money, but I always pay."

"Well the judge didn't give you a flexible payment plan," she hissed. "Your payments are due on the first of every month, no exceptions. I suggest you make them on time from now on or I might feel the need to take more drastic action."

The line clicked dead as she didn't even wait for his reply.

Mike put his forehead on the sun-heated steering wheel and took slow, easy breaths.

He suffered through things like that for Maria's sake, and thinking of her lifted Mike's spirits. Michelle might have dumped him, unable to handle his PTSD, but Maria had stood by him. On more than one visitation night, she'd come to his room and woken him from a nightmare like a lifeguard saving a drowning victim. One time he'd been so startled he took a swing at her. He'd missed, but what amazed him was her response. His then seven-year-old had kissed him on the forehead and told him it would be all right.

"You thought I was a terrorist. I won't tell Mommy."

That discretion, so unusual for one so young, had probably saved their visitations. And seeing his little girl was all that kept him sane some days. He couldn't stand the thought of losing her, too. That's why he was working a holiday—so he could pay child support, and still get her something for her birthday.

His cellphone buzzed, an alarm he'd set to remind him of his appointment. A few blocks away, an elderly woman was waiting for him to fix a leaking toilet, and he had ten minutes to get there.

Taking another deep breath, he started the truck and pulled back out onto Colfax. Sure, he was working Memorial Day, but if it helped him keep seeing his daughter, he'd work every holiday on the calendar.

Chapter Four

Annie sat on her mother's old Queen-Anne-style sofa, the white sheet that had covered it tossed on the hardwood floor, spotlighted by a beam of white sunlight with dust motes hovering inside. Legs stretched out in front of her, ankles crossed, fingers laced across her stomach, Annie stared into the beam of light, mesmerized and lulled into memories she didn't want to recall.

Through the crystalline filter of tears, she let her gaze wander around the room, ignoring the stacks of unpacked boxes, to the mantle over the brick fireplace. Before he'd left, her father had decorated the mantle every Christmas, using cotton as snow and lining up a whole light-up winter village. He'd do it at night, while she slept, so it would be there when she woke up.

Now the village sat packed in rotting boxes in the basement, replaced on the mantle by a maroon ceramic vase that had sat so long it had left a permanent ring on the mantle's white-painted pine. If she looked close enough, she could see the tiny, hairline cracks in the vase, the only indication that she, at age thirteen, had glued it back together under her mother's watchful, critical eye. She'd been dancing around the living room, showing her mother what she'd learned that day at ballet, and had knocked the vase off the mantle. Annie never saw her mother's backhand coming. One moment she was gaping at the shattered vase, the next she lay on her back, her lip already swelling.

Her mother made her glue each piece of the vase back in place, one each day, for the next two weeks. When done, the vase had looked good as new, but had leaked water, and never held flowers again.

Annie shook herself and decided to throw the vase away as soon as she was done unpacking. Maybe she'd put the village in its place, even though Christmas was far off.

She put her feet up on the couch, careful to leave the sheet in place between her black Converses and the cushion, another behavior her mom had driven into her. She told herself it was in case she decided to sell the out-of-date furniture later, but deep down she knew it was more than that.

A tall wooden bookcase stood against the wall beside the fireplace, its dark-stained wood gleaming in the sun. She had plans for those shelves, plans for them to hold her hardcover books, as well as a stash of them her mother kept in the attic, but right now one item stood alone on the shelf. Surrounded by a black frame, a photo of Annie in her high school graduation gown stood. Young Annie's smile—radiant and wide—seemed far away now, almost mythical itself.

Her mother had disapproved of Annie's choice to go to college out of state, unable to stand the thought of being alone. But Annie had moved away to Utah nonetheless, putting an entire mountain range between her and her mother.

Her mother didn't speak to her again until her deathbed.

Annie forced herself up off the couch. She needed to get to work. Unpacking sucked enough, but doing so into a home she'd spent her whole life running from seemed even worse.

She reached for the first box, but hesitated, and went to the kitchen instead, with its outdated green appliances and cabinets that had been repainted so many times the paint glopped in places. Her mother's liquor cabinet had been built into the kitchen, a narrow space against the refrigerator with lattice framing inside to hold bottles. She pulled out the only two bottles inside and held them up to the yellowed ceiling lights for closer inspection. In her left hand she held a bottle of Stolichnaya vodka, her mother's preferred drink. In her right, a bottle of Moscato Jason had given her as a housewarming gift.

She chose the wine, shoving the vodka as far back into the cabinet as it would go.

"One glass of wine," she told herself. "No more. I'm not like her."

She poured the sparkling golden wine into a clear plastic cup Jason had bought for the housewarming party he was convinced Annie needed. She could have used one of her mother's old wine glasses, but they likely needed a washing to be even somewhat useable.

Liking that idea, Annie put all the wine glasses, along with cups, dishes, bowls, and silverware into the old dishwasher. Pouring detergent into the cup, Annie eyed the peeling white interior and cracked rubber seal around the door. She thought for a moment that running the old thing might not be the best idea, but shook off the feeling and closed the door, sliding the old, chrome handle left to latch it closed.

As she reached for the start button, her cellphone rang. Caller ID read, "Unavailable," almost a sure sign of a telemarketer. She thought about ignoring it, but decided caution was her best bet. It could also be her boss.

"Hello?"

For an instant, only static answered her, but then Frank's voice blasted in her ear. "How's the old piece-of-shit house, Annie?"

He slurred his words, and sounded like he had cotton in his cheeks, but she knew his voice.

"Frank."

"Oh, I'm sorry." His drunkenness made him talk with a slight lisp. "Are you too busy to talk to an ex-boyfriend and ex-coworker? I'm sure you have a million things to do, all alone in your shitty, out-of-date kitchen."

A feeling like a hundred tiny snakes wriggled across her skin. She yanked down the blind, covering the window over the sink, and closed the curtains on the door to the backyard. She thought about turning off the lights, but that frightened her more than the thought of Frank spying on her.

"I'm trying to unpack," she said, keeping her voice steady, emotionless. She'd learned during their rocky year together that throwing fuel on his fire was unproductive. "And I'd like to get some sleep so I can—"

She caught herself, but not soon enough.

"Oh, that's right!" Malice spiked his words now, hard and sharp, like razor blades. "The bitch has to work in the morning. She has a job. I obviously wouldn't understand that, since I lost mine. Whose fault could that be?"

She covered the microphone on her cell and took a deep breath, forcing herself to remain calm. He'd conditioned her to react with passivity, and now, though she wanted to fire back, to eviscerate him, she found the old habit too comfortable to ignore.

"Do we have to do this right now?"

"Yes! Yes, Annie, we do have to do this. Did you forget that you got me fired from my dream job? Your lies cost me my job, my reputation, and my savings to pay that lawyer."

"You got a new job," she said. "Better pay."

"I don't care about the pay, Annie. I sell fucking cars. Used fucking cars. My boss is a jackass, I put in eighty-hour weeks, and I have to scrape, suck up, and kiss ass for every damned commission I get. That's *your* fault, Annie."

Retorts formed in her mind, fueled like rockets, ready to fire into his face. She thought of a dozen ways to tear him down, to prey on his already low self-esteem and leave him quivering with self-loathing. But they all stopped dead before she opened her mouth. Something inside her, some tiny, inescapable feeling, clipped her tongue and kept her fiery replies quiet.

Guilt. She knew it was stupid: he'd tried to rape her. He'd left bruises on her thighs from trying to pry her legs open, bitten her lip, even held his hand over her mouth so she couldn't say "no" anymore. Just because the cops and courts and even her boss Carol had blamed her didn't make it true.

And yet, that tiny splinter of doubt crippled her, rendering her helpless to even hang up on him now.

She could have complied. She could have consented and laid there like a dead fish while he got his satisfaction, like she'd done so many times before. Why had she chosen that night to make her stand?

"Are you listening to me, Annie?" Frank slurred. His high-pitched voice sounded even more pathetic and weak on the phone. "I'm talking to you."

"I'm listening, Frank."

He paused, and for a moment, all she heard was his breathing, sloppy and wet.

"Maybe we should get back together."

The absurdity of his words jarred her from her daze, snapped her wide awake, like a bungee cord snapping her back to the present.

"What?"

"Yeah, we should do that. You and I should get back together. Tonight. I can come over right now."

Annie's own burst of laughter startled her. She plopped into an old, vinyl kitchen chair, unable to hold herself upright with her sudden mirth. She laughed so hard and so long her sides hurt and her vision blurred with tears.

When she finally calmed, Frank remained silent on the other end of the line.

"Frank, that's the worst idea I've ever heard," she said, her voice low and calm now. "Look, leave me alone. Stay away from my house, stop calling, all of it. We're done, Frank."

"We'll never be done, Annie," he whispered. His voice brought the slithery feeling back to her skin. "Not until I say we're done."

Now her anger took over, drowning her conditioned conflict-avoidance in a storm of rage. Her words exploded from her almost on their own. "Look, Frank, if you call me again or come to my house or bother me in any way, I will get a restraining order against you. Are we clear on that?"

"Don't say that!" His voice rasped as he shouted. "Don't ever say that again!"

"Frank—"

Her cellphone shut off. As the display screen faded out, the "low battery" message died with it.

"Weird," she said to no one in particular. "I just charged this."

Flipping off the kitchen light, Annie went back to the living room. She was setting her cup on the coffee table when the front window exploded, shards going everywhere. Annie screamed and ducked behind the couch, dodging the flying glass. Something heavy rolled across the floor. She peeked over the couch and saw a rock amidst the shards.

Outside, a car started and peeled out of the neighborhood. She reached the window in time to see a red back-end fishtail around a corner.

"Frank, you son of a bitch," she muttered.

Resigned to not getting her unpacking done, Annie grabbed a roll of packing tape and an empty box to cover the window. Ghetto, sure. Mudge's worst nightmare? Yep. But it was all she had left in her that night.

When done, she picked up a yellow legal pad on which she'd written a list of things to fix. At the bottom of the list—about halfway down the page—she scribbled "front window."

With a heavy sigh, she dropped the pad on the table and went to bed.

Chapter Five

Annie peered over the tops of her cards to find Jason staring at her. A kind of dreamy half-smile curled his lips up at the corners, and he steepled his fingers under his chin.

"Okay, I know you don't like girls," Annie said, "so why are you staring at me like Floyd Bailey used to stare in second grade?"

She set the cards—a lousy hand—face down on the antique dining table and picked up her glass of Moscato. The wine tickled her nose and sent a wave of relaxing warmth down her throat.

"You're too cute to go cold-turkey on guys," Jason said, downing the last of his own wine. "Just get back on the horse ... or stallion. Bull. Whatever well-muscled guy-type you prefer. You'll forget about Frank in no time flat."

Annie rolled her eyes and took another, larger sip of wine. "Come on, Jason, we're supposed to be playing cards, not talking about my failed love life again. I told you—no more guys. I need to focus on work."

Jason frowned at his empty wine glass and stood up, his lithe frame moving with feline grace, and for a moment,

Annie wished again that he'd turn straight. She knew better, though. They'd been friends too long for that, and anything more would be awkward. But he'd have been quite a ladies' man if he didn't radiate gayness like a Lexus radiates snobbery.

"You can't swear off guys forever, you know." He moved toward the kitchen. "There are some good ones out there."

"Maybe," she said, "but you know what they say about one rotten apple spoiling the bushel."

Jason stepped through the door and out of sight into the kitchen. She hated the old house's closed floor plan. She'd liked it growing up here, but now, as an adult with a social life, the closed-off rooms seemed like prison cells.

"Oh no!" Jason's voice went up an octave. "Annie, you'd better get in here."

She rushed into the tiny kitchen to find him on his knees, sopping up water with a dish towel that looked way too small for the job. The puddle ran from under the archaic dishwasher and carried dark, ugly chunks with it across the faded linoleum floor.

The load of glasses. She'd forgotten about it until tonight, starting it just before Jason arrived an hour ago.

Annie tossed a handful of towels to Jason, then turned off the dishwasher.

"I'll call someone," she said.

*

"I don't care what they say," Jason whispered in Annie's ear, making her flinch. "Plumber's crack isn't always a bad thing."

Annie had to agree, even though the man squatting in her kitchen kept his faded blue t-shirt tucked into the back of his jeans, so no crack showed. That didn't spoil the view, though—Mike still had a great butt.

It had taken her an hour to find someone available for an emergency call, but Mike's website said he was a certified plumber in addition to a handyman, so she called. She reached him at home, but on hearing her problem, he dropped everything and made it to her place twenty minutes later. Jason had just about sprung his own leak.

Mike's eyes caught her attention first, as crisp and blue as the Colorado sky. Crow's feet wrinkled the corners, but instead of making him look old, they gave him an air of wisdom and toughness. His sandy-brown hair topped a face darkened by sun, and his strong jaw line sported a rough layer of stubble. He towered over Annie, and even over the five-foot-ten Jason.

Now he had the dishwasher pulled out, and his entire top half stuffed in the space where it had been. That left Jason and Annie to stare at his butt.

Jason caught her looking and kicked her in the shin. "You quit guys, remember?"

Annie slugged him on the shoulder, making him wince.

Mike backed out from the dishwasher space, blue eyes focused on something inside.

"Your drain hose is clogged," he said. "When's the last time you used the dishwasher?"

"Tonight's the first," Annie said. "This was my mom's place. I inherited it about a month ago and just moved in this week. It's just me, so I wash everything by hand."

"I'm sorry for your loss," he said, meeting her eyes. His gaze made her stomach flip.

"She died a year ago," Annie explained. "Honestly, I don't really like it, but in the end, a free house is a free house, right?"

Mike looked over his shoulder and pointed to his tool box on the floor. "Can you hand me that pipe snake, please?"

Annie handed it to him, trying not to eye the muscles in his shoulder. His right arm pumped, sliding the pipe snake in and out of the drain. A moment later, something made a soft plop sound on the floor.

"Found your problem."

He pointed and moved back so she could look. Flat triangles the color of wet ash covered the linoleum. She wrinkled her nose at a moldy smell wafting up.

Jason looked over her shoulder. "Are those leaves?"

"Miller moths," Mike said. "Must have crawled in during migration last May. They came right through this part of town."

"A year stuck in a drain would explain the smell," Annie said.

Mike rose and wiped his hands on his jeans. "Let me go get my wet-vac out of the truck. I should have this done in no time."

As soon as Mike left, Jason leaned on Annie's shoulder. "Now that's what I call a real *handy* man," he said.

She brushed him away. "He's hot, but he's just that: a handyman. I set my sights higher than that."

"That's your problem—your sights. Your vision is so narrow, all you see is what's in front of you. Expand your view a bit."

"He's probably a high school dropout," Annie said.

"Actually, I have two degrees," Mike said, appearing in the doorway, red vacuum under his arm. "Bachelors in Construction Management from CSU, and an MBA from Webster."

Heat rushed to Annie's cheeks. Jason clucked and muttered as he wandered away.

Mike kneeled again, grinning, and plugged in the vacuum. It roared to life, so loud Annie couldn't think. When he finished, Mike shoved the dishwasher back into place under the counter.

"Should be good to go," he said.

She dug in her purse. "Let me find my checkbook."

"I prefer a card," he said. "Electronic payment is more reliable. One of those things I learned in that MBA I don't have."

Annie winced at the jab and handed over her debit card. Mike snapped a reader onto his smartphone, swiped her card, then held it up to read.

"Annie Brown," he said. "I'm Mike Tolbert."

He extended his hand, even though she'd shaken it when he first arrived. She took it again, surprised by both the strength and the softness of his grip.

"Look, I apologize," Annie said. "For that remark. I shouldn't have assumed ..."

Mike shrugged. "I'm used to it. Most people overlook manual laborers until they need a lock changed or a short fixed. Or a drain cleaned."

Now his smugness irritated her.

"With that education, why aren't you sending other people to do the messy work while you sit in a cushy chair?"

Mike dropped the card reader back in his tool box with a clunk. "I tried management. Hated it. Mostly it's dealing with paperwork and other people's drama. I missed getting my hands dirty, but didn't want another boss. So I started my own business."

"How did you afford the loan?" she asked. "Taxes here are killer."

"Veteran's benefits offset a lot of the cost," he explained. "Made it all possible."

"You're a veteran?" Annie asked.

"Marines, six years. Two tours in Iraq, one in Afghanistan."

"I didn't see you as the military type."

Mike raised an eyebrow. For the first time, Annie noticed his roguish, lopsided grin.

"What exactly is a 'military type?'" he asked.

"Well, I dated an Army officer a couple years back." Behind her, Jason sniffed, as if offended. "He talked about drinking, war, and football—nothing else. And he ended about half his sentences with 'hooah.'"

Mike laughed. "Well, don't judge us all by one clown."

"Looks like I owe you another apology," she said.

Mike scratched the stubble on his chin. "Well, you could make amends by going to dinner with me."

A breeze hissed through the room, blowing out the candles. Annie reached to shut the window over the sink, but found it already closed. She stared, confused, at a tentacle of smoke winding its way up from the nearest wick.

"You should say yes," Jason whispered in her ear. "Or close your mouth."

She snapped her mouth shut, her mind scrambling for excuses. She wasn't going to date a cocky, smart-ass contractor. Or anyone else. "I, uh, have to—"

"I didn't say when." Mike said.

He had her cornered. "When?"

The heat seemed to flee the room, and Annie shivered.

"Thursday night," he said. "I want to try that new Italian place on West Colfax. It would be much more fun with company."

"Look, I've kind of sworn off guys." She winced, realizing how bad that sounded.

Mike didn't flinch. "Bad experience?"

"I'm not ready to start a relationship right now."

"I'm not asking for a relationship," he said. "Just dinner. And I'll pay. You get back some of your money."

No.

The whispered voice brushed her ear like a spider web, almost impossible to understand.

"Make up your mind." She turned, expecting to find Jason at her shoulder, but found no one. A chill ran down her spine.

She heard the voice again, and jumped this time. It had been a woman's voice, she thought, but she couldn't make out the words.

"Did you hear that?" she asked.

Jason appeared at Mike's side and the two exchanged glances.

Annie took a deep breath and regretted drinking so much wine. She was hearing things.

"Sure," she said. "Thursday's fine."

The garbage disposal whirred to life, grinding something inside. Even Mike jumped before flicking the disposal switch up and down. Nothing happened, so he reached under the sink and yanked the plug. The disposal ground to a stop, and the three of them stood, silent and staring.

Mike shook himself and handed her a receipt. "You should call an electrician for the disposal. I'm a certified electrician, by the way."

"Two hundred dollars?" she said. "To clean a drain?"

"Seventy-five per hour," he said. He closed the tool box, then lifted it and the vacuum. "Plus a seventy-five-dollar after-hours fee, and taxes. You're outside my normal operating area, but I waived the fifty-dollar fee for that, since you're in a tight spot."

"Last time I hire a plumber with an MBA," she said. She walked him to the door. Jason opened it for him.

"No it isn't." Mike stepped outside, then turned and flashed his crooked grin. "Ninety-seven percent of my customers are repeats. My satisfaction rating is outstanding."

Jason snickered and Annie elbowed him in the ribs.

"Well, I'm not easily satisfied," she said. "See you Thursday."

He opened his mouth to shoot back, but she slammed the door in his face.

*

Mike closed the truck door and took a deep breath. What had he done? He had a strict rule about dating customers—he'd been burned by it before. Like third-degree over one hundred percent of his body burned.

He gazed through the dark at the Victorians lining Ellsworth Avenue. Most had been restored, but a few sat vacant, faded memories of the grand homes they'd once been, waiting for someone to bring back their glory. Ancient oak trees lined the street on either side, their boughs forming a tunnel, as if to keep the city out.

Mike shook his head. A single woman Annie's age should be living in a downtown loft, going out at night instead of hiding in a drafty old house that looked like Uncle Fester lived in the basement. But Annie seemed nutty as a Payday bar, anyway. Talking to herself, hearing voices, gay friend—the proverbial hot mess. And who swore off dating like booze after a bad hangover?

Yet something drew him to her, as if those moths had been an act of God, designed to bring them together. He couldn't explain it. Her beauty wasn't traditional, like Beckinsale or Theron, but those green eyes captivated him from behind her red horn-rims, and when she smiled, she tilted her head to the side, as if peeking around a corner. Her ebony hair fell in mischievous waves past her shoulders, impish and playful.

He thought he'd spotted tattoos, as well. One on each shoulder, though she kept them covered with a wrinkled white blouse straight out of her dead mom's closet. A professional business woman with tats—that added an instant ten hot points.

He sighed and was about to start the engine when his cellphone rang. He groaned when he saw the caller ID, then answered.

"Hey, Michelle. I know I'm late with the check. I have it with me. Just been busy across town."

"Don't bullshit me, Mike." Her voice grated on him like fingernails on a chalkboard. "You were on our street yesterday, fixing Harry Chambers' toilet. You could have dropped it by then."

"I wasn't sure you were home," he lied.

"It's not like I can work, since I'm home raising our daughter. You remember Maria, right? Eight, blue eyes? Birthday this weekend?"

Yeah, you were at Pitt's and you know it, he thought.

He longed to say it, to throw her hypocrisy in her painted, perfumed face. It had been three days since their fight, and his pride still hurt. But he couldn't lose it again. If she took him back to court, his child support would double. He took a deep breath and calmed himself.

"Would you like me to bring it over now?" he asked.

"That works." Her tone softened. "You could stay for a movie, if you wanted."

He froze as if realizing he'd wandered into a mine field. "Is Maria there?"

"No, she's at Chloe's house, spending the night ..."

She let the sentence dangle like bait, but Mike didn't bite. A barbed hook hid in there somewhere.

"I'd better not," he said. "I have an early call in the morning."

"Whatever." She hardened again. "Don't forget to bring the full amount this time. And the part you didn't pay last month."

"Couldn't pay. I can't give you what I don't have."

"Christ, Mike, don't make me report you as a deadbeat dad. You know I'll do it."

She would. "I'll be there in twenty minutes. I need to withdraw the rest."

And write out a receipt to cover my ass, he thought.

She hung up without replying, and Mike tossed his phone on the passenger seat. He grabbed the vinyl steering wheel with both hands, twisting until he thought it might snap.

Thursday's dinner wouldn't be cheap, and he'd hoped to take Annie out for a drink afterward. Now he couldn't afford drinks, and dinner had just become a question mark.

He picked up the cellphone. Annie's number remained on the call list. He tapped it with his finger, hesitated, then hit cancel.

He thought of Annie's pixie smile, the sarcasm behind her eyes and the tattoos hiding coyly on her shoulders. Thursday seemed like the most important date on his calendar. He couldn't cancel.

If it meant charging dinner, so be it. Debt could be paid back, but a missed opportunity never returned.

*

Annie stood in her living room, peering out the window at the white work truck pulling away. She'd watched his whole conversation, followed the angry gestures, and even flinched when he tried to strangle the steering wheel. Someone knew how to push his buttons.

"Honey, I'm leaving now," Jason said from the kitchen. "You should stop staring. He'll think you're a stalker-freak."

"I heard voices," she said. "He already thinks I'm a freak."

She remembered the flash of confusion on his face, the second thoughts about her that flickered for an instant in his eyes.

With a sigh, she hugged Jason. He kissed her on the cheek. "If you don't jump him Thursday," he said, "I'll be waiting to do it Friday morning. Then you'll never have a shot. You remember what they say, right?"

She laughed. "'Once you go gay, you'll never stray.' I remember."

Annie locked the door behind him, made sure all the candles were out, and trudged up the creaky stairs. Typical Monday: her kitchen flooded, she heard voices in her head, and her boss had chewed her out.

Her boss. Crap.

It was almost eleven o'clock, and she needed to be at work by seven the next morning. Time for bed.

She stopped at the first door on the left, ignoring the dark, wooden door of the master bedroom on the right.

She'd moved into the room farthest from her mother's, turning her childhood room into an art studio to gain separation from the master.

Annie pushed open her own door and peered inside. A single window faced north, and when the wind blew, cold air slipped in like a snake, making the room drafty and cold. An electric blanket helped, but it couldn't make the room bigger. Her dresser dominated one wall, crowding close to the foot of her bed. Clothes, handbags, and shoes spilled from the tiny closet. An adult's life crammed into a child's space.

She walked back to the master, nudging open the door, holding her breath as she took in the silence. She clicked the light switches, illuminating the room and making the ceiling fan whirl to life. Her mother's titanic bed stood against the back wall, all four posts almost scraping the ceiling. The fan blades reflected in the glass of the Wyeth print hanging over the headboard. To the left shone the gleaming subway tile of the master bath.

A bath sounded good—just the thing to end a long Monday night. She hadn't used the tub since her mother died, showering in the smelly second bathroom instead. Now it seemed silly—she wanted to soak.

She took a step and stopped. Had something moved in the closet? Had a shadow shifted from dark to darker? Of course not, but she backed out of the room nonetheless, closing the door behind her. She leaned her back against the door and sighed.

A shower would have to do.

Chapter Six

Mike leaned back against the hard wood of the bench built into Pitt's back deck, stretching his legs out in front of him, trying to mask the discomfort stirring his guts up like a blender.

Maria dashed past, dodging a water balloon heaved by another girl. Her pink shorts and white tee-shirt clung wet to her body, and her hair lay matted to her head, but the grin on her face drowned Mike's worries that she might be cold. Besides, with the late afternoon sun pressing down on the crowd like a massive hand, Mike wished one of the water balloons would hit him.

And that about ten would hit Pitt, in his designer khaki shorts. A typical douchebag divorce lawyer, Pitt stood at the grill, *supervising* one of the other dads as he flipped pre-made burgers and sizzling hot dogs. Mike would have bet money that Pitt didn't even know how to light the expensive gas grill—that was probably Michelle's job. The Blackberry-connected Bluetooth earpiece permanently attached to Pitt's head seemed more engrossing to him than the party, as he'd chattered on it for the last hour.

Pitt's backyard was bigger than Mike's entire apartment, a sprawling quarter-acre of lush green grass, pavestone walkways, and mature aspen trees, surrounded by a six-foot cedar privacy fence. The deck itself probably took up two hundred square feet, enough room that he'd been able to find himself a quiet corner, away from the other adults, to watch the girls run and play.

Maria streaked past again, this time with a rifle-sized water gun in her hands, shooting at the girl who'd pelted her, giggling the whole time. Mike smiled. He hadn't seen her this happy in months, pretty much since he and Michelle had split up.

A shadow fell over him, and he looked up to see Pitt's green Polo-shirted gut in front of him.

"Hey, Tiger, what's up?" The Bluetooth device still flashed, meaning the other party could hear everything. Pitt's beard remained as perfectly manicured as his lawn, and his deep voice dominated whatever conversation he joined. It had served Michelle well during the divorce proceedings, often talking over anything Mike's much less aggressive attorney said.

"Just relaxing, Pitt," Mike answered. Even seated, his head came almost to the lawyer's shoulders. "Don't let me interrupt your phone call."

Pitt winked, his brown eyes darting to a nearby cooler. "Have a beer," he said. "Don't worry, I'll add it to some future alimony payment or something!"

Mike gave him the most deadpan stare he could manage without looking hostile.

"No, I'm just kidding, Tiger. Help yourself. My castle is yours."

Mike couldn't help but notice the smug grin as Michelle's boyfriend turned away, satisfied he'd won the role of alpha male for the time being.

Mike strolled to the cooler, none too eager to let Pitt see him doing as he'd been told. In truth, a brew sounded just right to cool him off, and to take the edge off his anxiety. Mike didn't do well with crowds, another side effect of his PTSD. They didn't scare him so much as make him feel claustrophobic, like he had no way to get out if something went wrong. He'd get restless, squirming and shuffling toward whatever open space he could find. He didn't want to do that in front of Pitt, so a drink was just the prescription to help.

He found a collection of craft beers—not his normal fare, since he preferred good old American lager—but he grabbed one that looked lighter than the rest, cracked the top off on the deck rail, and grinned at the tiny chip he'd left in the wood. Maybe water would get in and the deck would rot. Of course, Pitt would pay to fix it by fleecing some other man going through a divorce, so Mike felt terrible almost immediately.

He was just sitting back down when Michelle came out of the house carrying an armload of presents. She looked fantastic, her blue eyes shining like slices of the summer sky under her sunshine-gold bangs. A yellow sundress showed off her figure, with the top two buttons open to display her cleavage. As she set the presents down, their eyes met, and for a single frozen instant he thought she might smile.

When the moment ended, though, she frowned, her disappointment in him showing through. And even though it shouldn't have, it drove a dagger into Mike's heart, just like it always did.

He turned his back on her as Maria ran shrieking into his arms. He scooped her up, even though she soaked his t-shirt, and squeezed her to him. She buried her head in his neck, then looked back at her friends and stuck out her tongue.

"Ha ha, now you can't shoot me. I'm on base!"

"Hey, how did I get selected as base?" he asked, spinning her around. "I'm neutral in this war."

She wrinkled her nose and whispered in his ear. "It was you or Pitt, and I chose you." His heart soared. Moments like this could keep him smiling for a week or more. "Pitt hates to get his silly Blackberry wet."

"He doesn't have much of a sense of humor, does he?" Mike asked.

Maria shook her head, but Michelle's voice behind him froze Mike's blood and dashed his momentary joy on her own personal iceberg.

"Mike, can I talk to you? Alone?"

Shit.

He put Maria down and followed Michelle to an oak tree a few feet away.

"I thought we agreed no bashing Pitt," she said. Her eyes had gone from summer-sky-warm to arctic-cold in no time flat, slicing into Mike like daggers of ice.

He took a deep breath, swallowed his pride, and nodded. "You're right. My bad."

"She'll never learn to accept him if you don't," she scolded. She knew just how to make him feel nine years old again. It had taken him seven years, but he'd eventually figured out she was more like a stern mother to him than a wife. "You need to build him up, so she can see the good in him."

She'll need a microscope to see it, he thought. Instead, he replied, "I will. I didn't mean anything by it."

Michelle nodded and turned to the crowd. "Okay, everyone. Let's do presents!"

As usual with kids, the process of opening presents went something like keeping cats on a roller coaster. No sooner would Maria get enthralled with one present, surrounded by the jealous exclamations of her friends, than someone would put something more exciting in front of her, making them all forget about the last thing. So when Mike's present was one of the last two remaining, he held his breath and hoped Michelle left it for last.

She didn't.

The box from Pitt, wrapped in expensive-looking silver paper with a fancy, curly-q bow, was much smaller than Mike's, with its unicorns, stars, and rainbows. Michelle wrinkled her nose as she handed the gift to Maria, who beamed at her father without even opening it.

She'd demolished the other wrappings, shredding them as she tore into their contents, but with his, she took it slow, folding the paper back on itself, as if she might reuse it. When the paper lay in a neatly folded stack, she slit the clear tape on the plain cardboard box inside and opened the flaps.

A smile blossomed on her face like a flower opening in spring sunlight. Her blue eyes brimmed and met his, the corners of her lips curling up, trembling slightly. She pulled out the stuffed bear, held it up as if inspecting it, then wrapped it in a hug so tight Mike almost felt it himself.

"You remembered," she told him. "I thought you'd forget."

"Never," he told her. Everyone else gaped at them, realizing they'd been left out of some hidden meaning. Mike explained. "She saw this at the Cheyenne Mountain Zoo down in the Springs last year. We went there for a daddy-daughter day, and she wanted this. I didn't have the money then, but I saved up and went back last week. I lucked out—they still had them."

Mike fought back his own tears at the unanimous round of "awwws" and "ooohs" from her friends. Michelle even smiled at him, something rarer than a black diamond.

Maria ran into his arms, squeezed him harder than she had in a long time, and kissed him on the cheek.

"You're not too old for it?" he asked.

"A girl is never too old for teddy bears," said a woman in the crowd. Mike had no idea who she was, but he didn't care. For once, he'd done well.

"Okay, well, there's only one more," Pitt said, looking at Mike with something akin to worry in his eyes. "Mine can't possibly match that, but I hope you like it."

Maria pulled away from Mike, her eyes mischievous with the enigma of her last present. Mike grinned when she ripped the wrapping paper apart like she had the others, but his joy ended as soon as her eyes popped open wider than the water balloons she'd thrown. Her mouth formed a silent "O" and her hands flew up to hide it.

Inside the paper was a box with the newest smart cellphone.

"But our contract isn't up for another year," she said, eyes still wide.

"It's all right," Pitt said. "I paid the early fees and upgraded you anyway. You're nine now. You shouldn't be using an archaic flip phone anymore. All your friends have smartphones, so you need one too."

Fantastic logic, Mike thought. *Hope all her friends don't get Porsches. Or boob jobs.*

As if reading Mike's mind, Pitt turned and winked at him, then opened his arms so Maria could rush into them. Her hug was at least as tight as the one she'd given Mike, maybe even tighter.

In a heartbeat, Mike went from elated to miserable, from feeling like a hero to feeling like an outsider. He'd never be able to give Maria that kind of birthday gift, at least not on a handyman's salary, and not while Michelle drained every last drop of alimony she could get from him.

He took a long pull on the beer and stood, moving away from the group.

By the time food was served, he'd moved to a solitary position in a folding lawn chair under a Norway Maple in Pitt's backyard. He'd moved on to beer number two, and his feeling of alienation had started to fade. He craned his neck backward, staring up into the canopy of the tree as a gray squirrel skittered from branch to branch, studiously watching for dropped food from any of the guests.

A loud "bang" sounded, and Mike dove to the ground. In a heartbeat he found himself in Fallujah again, bullets ripping through the hot, dry air, ricocheting off buildings and cars. For a moment, for a fleeting, ethereal instant, he stared down the barrel of an AK-47 again, waiting for it to fire and rip his life from his body.

"Daddy? Are you okay?"

Maria's voice brought him back, and when he opened his eyes, he lay under the maple tree in a fetal position, his hands over his ears. Gathered around him, the rest of the party stood, whispering to one another. Maria put her hand on his shoulder, her touch feather light, warm.

"I'm all right," he forced out, though his voice shook. He unfolded himself and sat up. Maria took a step back. "Just startled me, that's all."

He rose to one knee and found a hand there, waiting to haul him to his feet.

"I apologize," Pitt said, his hand out. "I should have warned you about the firecrackers. Totally inconsiderate of me."

Mike ignored his hand and rose on his own. "No problem. Don't walk on egg shells because of me."

Pitt looked at his shoes, and for an instant, Mike thought he might be sincere, but when he met the lawyer's gaze, the tiniest smirk told him all he needed to know. This had been intentional.

After a minute the crowd dispersed, and Mike plopped back down in his folding chair, putting his head in his hands. Michelle's white pumps appeared in the grass before him, and when he looked up, she had her hands on her hips.

"Had to make it about your PTSD again, didn't you?" The frost had returned to her voice.

"What are you talking about?"

"Come on, Mike. Pitt's gift showed yours up, so you had to regain the spotlight by using the war. This is getting old."

Mike reeled like she'd thrust a knife into his chest. She'd never been able to handle his condition, but she'd never been mean about it either.

"I'm not even going to respond to that," he said, turning his back on her. A moment later he heard her stomp away.

Mike's phone rang just as Pitt's lackeys started serving burgers and dogs. Mike moved a bit away and answered. One of his regular customers had a busted garage door opener and needed it fixed right away so she could go on vacation. Mike hated the thought of leaving the party early, at least when he thought of Maria. Once weekly visits and one overnight a month made him cherish every moment he got with his little princess.

Still, judging from the heated glare Michelle was burning into him right now, his welcome here had worn out. He agreed to fix the door, promising to be there in thirty minutes. As soon as he put his phone away, Maria grabbed his shirt tail and gave his ribs a light punch.

"You're leaving, aren't you?"

She put on her best kitten eyes, trying to charm him into staying. It almost worked. Then Michelle opened her mouth.

"So you're taking off? You can't even stop working for your daughter's birthday?"

Mike took a deep breath to calm himself. "You know how it is, Michelle. I run a business that depends on repeat and regular customers. This one's been with me a year now and I can't afford to lose her."

"Oh, it's a woman? That explains it."

Maria wrapped her arms around her mother's waist, squeezing like she wanted to force the words to stay inside.

"It's okay, Mom. The important part is over anyway."

Mike knew his daughter was trying to keep the peace, but he wasn't going to let Michelle have the last word, especially when it involved an implication like that.

"She's seventy-five," he snapped, resisting the urge to point his finger at Michelle's chest. "She has a walker and I'm pretty sure she wears adult diapers. She's not my type. I need the money, that's all."

Michelle stepped forward, her chin jutting like it always when her pride was in charge.

"You're choosing money over Maria? That's so much better than meeting a girlfriend."

Maria put herself between them, a hand on each one's stomach. She shook her head, but said nothing.

"I wouldn't need so much money if some vampire wasn't sucking the blood from my bank account every month. How much of that do you actually spend on Maria, since Pitt here seems to be doing most of the spending on her?"

Michelle drew herself up to retort, but Maria cut her off. Tears flowed down her cheeks, and her voice shook.

"Not today! I can't believe you guys did this on my birthday!"

For the first time, Mike noticed the crowd that had gathered to watch the fireworks, including adults and kids. He felt like hiding under a rock.

Maria let out one last wail of despair and dashed for the house, her friends in a line behind her.

"Maria, wait!" Mike called, moving after her. "I'm sorry, let's talk."

Then Pitt stood between him and his daughter, one hairy hand on Mike's shoulder.

"Let her go, Ace. Her friends will talk her down."

Mike stared at Pitt's hand until the lawyer removed it, backing up a step.

"I am going to talk to my daughter," Mike said. He turned to go around Pitt, but the lawyer stood his ground.

"Not in my house you aren't. I think you should go."

Mike's fists bunched at his sides. He took a step toward the smaller man, teeth gritted. Before he could do anything, Michelle appeared.

"I'll talk to her," she said, putting her arm between the two men. "Just go, Mike. You can call her later, when she calms down."

Mike's temper ebbed enough that he unclenched his fists. He poked an index finger at Pitt's chest.

"Don't call me 'Ace,'" he growled. "Or 'Tiger.' And don't ever come between me and my daughter again."

As Mike stormed out of the yard, Pitt called after him, "Are you threatening me, Mike?"

Mike knew better than to answer. After all, the guy was a lawyer.

Chapter Seven

"Morning, Annie!" Veronica sidled into her cube, plopping her skinny butt into the chair opposite Annie's. "You're in early."

Stifling a sigh, Annie tore her attention from the proposal she was writing and smiled at the intern. Veronica's red-painted lips turned up in a smile like they did anytime someone looked at her. Her blonde hair had been sprayed stiff, to the point it looked like a helmet made from gold strands.

"So are you." Annie tried to hide the disappointment in her voice. So much for getting work done.

Annie's cubicle sat directly in front of the door to the giant, fluorescent-lit room housing the cubicle farm, so anytime someone entered the office, they felt it necessary, polite even, to stop and chat. Most would hang over her low cubicle wall and chat about their kids, sports, dogs, cars, lovers, or whatever was foremost on their minds. Thus, Annie accomplished far less than most of her other coworkers. Coming in early usually gave her two uninterrupted hours to work before the daily sabbaticals to her desk began.

"What are you talking about, silly goose? I always come in at this time."

Annie glanced at the clock in the lower right corner of her monitor. Eight fifty-six.

"Where did the morning go?" She'd written only three pages of a six-page proposal. This was not going well.

Josh—the other intern at the agency—strolled into the room, waving as he passed her desk, but did not stop. Josh was personal assistant to Carol, their manager, and always seemed more stressed out than a twenty-year-old intern should be. Especially a paid intern.

Veronica watched him round the corner into Carol's office with its view of the mountains, then whispered to Annie, "Josh told me Carol has a big announcement to make. Something about moving people around. Promoting some, even."

Annie's heart jumped into her throat. She'd been working three small accounts for two years now, and they weren't enough to make her crucial to the company or keep her truly busy. She was ready to pick up a major account.

Before she could ask Veronica for details, Carol hustled into the room. Another disadvantage to Annie's cube—her boss would see her desk anytime she entered or left. If Annie's cube sat empty, Carol would undoubtedly ask her about it later.

Carol saw them talking and stopped. Her tiny frame shouted efficiency, with short, styled black hair and eyes that seemed to take in everything at once, noting even the smallest of details. Lines had started to crease her cheeks and brow, but she covered as much as she could with glopped-on makeup, and her brown eyes sparkled with a hint of mascara-crusted cruelty.

She smiled, and frost seemed to settle over the room, as if her breath itself was made of pure winter.

"Good to see you ladies in early," she said, her smile barely changing as she spoke. "Even if you are just sitting around. It's not quite nine yet, so that's okay."

She stuck her head into the cubicle, keeping her body outside, as if she might catch something if she touched one of them.

"We'll be having an all-hands meeting Friday morning, so mark your calendars and tell anyone else you see. We're realigning some responsibilities. You'll both want to be there."

And with that, she was gone, practically fast-walking to her office, where Josh waited outside the door, her coffee mug steaming in his hand.

When they both disappeared inside her office, Annie let out a deep breath. "It's about time!"

Veronica's brow furrowed, her lips pursing. "Time for what?"

Annie lowered her voice to a near whisper, even though she knew it didn't really matter. One thing about cubical farms—they're acoustically perfect, carrying every little sound all the way across the room, especially the sound of a whisper.

"I've been working these three puny accounts for two years," she said. "They're not even five percent of the company's income, and I feel like I deserve a larger account. When they brought in the Sterns Company as clients, I thought for sure she'd give it to me, but Mark got it instead. Frustrates me."

"You're really good, no doubt," the perky blonde said. She cocked her head to one side, her hair remaining perfectly still despite the shift in gravity. Annie noticed too that her makeup leaned toward the heavy side, with so much on her eyebrows that they almost looked like tattoos. "Have you told Carol you want more responsibility?"

"Repeatedly," Annie said with a nod. "Every time we do a sit down feedback session. She tells me what a great job I'm doing, and I ask for a bigger account."

"And?"

"And at first it seemed like she listened. She gave me some committees to work on, some social events to plan so the higher-ups would notice me. Then it just stopped as soon as Frank and I ... split up."

She didn't know if Veronica knew the whole story and was not about to volunteer the information to a known gossip.

The intern frowned. "Well, Josh did mention something about that ..."

She let the sentence trail off like a path into a dark woods. Annie, of course, walked right in.

"What did he say?"

Veronica looked around, then leaned in close. "Carol's not going to promote you or give you big accounts, Annie."

"Why not?"

"Because she's trying to get rid of you." She sat up with a jerk, glancing around again, then leaned in again, her voice a hoarse whisper. "She blames you for Frank being fired."

"Well, I did get him fired, but the company supports me in the matter. Did Josh tell you *why* Frank and I split up? *Why* he lost his job here?"

"He told me what Carol told him, that you exaggerated something that happened on a date. That you led him on, then changed your mind."

Annie's temper boiled, and she gripped the foam rubber armrests on her rolling office chair until her knuckles turned white. She fought to keep her voice to a whisper. "He wouldn't take no for an answer until I clocked him on the head. How can she possibly blame me?"

Veronica held her finger to her ruby lips, her blue eyes narrowing with worry. "Keep it down! You can't tell anyone I told you this. Promise, or I keep the rest to myself."

"There's more?"

"Not unless you promise!"

The intern looked frightened, like her dream job was in jeopardy. As much as it went against Annie's instincts, as much as she doubted Veronica's credibility, she nodded.

"I promise."

"Good. Now, what she told Josh is that she was grooming Frank to replace her. He was her golden child, and since you got him fired, she got yelled at by the CEO. Now she's pissed at you and plans to drive you out of the office."

"She's going to need more than her own version of what happened to do that," Annie said. She didn't know whether to be angry or hurt, so she felt a little of each.

"No, she won't," Veronica said. "Colorado is a work-at-will state. I know a woman who got fired from a software company just because her manager didn't like her. As long as her boss supports her, that's all she needs."

Annie took a deep breath and leaned back in her chair. "Why would she tell Josh all of this?"

"She'd been drinking. She does that sometimes. Takes him out for dinner and drinks. She uses him as her own personal designated driver."

Annie mulled things over in her mind. Carol had been colder and more distant with her since Frank's firing. For Annie's first two years with the firm, she'd been a hero, far exceeding Carol's expectations, skyrocketing up. Only Frank had outpaced her, but since they got along, it didn't bother her. Carol had been friendly then, often hugging Annie when she saw her, and giving her cards to tell her how much she appreciated Annie's hard work.

Now that she thought about it, though, all that changed with Frank's firing. Annie became a problem child. Instead of hugs and thank you cards, she got cold shoulders and angry glares. She knew Carol had some issues in her personal life, too. Her husband was ill, her son having trouble in college. She'd assumed the change in Carol's behavior had to do with those things, but now she wondered. Was Carol really spiteful enough to blame Annie? To try to get her fired?

Something didn't add up.

Before she could question it, Veronica changed the subject.

"You really need to get a life outside this office," she said. "You're always here when I arrive, still here when I leave. Why put so much effort into a place that isn't going to put it into you?"

"I do have a life," Annie said. "I have my house, my painting, Jason ..." She tried to list more, but found herself embarrassed that the intern was kind of right. She needed a life.

"Jason?" Veronica said, clapping her hands in typical cheerleader fashion. "A guy?"

"It's not like that. He's my best friend."

Veronica raised her eyebrows, then winked. "That's the best way to start a relationship. Builds trust."

"No, you don't understand," Annie explained, "Jason doesn't like girls. He's actually attracted to the guy I'm seeing Thursday—"

"You're seeing a guy Thursday?" She looked like a kid seeing the presents under the tree on Christmas morning. "Oh, tell me about him!"

Annie went through the whole night she met Mike, and when she finished, Veronica moved to stand behind her.

"Pull him up on Facebook," she demanded. "I need to see this hunk of yours."

Annie reached for her mouse, then stopped. "I, uh ... I don't remember his last name."

Veronica put her hands on her hips and looked down at Annie. "You're going on a date with this guy, and you haven't Facebook-stalked him yet? You really aren't very good at this, are you?"

Annie frowned.

"So you said he owns his own business," Veronica said. "What's it called?"

"More Than Handy Man," Annie told her, somehow embarrassed at the name's implications.

"So hit his website. I'll bet it has his name."

Annie almost face-palmed herself. She should have thought of all this last night.

She found the website, clicked on the "About" link, and sure enough, right at the top was a bio, complete with Mike's picture.

"Tolbert," she muttered. "Mike Tolbert, that's right."

She proceeded to *Facebook-stalk* him, feeling more than a bit guilty about it.

"Okay, I'm impressed," Veronica said, as Annie clicked through several pictures of Mike. Most of the profile was hidden, though, only visible to his friends.

Annie hovered the pointer over the "Add Friend" button.

"Do it," Veronica said. "You need more intel on this guy so you know he won't ..."

Her hesitation caught Annie's attention.

"Won't what?"

Veronica shifted on her feet, looking at the floor. "You know," she mumbled. "Pull a Frank on you."

Annie closed the browser and stood. "That's all for now," she snapped, more heatedly than she intended. "Time for us to get to work."

Veronica looked sad for a moment. She opened her mouth as if to say something, then decided against it and left the cubicle. Annie plopped into her chair again.

Her mind felt like it might explode. Her boss hated her. She was going out with a guy she barely knew. And she'd just confided in the office gossip.

She really did need to get a life.

Maybe that process would start on Thursday.

Chapter Eight

Mike had been to the Landry's restaurant in Denver many times, so he trusted the wait staff and knew the food was excellent. Sitting just east of Interstate 25, on the very south end of town, the place had been quite a drive for both of them, but Annie hadn't balked when he suggested the change.

They met in the parking lot at seven, as the sun started its dip toward the western peaks, painting the sky a montage of red, orange, yellow, and purple. The night air surrounded them, smothering them with heat cooked even higher by the highway a football field away. Normally this time of year, Denver would get showers and storms in the afternoon, cooling things down for evening, but today remained dry and roasted.

Air conditioners kept the interior cool, though, and the hostess led them to a booth in the back corner, a place Mike had called ahead to arrange, so he could see everyone coming and going from the place. The décor was predictable for a steak and seafood place, with brick columns sporting large trophy fish, rough-hewn wood ceilings, and a square bar smack in the center of the floor. The sound of glasses clinking mingled with the low hum of conversation, while the smell of wood smoke and fish wafted through the air, tempting and taunting.

Annie looked amazing as she slid into the black leather bench, resting her elbows on the polished sheen of the table. She'd dressed in a simple white blouse, left open at the neck, and faded blue jeans just tight enough to show off her figure, but not enough to look painted on. Her ebony hair fell in ringlets to her shoulders, and her green eyes sparkled through her red tortoise-shelled glasses. When she smiled, Mike nearly stumbled into his seat, making her giggle. The laugh enhanced her pixie look, holding an almost musical quality.

"I'm glad you went with jeans," he said, realizing too late how bad that sounded. She grinned at him, mischief dancing in her eyes. "I almost changed into something more formal before I left the apartment, but now I'm glad I didn't."

"I dress formally all day at work," she said as the waitress put menus in front of them. "I'm not big on doing so after work."

Mike nodded at the server—Zoey was her name—and took his menu.

"They have some amazing seafood here," he said. "About as fresh as you can get it this far inland."

"I was thinking a juicy steak sounded good," she said, stealing a glance over the top of the menu to gauge his response. "Maybe the T-bone. Medium-rare."

Mike kept the menu up to hide the grin spreading across his face. A woman who liked red meat still mooing was a rare find. So far, so good.

The server took their drink order, with Mike ordering a Coors and Annie sticking with water.

"I'll tell you up front," she said, her mischievous look hiding behind seriousness for a moment, "I don't drink much. Alcoholism runs in my family. I don't want to end up like my mother was for many years."

"No problem," Mike said. "I can do water, too."

He changed his order, mentally marking the "one strike" box in his mind. Genetic alcoholism.

"You didn't need to do that," she said. "I don't mind other people drinking, and I have been known to have the occasional glass of wine, but just not tonight."

"I get it. First date with a guy you don't know—you have to be careful. Honestly, I'm a bit relieved to be drinking water. I was worried you might get me drunk and take advantage of me."

He grinned at her, but she didn't look up from the menu. He kicked himself for making the joke. He didn't know her that well yet. She could be a devout Christian or one of the many Mormons in town, uncomfortable with innuendo.

They ordered their food, Annie sticking to her guns about the T-bone, and Mike choosing the New York strip steak. When the server left, Annie still wouldn't meet Mike's gaze, looking instead at a big screen TV playing a Rockies game.

"You like baseball?" he asked.

"Love it," Annie said. She kept her eyes on the game. "It's America's pastime, how could I not?"

"We should hit up a game sometime. They look like they could be good this year."

She nodded, finally meeting his eyes. To his surprise, hers glistened.

"Hey, I apologize for my joke earlier," he said. "I didn't mean to offend you."

She dabbed at one eye with her cloth napkin, put her hands in her lap, and took a deep breath. "It's not your fault," she said. "Unwanted sexual advances are a sore spot with me. You couldn't have known that."

"I assume that's why you'd sworn off guys? The whole bad experience thing we talked about?"

She nodded and sniffled, but seemed more under control. "Yeah. My last boyfriend...well, things went a little rough at the end of our relationship."

"You don't need to tell me about it," Mike said.

She shrugged and smiled, a bit of the mischief back in her eyes. "You might as well know. Apparently it's the talk of my office."

"How did that happen?"

By the time she'd given him a rundown on the situation with Frank and her job, Mike was grinning like a fool. Annie was a strong woman who made her own decisions. She hadn't let Frank force himself on her, and had suffered for it. But she still had the courage to go out with Mike.

"So there you go," she said as their food arrived. "You now know you're on a date with a potential drunk with shitty taste in men. Congratulations, you scooped up a winner."

Annie watched Mike's face for any reaction, but if her comment fazed him, he didn't show it. His blue eyes met hers, and electricity crackled between them.

Then his cellphone chimed, and he looked at the screen. Frowning, he shook his head and stuffed the phone back in his pocket.

"Nothing important?" she asked.

He smiled, making the crow's feet around his eyes crinkle. She felt the tiniest tickle in her stomach.

"No *one* important," he answered. He flicked his gaze at her steak. "You sure you can handle all that?"

Annie grinned and dug in, suddenly ravenous. Across from her, Mike dipped a steak fry in ketchup, then popped it in his mouth.

"Well, in the interest of full disclosure," he said, "you're not exactly dating a blue chip prospect."

She paused in mid-chew and studied his face. One corner of his mouth had turned up in a sly grin, but his eyes told her he was serious.

"I don't know. A veteran who runs his own business. You seem pretty together from my point of view."

"I must do a good job of acting then," he said. He took a drink of water and kept his eyes on the table as he put it down. "I have my own closet full of skeletons that you should probably know about."

He hesitated, uncertainty flickering in his eyes, then took a deep breath and opened the floodgates. He told her about Afghanistan, his friend Kyle, his PTSD, even his divorce. The words seem to explode out of him, as if he were a soda bottle shaken and punched with a nail. His ex-wife was living with her divorce lawyer, fighting him for custody of their daughter. He couldn't get to counseling enough because he was too busy working to pay child support and alimony. He told her how he stumbled from depression to paranoia to normalcy, sometimes in the span of a day. In the whole time he spoke, he kept his eyes on the table, only meeting her gaze when he came to a close.

"So there you go," he said. "You're dating a real winner."

"Sounds like this was meant to be," she laughed. "Two hot messes out on a date, complaining about their lives. It's almost therapeutic."

They talked all through dinner, and the more she learned about him, the more she liked. Sure, his life wasn't perfect, but whose was? He ran a successful business, helped raise his daughter, and dealt with all the other issues on his own. He'd watched his best friend die in his arms, and yet he didn't seem bitter or jaded. If he hadn't told her, she never would have known he had PTSD. It put her own life into perspective, and made him feel like her comrade-at-arms against life's injustices. She found herself picking at her food, trying to prolong the meal. She wanted more time with him, to hear him talk and feel his voice roll over her like waves on a beach.

She caught herself staring into his stunning blue eyes and took one last bite of her steak to cover it. As she put her fork down, Mike's phone chimed again.

"Shouldn't you get that?" Annie asked.

"Nope. That's the aforementioned ex-wife, probably nagging me for her payments. She can wait—I still have a few days."

The server came to clear away their plates and asked if they wanted dessert.

Annie shook her head, patting her stomach to show she was full. Disappointment flickered on Mike's face, and she knew he wanted the meal to last longer, too. It all seemed too good to be true. A good-looking guy with a secure job who actually knew how to listen. She almost pinched herself to see if she was dreaming.

He declined dessert and asked for their check.

"I don't know about you," he said, "but I'm not quite ready for this date to end."

The look of mischief he gave her made her stomach do a flip.

"I agree," she said. "It's been a long time since I found a guy I could talk to like this. It's weird, and don't take this the wrong way, but you're as easy to talk to as Jason. And just as good-looking."

"Your gay friend from the other night?"

She nodded.

"I'll take that as a compliment," Mike said. "Jason is a damned good-looking guy, though you shouldn't tell him I said that. Those gold eyes of his might steal me away from you."

Her laugh jumped from her throat before she could stop it, a barking, uncontrolled sound that made several people around them glance in her direction. It didn't seem to bother Mike, though, as he smiled and laughed too.

"Let's go get drinks," he said. Her laughing died and she felt her neck muscles tighten. "Don't worry, we can make it milkshakes if you want, or coffee or whatever you're comfortable with. As long as I get to keep talking to you."

He couldn't have said anything more perfect. Tension drained from her.

The server brought the check and Mike handed her a platinum card, cutting off Annie's attempt to get her card out of her wallet.

"I told you I'd cover dinner," he said, "so let me cover it. You can pay for drinks."

"I didn't agree yet," she said, eyeing him playfully over folded hands.

"You didn't say no, either, so until you do, I'm assuming it's a yes."

That self-confidence disarmed her, lowered her defenses and made her feel helpless. All she could manage in reply was a smile and what she thought was a smoky stare.

They talked while the server handled the bill, but when she didn't return right away, Annie noticed worry creeping onto Mike's face.

A moment later, the girl returned and whispered in Mike's ear.

Annie fished in her purse, pretending she didn't see what had happened. She'd had cards declined before, and she knew how embarrassing it could be. Mike handed the server a second card and shot Annie a worried glance.

"I gave her the wrong card."

This time, the flutter in Annie's stomach felt more urgent, a warning rather than a moment of elation. The sweat beading on Mike's forehead told her he felt the same. Something wasn't right.

The server came back a moment later, a manager in tow, a short man with a comb-over and no chin. He handed Mike's card back without smiling.

"I'm sorry, sir," he said, "but both of your cards were declined. Would you like to pay by check or cash?"

Mike paled, and when he took the card back from the manager, his hand shook. His face scrunched, deep in thought for a moment, then his eyes opened wide and he pulled out his cell phone.

"Just a moment," he said. A moment later, he groaned.

"What's wrong?" Annie asked, already reaching for her credit card again.

Blushing, Mike showed her the first text message:

Trying to rebuild credit score. Closed our old cards. Don't try to use them.

Annie watched as embarrassment morphed into rage on his face, the red changing to purple, his blue eyes turning storm-cloud gray. The way he held himself, fists clenched at his sides and jaw set, told her she did not want to be Michelle the next time they talked. Hoping to calm him down, Annie handed her card to the manager and offered Mike a sympathetic smile.

"Exes suck, don't they?" she said.

He nodded, but said nothing.

The manager returned with Annie's card, and Mike fished a twenty out of his wallet.

"I'll at least cover the tip," he said.

Annie nodded, but didn't make eye contact. She couldn't believe the sudden change, the shift from smiling and happy to wound tight with fury. If that was PTSD, Annie wasn't sure she could handle it.

"You know," she said as they stood, "I'm actually kind of tired, and I need to be at work early tomorrow for a meeting. Can I get a rain check on the drinks?"

Mike nodded and looked like he was holding back, a bomb trying not to explode. He walked her to the door, where she stopped and gave him a quick hug.

"I'm sorry that happened," he said, easing away from her. "Sometimes, I think she tries to ruin my life."

Annie smiled and shook her head. "Don't mention it. It happens. I'll call you about drinks sometime, all right?"

He nodded, but Annie could tell he didn't believe it. And Annie wondered if she meant it. The good side of Mike seemed better than anything she'd ever had, but the transformation had reminded her a little too much of Frank.

Chapter Nine

"We're realigning some responsibilities." Carol's space-saving frame moved around the end of the gleaming, cherry conference table. Her cropped, jet-black hair didn't move, and she'd painted her smile so well it almost looked real. "I've heard some of you want more responsibility, and I want to encourage that initiative."

Annie's heart leapt.

Carol stopped at the head of the table. Tall, willowy Sabrina, her newest pet, sat closest to her, with the two fresh-faced interns—Josh and Veronica—on her right. Across from them sat stern-looking William (never Bill), and the ditzy brunette, Jenny. Only Annie sat a few chairs apart.

Annie's cellphone chimed on the table, drawing glares. A quick glance showed her a text from Mike. She set the phone to vibrate only and stuffed it in her purse on the floor.

"If we can continue," Carol said, "I want to thank Sabrina for wrapping up the Stanbridge Brothers account so quickly. The coffee chain is now the third biggest account we have, and will bring in more quarterly than most others combined."

Annie rolled her eyes. Sabrina had led the charge on Stanbridge Brothers, but Annie had done most of the legwork.

Carol went on. "William and Jenny, your workload seems steady but manageable, do you agree?"

Both nodded.

Annie's cell vibrated in her purse.

"However, our interns really don't have much to do." Carol's tone told Annie she'd heard the cellphone, too. "They can't learn the business if we don't empower them. So I am giving them each an account to work, with supervision from one of us."

Annie gripped the table. *Supervision? Yes!*

"William, you will be working the Denver Public Schools account, with Josh supervising, and Veronica, you'll be working the BHE account, with Sabrina supervising."

Annie's jaw fell open. She'd just lost two of her three tiny accounts. The third consisted of a tiny local clothing chain and made her company almost no money.

"Excuse me, Carol." She fought for composure. "I have experience with those accounts. Wouldn't I be the logical choice to supervise?"

Carol's eyes frosted over and she put her hands on her hips. "You've only been with us a couple of years, Annie. We don't see you as a supervisor."

"It's been thirty months, actually," Annie said. "I was hoping to expand my responsibility. I don't want to stagnate."

Carol smiled, a cool, oily expression that left Annie wanting a shower. "We need you to apply yourself fully to the Halloween party. You did such an excellent job with the picnic, Charles wants you to handle it."

Great. Charles, the CEO, knew Annie as the picnic planner.

"In fact, he'd like you to handle all the events. The Halloween party, Thanksgiving potluck, and of course, the annual holiday party. Congratulations."

The last word dripped with sarcasm. Annie drew herself up to retort, but her cellphone buzzed again.

"You should answer that," Carol said.

Fuming, Annie snatched her phone out of her purse and marched out, slamming the door behind her. She stood, phone clutched like a knife.

What a bitch!

Her phone buzzed again. Four texts in five minutes. She stomped past the cubical farm and into the break room. She couldn't believe this was happening. First he'd stuck her with the bill last night, now he'd gotten her thrown out of a meeting with Carol. Mike was turning out to be another in a long series of bad choices. It was time to end the pattern.

She didn't even read the messages, she just dialed his number. He answered on the first ring.

"Hey, Annie, I just wanted to—"

She cut him off without hearing another word. "Mike, not all of us work for ourselves. Some of us have real jobs, with managers on our butts every second. You just got me booted from a meeting with my boss, so I figure that combined with last night's disaster precludes any further social interaction. Stop texting, don't call, and let's forget last night even took place!"

"Annie, I'm—"

And she hung up.

Behind her, someone cleared their throat. Annie turned, mortified, to see Sabrina holding her purse while the rest of Marketing gave her performance a polite golf clap. Carol stood in the conference room door, arms crossed, grinning like an evil clown.

Annie wanted to curl up and die.

*

Larry Collins leaned back in his padded leather chair, rested his hands in his lap, and studied Mike with soft, brown eyes.

"Looking at it now," he said, his voice soft and neutral, "do you think texting Annie was a good idea?"

Mike rolled his eyes, groaning. He hated the Socratic approach, with its targeted questions. "Of course not. I should've called her tonight, after work."

He'd gotten Annie's call just an hour earlier, her words hitting him like repeated slaps to his face. Her rebuke had knocked him down so low he'd flashed back to Fallujah, frightening himself enough to call Larry for a same-day appointment.

"Are you sure all that was really directed at you?" the counselor asked. "Or do you think other frustrations like her house and her work might have been responsible?"

"I know she's not completely mad at me, but I got her thrown out of that meeting. I knew how important that was for her. We talked about it last night. I'd put it on par with my visitations with Maria."

"And if Michelle made a problem for those visitations because she's jealous of Annie, would that be Annie's fault?

"No, of course not," Mike said, "but this is different. I'm a man."

Collins raised his eyebrows, forming a near-perfect arch on his forehead. "So, because you're a man, you're supposed to take the blame for something your ex-wife did?"

"I'm supposed to have my shit together."

"I'm sure Annie likes to think she has her stuff together, so what's the difference?"

Feeling trapped, Mike looked out the window. After a few minutes, Collins changed the subject. "Do you feel ready for a relationship, especially a serious one?"

Mike sucked in his breath like he'd stuck his hand under scalding water. In fact, the sensation was similar. "I think I'm more ready than I was a year ago," he answered. "I think I'd like to try again, at least."

Collins put on a pair of wire-rimmed reading glasses and looked down at his notes, scribbled on a yellow legal pad in his lap. Mike didn't know why the man had a desk, since he never used it. He took notes in his lap, read things in his lap, even put the phone in his lap when talking on it. His desk seemed superfluous.

"From what you've told me, it seems Annie has some problems of her own. What kind of match do you think she is for you?"

"Birds of a feather ..." Mike let the saying hang between them.

"Do you think she's confronting the true source of those issues? Is she really making headway against it?"

"I think so," Mike answered. He'd thought about this last night, lying awake in his bed, unable to sleep or even doze. "I think she will avoid guys like Frank in the future, and she certainly seems to be strong enough now to stand up for herself."

"So you think her problems stem from the attempted rape?"

Mike knew a trap when he saw one, and he knew he'd fallen right into this one. "They don't, do they?"

Collins motioned with his hand for Mike to finish the thought.

"So, if the assault isn't the true basis of her insecurities," Mike said, reasoning things through in his mind, "it must be her mother somehow."

"Adult children of alcoholics are a unique breed," Collins said, walking to a bookcase against his wall. He pointed to a cluster of books there. "There's a whole field of study, with book upon book dedicated to helping adult children of alcoholics. One of the consistent traits of ACAs is that they struggle with intimate relationships. They have no basis for 'normal' in their life, no example from which to model their own behavior. They also fear deeply being abandoned, since their parent or parents abandoned them for a bottle."

"I guess I can see some of that in her," Mike agreed. It made sense, now that he thought about it.

"Know anyone else with that issue?" Collins asked.

That took Mike aback. He was used to talking about his tendency toward depression, anger, and even violence, all parts of PTSD. But he'd never thought of himself as being afraid of a relationship before.

"You mean since Michelle abandoned me, I'm afraid of being abandoned, and of letting Annie in my life?"

"Could it go deeper than that?" Collins said in that voice that whispered, *I want you to tell me the rest.*

Mike thought about it, wracking his brain, but knowing all along what the counselor wanted to hear. Knowing because in his heart, he knew it was—at least in part—true. Finally, he blurted it out.

"You think I sabotaged my date with Annie?"

The same satisfied smile crossed Collins' face. "That's your conclusion?"

"No way," Mike said. "I didn't cancel those cards. Michelle did."

"But she hinted about doing this," Collins said, returning to his chair. "You could have prevented it by simply taking her off the accounts, but you chose not to. Why?"

"I didn't think of it."

"It's one of the first things you told me you were going to do, right after the divorce."

Mike's jaw fell open, but he managed to snap it shut before any words fell out. Collins was right—they had discussed it the week after the divorce went final. Why hadn't he removed her?

Seeing Mike's shock made the counselor grin again. "Do you think this could relate back to your experience in Fallujah?"

Mike knew where he was going with this. "You mean Kyle's death?"

"Survivor's guilt could cause you to avoid getting close to someone for fear of them abandoning you, too."

Mike jumped to his feet, his temper leaping to a boil. "Kyle didn't abandon anyone!"

"You told me over a year ago that you felt guilty for surviving when Kyle died. You felt alone, like you should've died instead of him."

Mike sat back down, staring at his feet.

"Who's the only person you let get close to you?" the counselor asked. "Who do you feel will never leave you?"

The answer came lightning-quick. "Maria."

"And you don't think that somehow impacts your other relationships?"

That question hit a little too close to home for Mike's comfort, so he changed the topic.

"Doesn't matter anyway," he said. "You heard Annie: she wants nothing more to do with me."

"And you think giving up is your best choice?"

"I think it's my only choice."

Collins shifted in his chair, leaning forward and putting his elbows on the desk. "Mike, I'm concerned that your PTSD symptoms are starting up again. We stopped treatment earlier than I thought we should last time. I'd like to resume it. I'd like to try prolonged exposure therapy."

"Doc, I'm so busy," Mike said. "I have to work so much just to make payments."

"There are also medications—"

"No way!" Mike burst. "I'm not medicating. I'm not putting a bunch of chemicals in my body and hoping they fix things."

Collins frowned, then hid it quickly. "Someday you'll have to commit time and effort, then."

"And I will," Mike said. "Someday. I just need to get my life to a point where I can."

"If you don't put in the time, your life may never reach that point."

His tone reminded Mike of how his father sounded when he'd lectured him as a boy. Collins usually didn't do that, let his frustration slip through. He was usually more emotional mirror than a window.

Mike decided to change topics again. "There is one more thing, Doc," he said. Collins wasn't a Ph.D., but Mike used the term anyway, mostly because it made the counselor shift in his seat and adjust his hair. "Michelle has been showing interest in me again."

Mike told him about her asking him to come over to her place, and about her attention at the party. When he finished, Collins leaned in close, his brown eyes intense.

"What do you think about spending time with her?"

Mike shrugged. "It would be good for Maria."

"Would it?" Collins leaned back, checking his watch once more. "Have you changed your mind about Michelle being toxic for you?"

Mike looked at his hands where they rest in his lap. "No."

"How do you think Maria is going to see this?"

Mike hesitated, knowing the answer but not really wanting to speak it aloud. "She get her hopes up. She'd think we were getting back together."

"Do you think that's good for her?"

Mike shook his head and stood. "No, I don't. It's just tempting. Things would be so much simpler."

"The simple course is rarely the right one. Think about what I said. Prolonged exposure therapy might help you get your PTSD under control before it hurts someone important to you."

Mike left without saying a word.

Chapter Ten

Annie sat back on the old, worn sectional she'd had shipped over from her apartment. Its contemporary look didn't fit well with the Victorian décor throughout the rest of the living room, but she couldn't bring herself to keep her mother's old-style couch. She didn't care about the appearance—her sectional looked like the moving truck had run it over—but her mother's old furniture was about as comfortable as sitting on a pallet. Besides, it still smelled like her mother, like mothballs and hairspray and alcohol. So she and Jason had moved all of the Victorian-style furniture into the unfinished basement, replacing it with Annie's worn but more modern pieces.

"How pathetic am I?" she muttered, putting her head in her hands. "Saturday night, and I'm home alone in my dead mother's house."

Through the open windows came a distant roll of thunder, a subtle, almost comforting sound that carried only the slightest hint of a warning. Annie took a breath and relaxed, resting her head on the couch back, cradling a glass of chardonnay in her lap.

It wasn't like her furniture had to impress anyone. Jason had company in town, and her love life had gone extinct with Mike's flubbed attempt at courtship. She didn't even care that half her living room hid behind still-unpacked cardboard boxes, like a half-finished fortress erected around her flat screen TV on its black-lacquered stand.

"If you hadn't chewed Mike out, he might be here right now," she told herself.

As if in answer, the TV burst to life, white noise blasting through the speakers while the screen showed an electronic snow storm. Annie jumped, then pushed the power button on the remote. Nothing happened, so she tried again with the same result. She slapped the remote on her palm, but even that didn't help, so she crossed to the TV and turned it off there.

The eerie silence that followed made her feel alone, tiny and weak, until distant thunder pealed again, this time more foreboding. Suddenly, Annie didn't want to be alone any more.

She tossed the remote on the couch and meandered toward the kitchen, grabbing her wineglass on the way, letting her thoughts stray.

Mike's credit card issues at dinner weren't his fault, and she knew she shouldn't judge him for it. Sure, it demonstrated that his crazy ex-wife still had too much control over him, but Annie wasn't exactly free of her ex either. It was one more thing they had in common, one more piece of the puzzle that had clicked right together like it was meant to be.

The bottom line was that they'd had a blast together. It had been a long time since she had sat back and enjoyed a conversation with a guy over dinner, since she felt so at ease with a man. She couldn't hold one bad date against him forever.

She wrinkled her nose as she entered the kitchen. The room still smelled musty and damp, a stench that started the day Mike pulled the moths from the dishwasher drain and hadn't lessened much since. Pausing by the sink, she looked at her glass, holding it up to the light and swishing it around, admiring the way the bubbles sparkled like gems in the wine.

"Now I'm fantasizing about alcohol," she said, pouring the wine down the sink. "I'm hopeless."

Back in the living room, she picked up her cellphone. "I'll call Mike, apologize, and see if he wants to meet for that drink. It's better than being alone, right?"

As she dialed his number, her screen blacked out and her phone died. Just shut off.

"This is ridiculous," she muttered. "A new battery should hold a charge longer than this."

She added "get new phone battery" to her To Do list, plugged the cellphone into its charger, and left it on the coffee table.

It seemed she was destined to spend the night alone, so she set her mind on at least being productive. She marched up the stairs and into the third bedroom at the end of the hall, the tiny room she'd slept in as a child, the room now set up as her painting studio.

Flipping on the light, her heart almost stopped. A painting sat on an easel, a work she'd started by photographing an old woman at a nearby strip mall. She'd brought the photo home and was turning it into a portrait. Except as she looked at it now, the painting had a crucial flaw—she'd given the old woman the wrong eyes. Her mother's eyes.

Annie kicked the leg of the easel, then watched the painting tumble to the floor. She wanted to stomp on it, put her foot through the canvas and destroy it the way her mother had destroyed everything. Instead, she picked it up, turned it around so she couldn't see the front, and leaned it against a stack of paintings. Paintings that all reminded her, somehow, of her mother. She felt like screaming, shredding every painting in the stack. Why, at twenty-eight-years-old, did she still let her mother rule her life?

"Thanks, Mom, now I can't even paint. Anything else you'd like to take from me?"

She turned to leave, but at the outer periphery of her vision, she noticed something in the window. She spun, but the object disappeared. Had it been a face? A man's face?

"Impossible, this is the second floor," she told herself. But a tall elm tree grew outside the window. Even as a girl she'd used it to sneak out more than once.

She tiptoed to the window, leaned down, and peered outside into the darkness. Far to the south, lightning flashed in heated silence.

A sudden brush of cold air on her neck startled her, made her feel like someone was watching her. She stumbled backward, tripping over her chair. She grunted as her bottom hit the hardwood floor, but scrabbled back from the window, her breath coming in rapid gulps, her heartbeat pounding in her ears.

Something beat against the window panes, feathers and beak, huge golden eyes. When the owl flew away, Annie watched it swoop across the street, light on a power line, and stare at her. The feeling of being watched struck so hard she yanked down the shade before leaving the room, flipping off the light on her way.

Even animals liked to torment her.

She closed the door to the studio and marched downstairs to the kitchen. She grabbed her largest kitchen knife—a serrated eight-incher with wood handles and flecks of rust—and caught her breath. Sure, it had been an owl, but she'd feel better with a weapon beside her bed tonight, since she couldn't have someone to sleep with.

*

Mary stood outside the closed door to Annie's room, her rage swirling like a swarm of locusts, bouncing off the door without effect. She screamed, head back and mouth open like a chasm, her frustration boiling over like lava from a volcano.

Foolish girl would not listen. She tried to warn her, tried to show her the man was there, was dangerous. But Annie only saw what Annie wanted to see, and only heard what she believed could be said.

He'd been so close, just inches away, close enough to slit her throat had she stuck her head out the window. All because Annie refused to listen.

She returned to the art room, drifted to the window, and pressed her face through the glass, its cold, sharp edges sending stabs of pain through her. The bad man was gone, run away like he always did, leaving only some scuffed bark in the tree where he'd climbed up to peek inside.

Annie didn't understand how dangerous men were, how they'd tear her heart out and stomp on it like dirt. Annie should have known, should have understood the danger. She'd been hurt by their anger and rage and violence, and had let them walk away.

But she refused to listen. The blackness of anger and the ice of resentment shrouded her heart, making her unable to hear what her mother told her. Mary felt Annie's rage like a hot poker thrust into her heart, but did not understand. From where did the anger grow? What caused it? Was she that bad a mother, that her own daughter hated even the thought of her? That she allowed that hatred to blind her to Mary's warnings?

If Mary could have talked to her, she would have. But a curtain divided Annie's world from hers, a veil thin enough to see through, but thick enough to block sound, to stifle all but the loudest screams. And those screams hurt Mary, tore at her like razor-sharp claws that threatened to shred her very being.

She could not touch, either, for touch endangered Annie. The dead world must never touch the living, for death can spoil life, but life cannot reverse death. Touching her daughter would have left a mark like that of a spider bite, where the flesh sloughs off, rotten and putrid and dead. No, touch was not the answer.

Somehow, Mary still smiled. As frustrated as her daughter made her, she knew her purpose now. Annie still made bad decisions, especially about men. She needed her mother, required her guidance and control to force her life in the right direction.

That was Mary's purpose in being there, tied to the house. She was sure of it. She was there to do what she'd always done, to be what she'd always been: Annie's mother.

*

Annie woke to the smell of smoke. Not just any smoke, but the crisp, acrid smell of an electrical fire.

She jumped out of bed, tossing her blankets to the floor, and grabbed her cellphone from the nightstand. She stood, sniffing, turning her head to try to gauge where the smell came from. A quick assessment made her follow it to the hallway, where the scent grew stronger. Light flickered in the guest bathroom, orange then white then orange again.

She ran to the door to find flames leaping from the plug over the white porcelain pedestal sink, the one where her nightlight remained plugged in. Above it, the striped wallpaper started to catch, flames working their way up from the outlet.

Grabbing a towel from the rack, she swatted the flames until they no longer climbed the wallpaper. She thought briefly about water from the sink, but decided against mixing water and electricity. She needed the power off.

She dashed down the stairs, trying to remember where the breaker box was located. She hadn't seen it in the basement, so she guessed it had to be in the one-car garage.

When she found it, she couldn't tell which switch went to the bathroom. The labels—written decades ago in pencil—were faded, some even gone. So she threw the main one, killing power to the whole house.

That plunged her into total darkness, unable to make out even the shape of her tiny Ford Fiesta, which should have been right in front of her. For a moment, she felt like someone watched her, the clammy fingers of their gaze moving down her spine. She activated her cellphone's screen, throwing light around her, and the feeling fled.

She found the flashlight app on her phone and turned the tiny flash for the camera into a light. Guiding herself back upstairs, she returned to the bathroom, a box of baking soda in her other hand. But flames no longer leapt from the outlet, replaced by a tiny tendril of smoke.

"Now what?" she asked herself. She couldn't read the fuse box labels, so turning any power back on was out of the question. But she wasn't going back to sleep with no power, not in this house.

She looked on her cellphone's call list. Mike's number sat third down. His website said he was a certified electrician, and he did emergency calls. And even though he was a jerk, he was a trustworthy jerk.

She sighed. "It's better than having a total stranger in my home at this time of night."

She touched the screen to call him back, but as she did, the battery meter went from full to empty in an instant and her phone shut down. She shivered as a wave of frigid air slithered over her skin.

"Damned battery," she muttered. Having no land-line, she had only one other choice. In the dark, her hands groping in front of her for unseen obstacles, she worked her way through the kitchen, grabbing her car keys.

She whacked her knee on the front license plate, but made it to the car, started it up, and plugged her phone into the charger. Taking a deep breath, she dialed.

Chapter Eleven

Mike panted, his back slammed against the asphalt street. The thunderous crack-crack-crack of AK-47 fire sounded around him as bullets whizzed past, ricocheted off the street, and tore into vehicles.

He rolled over to find Kyle, sprawled on the street, his right leg gone from just above the knee, a jagged white tip of bone jutting out from the bright red of sundered flesh. Kyle's arm lay twisted underneath him, not recognizable anymore. They were two pieces of meat left to cook on the pavement.

Mike dragged his friend by the flak vest around a corner, behind a concrete wall. Bullets cut through the baked cement, sizzling through the air around his head. When he looked up, he found himself staring down the barrel of an AK-47, the blued metal less than an inch from his face.

A cellphone rang.

Mike searched his pockets, trying to dig out his phone. He patted his chest pockets, his hips, even his sleeves. No phone.

It rang again.

He checked Kyle's pockets; still no phone.

The barrel of the AK pushed closer to his head, the gunman's finger tightening on the trigger.

It rang a third time.

Mike sat bolt upright in bed. He found himself alone in the dark of his bedroom, his sweat the only remnant of the Fallujah heat. Despite the sweat, he found himself shivering.

The phone rang again. He grabbed it off his night table, and without checking caller ID, he answered.

"Hello?"

"Hi, uh, Mike." It took him a moment to recognize Annie's voice. When he did, he sat up taller and rubbed his eyes as she went on. "I'm sorry to bother you so late."

Her voice brought back the pain he'd felt during their last conversation. He said nothing, so she continued.

"I had a little problem with the house tonight. An electrical fire."

His heart beat a little faster. Something in her voice had changed. She sounded softer now. More vulnerable. He'd never heard fear from her before, and it awakened something in him that sought to protect her, but he managed to keep his teeth firmly embedded in his tongue.

Annie sighed. "Look, I know you're pissed at me, but I don't want to turn the power back on until I know it's safe. Could you come take a look?"

So she needed a handyman, not a date. He wasn't letting her off the hook that easily.

"This is my personal cell," he said, keeping his voice as flat as possible. "I don't conduct business on it."

On the other end, Annie took a deep breath, then the line went dead.

Almost a full minute later, his work cell rang on the kitchen table. He took his time putting on his robe, then ambled out of his bedroom and into the kitchen. He picked up the cellphone on the fifth ring, just before it went to voice mail.

"More Than Handy Man," he answered, emphasizing the last word. "The handiest man you'll ever need."

He added the last part on a whim—he didn't have a catch phrase.

For a moment, she said nothing. When she did speak, the vulnerability in her voice had been replaced with cold, sharpened steel.

"Is that supposed to be funny? I thought I was calling a professional contractor, not a teenager playing grown-up games."

Mike choked back a chuckle, not about to show her an opening. "I'm sorry, ma'am, we're closed for the weekend. Call us back on Monday."

As he lowered the phone from his ear, the panic returned to her voice.

"No, Mike, please!"

He rolled his eyes. He'd always been a sucker for a damsel in distress. "Tell me what happened," he said.

As she told him about the fire, he heard it again, the vulnerability. This time, it came as a slight tremble in her voice, a vibration that sounded out of place. Like a songbird out of key.

Five minutes later, he closed his apartment door behind him.

*

A flashlight in one hand, Annie took a deep breath, ran her fingers through her hair, and yanked her front door open. Mike stood there, hair tousled, jawline stubbled. In his left hand he held a green canvas tool bag, and in his right, a single yellow rose, which he extended to her.

"It's not an olive branch, but truce?"

A smile popped onto her face before she could stop it. "I should be making the peace offering," she said, stepping aside to let him in. "I acted like a total bitch on the phone the other day. I'm sorry."

She took the rose and put it in an empty vase on a table inside the door.

"Yes, you did," he said, "but I deserved it. We can talk about it another time, if you want. Let's take care of this electrical problem."

She nodded, hiding the relief that flooded through her. She'd been dreading this conversation, and wasn't ready for it. In a couple of sentences, he'd removed the stress and awkwardness. She smiled as she led him up the stairs.

Annie told him again what had happened, and shone the flashlight on the outlet while Mike used a screwdriver to remove the scorched ceramic cover and peer inside.

"Well, the good news is that your fire is out," he told her.

"And the bad news is?"

"I'll have to look at it more closely, but it looks like your wiring is all out of code. Looks like some of it might be original to the house. When was this place built?"

"1910," she answered. "But I think Mom had some renovations done in the seventies."

"That's still over forty years old, probably ten out of code."

He stood and put his hand in front of his eyes. Annie realized she was shining the flashlight in his face and lowered it.

"So, am I looking at a huge cost?"

He shrugged. "We'll take it one step at a time. Let's start by getting your power back on. I'll need to figure out which breaker controls the bathroom. Where's the box?"

A few minutes later, after running back and forth to find the right breaker, Mike had her power back on, except for the second bathroom. He trudged back in from the garage, wiping his hands on his jeans. Annie watched the way his t-shirt hung loose across his flat stomach, admired the way the muscles in his arm moved as he brushed himself off.

When he saw her watching him, he smiled. "I found the breaker for the second bathroom. You should be safe with your power on, as long as the bathroom breaker remains off. I won't be able to turn power back on in there until I fix the wiring. That'll require a more detailed inspection, which I should be able to do mid-week?"

Annie nodded, her insides roiling. "So until then I need to use the master bathroom?"

"Right. Is that a problem?"

She didn't want to tell him it was, didn't want him to think her nuts for still fearing her long-dead mother, so she turned away. "No, that should be fine."

"The master bath works, right?"

She nodded and changed the subject. "How much do I owe you?"

"This one's on the house," he said. "Consider it pay back for me botching dinner."

"This more than makes up for one rough night. Let me pay you something, at least."

"There is one thing," he said, one corner of his mouth curling up. "Maybe we'll try again someday?"

His smile disarmed her, dropping her defenses in a heartbeat.

"Yeah, maybe. Once I get some work stuff resolved, so I'm not as stressed out. I kind of dumped on you for something that wasn't your fault."

She motioned to a wooden dining room chair, and to her surprise, he sat. She'd expected him to excuse himself and go home.

"What happened?" he asked.

Annie dropped into the chair across from him and explained what happened at work the day after their date. Mike listened, asking questions from time to time. His eyes never left hers the whole time, and by the end of the tale, she had to look at her hands to break eye contact. Having someone listen to her that intently was unnerving. But she liked it. A lot.

"Bosses like Carol are the reason I started my own business," he said, squeezing her forearm. A tiny spark jumped from his fingertips to her skin. "It sucks you have to deal with her. You ever think about painting for a living? "

She raised her eyebrows at him.

He pointed upstairs. "When I was checking breakers I looked in your studio. Flipped the light on to test it and saw your paintings."

She laughed, in part because she was flattered, and in part due to embarrassment. Had he noticed all the paintings of her mom?

"Thanks," she said. "But the income of an artist is hardly steady enough to support myself and pay for this house."

"I thought this place belonged to you outright?"

She brushed back a lock of her black hair and rested her chin in her hand. "It is, but the utility bill is sky high, I need to get the outside back into covenants in eighty days, and now I have an electrical system to replace. Maybe I should just skip all that and let the place burn down. Collect insurance."

"Sounds like you need a good handyman for a long-term contract," he said, grinning like a coyote in a henhouse.

"Well, assuming you're actually talking about handyman work right now, I could."

Annie picked up the yellow legal pad with her repair list on it and gave it to Mike, telling him about Mrs. Mudge and the Historical Society. He looked it over, scratching the stubble on his chin.

"What happened to the window?" he asked, not looking up from the pad.

"I can't prove it," she said, "but I think my ex threw a rock through it. Under my deductible for homeowner's insurance, too."

He studied her, blue eyes intense, then nodded. "Shouldn't be too bad," he said. "Most of this is cosmetic. I know a good painter who's done some old Victorians like this. I can handle most of the exterior stuff pretty cheap, at least enough to get the Historical Society off your back."

"What's your idea of cheap?" Against her better judgment, she liked the idea of having Mike around a lot. At least it might keep Frank at bay a little.

"Won't know for sure until I look at everything, but if it's all really superficial, you should be talking under five thousand. The front window will be the worst, since it's old and no one makes windows like that anymore."

He stood and she stood with him, surprised at how close they were. Her heart thudded in her chest and she took a half-step back so Mike wouldn't feel it. He extended his hand.

"But let's handle the bathroom wiring first," he said. "Take things slow."

Warmth from his hand ran up her arm as they shook.

"Slow. Got it."

She looked up and stared right into his huge, blue eyes, feeling drawn in closer to him, as if he had his own gravity she couldn't escape. Their handshake lasted a second longer than normal before he let her go.

"If you're good in the bathroom," she said, "I'll hire you for more."

She realized a moment too late the innuendo she'd dropped and wondered where it had come from. Mike laughed.

"And maybe we can take a second shot at dinner someday."

She smiled before she could stop it, grinning like a foolish schoolgirl, asked out by the school quarterback.

"Yeah, I think I'd—"

A car alarm sounded outside, making them both jump. Mike listened a moment, then cursed.

"Damn it, that's my truck!"

He grabbed his tool bag and ran.

*

Mike sprinted as fast as he could, his tool bag slapping his thigh as he ran. His work truck sat at the curb, horn honking on and off, lights flashing, alarm whistling. He pressed the off button on his remote.

Nothing happened. A light came on next door.

He pressed off again, closer this time. Still nothing, as someone cussed at him from the dark.

He reached the driver's door, shivering in the sudden chill of the night, unlocked it and tore the door almost off its hinges. Jumping in, he started the engine, which killed the alarm.

Letting out a sigh, he noticed Annie standing on her front porch, laughing, hands on hips. He paused, unable to take his eyes off her. Her smile touched her eyes and her hair blew sideways in the light breeze. In the yellowed light of the porch, with her green eyes glittering, she looked like an impossibly beautiful elf, a creature used to luring men into the forest with only a smile.

He shook his head and shut off his truck. Getting out, he slammed the door and strode toward Annie. He'd gone just a few steps when the alarm went off again, making his heart jump almost out of his chest.

He unlocked it again, reached inside, and started the motor. This time, ice cold air blew through the vents, blasting him in the face with the stench of a rotting corpse. He went to turn off the air conditioner, but paused, confused. The dial already pointed to the off position.

He twisted it left to "Max AC" then back to off. This time, the fan died.

"What the hell?" he said. "Don't you start flaking out on me too, baby. Two crazy women in my life is more than enough."

He shut the door again, ready to leave the truck running long enough to talk with Annie, but she waved, laughed again, and went inside. The whole street looked darker with her gone, lonelier. Almost desolate.

He swung the door open and climbed into the cab. Everything worked as it was supposed to this time. Mike rubbed his temples—he'd owned the truck for three years, and it had never done anything like that. Why did weird things always happen around Annie? He'd only been half-truthful about her wiring. Yes, it was out of code by a couple of decades, but he didn't think that had caused the fire. In fact, except where burned, the wiring looked like it probably had the day it had been installed. Normally in a bathroom fire, absent an obvious bad connection or short, he'd expect to see signs that water had leaked into the wiring, hitting exposed copper and causing the fire. But the wall itself showed no signs of saturation. As far as Mike could tell, the fire had just started. He'd know more once he did the work to replace it, but for now, he had to blame it on old wiring.

He swung a U-turn on her street, careful not to mess up anyone's curb, and pulled away. He took one last look at the house in his mirror and spotted her. She stood in the upstairs window—the master bedroom—silhouetted against the dim light, holding back one curtain. As he drove off, she let the curtain drop and disappeared.

*

Annie leaned against the inside of her door, her heart pounding, as the sound of Mike's truck rumbled off down her street. She'd planned to keep him at arm's length, business only. Just a handyman. But the moment he'd smiled his roguish smile, the instant her eyes met his, her knees had turned to jello, and her willpower to dust. He'd been much more than a handyman in a flash. How could a guy do that to her?

She took a deep breath, let it out, and walked to her living room. Especially a guy who needed to get his shit together as much as Mike did. He was emotionally unstable, had a daughter, and still jumped when his bitch of an ex called. She'd be nuts to go back to dating him.

So why did she hope he called her that night to ask her out?

She looked at her clock: two twenty-nine a.m. She yawned, flipped off the downstairs lights, and trudged up the stairs. Mike had left the light on in her painting room, so she passed the closed door to the master and peeked inside, half-hoping he'd left her some sort of note. She kicked herself for being silly.

"Mr. Handyman, get out of my head," she mumbled, "and into my bed."

As if on cue, her easel collapsed backward, the canvas falling and knocking down a landscape. That uncovered the portrait of her mother, and Annie gasped. Her mother's eyes seemed to glow red hot, the painting itself looking three-dimensional, as if her mother might crawl off the canvas and slap her across her face for saying such a dirty thing.

Annie squeezed her eyes shut and shook her head. When she opened them again, the portrait looked normal, like nothing had happened.

"I know what I saw," she said, switching off the light and closing the door with a slam. "I might be going crazy, but I know what I just saw."

She had to pee, but the thought of using her mother's bathroom felt like a knife held over her heart, so she ran to her room, jumped in bed, and pulled the blanket up to her chin.

So much for sleeping.

Chapter Twelve

Mike swung his truck into a parking slot and jumped out into the drizzle. Water splashed up, soaking his socks and drenching his pants legs, but he didn't stop. He jogged around the other cars, dodged a mom leading her son by the hand, and dashed up to the elementary school door. He stopped, looked into the security camera, and rang the bell.

On most days, the secretary Norma would greet him over the intercom. Today, she just buzzed him in.

He popped into the office and signed in. Norma looked at him over the top of her thin, wire-rimmed glasses. Her skin was the color of cherry wood, her lips bright red.

"Bell rang thirty minutes ago," she said. "Principal took her to the library."

Mike thanked her and ran down the hallway, acutely aware of breaking the no-running-in-the-hallway rule. He burst into the library thirty minutes late, but that thirty minutes seemed more like an eternity.

Maria—and every other student in the library, about fifteen total—looked up as Mike slid to a stop, panting from the exertion of sprinting at 5,280 feet above sea level. Even the principal—a stout, graying woman in a cardigan—glared at him, holding her finger to her lips and shushing him. Mike felt color rising in his cheeks, and noted the same on his daughter's normally pale face. Her mouth stood in a silent "O" and her left hand jumped to cover it. Before her, books and notebook paper spread out on a table.

Mike gathered his composure and stood before the principal's desk, still puffing a little. The principal shushed her students, stood, and waved Mike off to one side, behind a low bookshelf.

"Mr. Tolbert," she said in a hoarse whisper that Mike was pretty sure the kids could still hear, "you're a half-hour late. You're lucky we had a detention class today, so I could keep Maria safe, but if you cannot get here on time reliably, you and your wife will need to make other, more dependable arrangements."

"My *ex*-wife," Mike explained. "And I apologize. I had a job run late. I got here as soon as I could."

"Explain it to your daughter," the principal said. "And your...daughter's mother. She's on her way."

"You called Michelle?" Mike's gut twisted, trying to do a flip.

"I had no choice. I had no one to pick Maria up. I couldn't risk—"

Mike wheeled away from her and walked to Maria. "Let's go."

Maria looked at him, confused.

"Come on, let's go," he repeated. "I need to get to my next job."

"Dad, I don't want to go to work with you," she whined, gathering up her books. "I'd rather stay here and do homework until Mom comes."

"There's no time for arguing," he told her. "You don't have detention, so let's go."

She rolled her eyes and shoved her books in her backpack. "It's so boring waiting while you work," she complained. "There's nothing to do."

"You can do your homework there," he said. "We'll be at a friend's house, so if you behave while I fix her bathroom wiring, you and I will do a movie and pizza later."

She perked up, but it had nothing to do with pizza or a movie. "We're going to Annie's house?" Her face lit up like a tiny Christmas tree. "Cool!"

Mike led her from the library, walking fast. He couldn't risk running into Michelle.

"How do you know about Annie?"

She grinned at him, a knowing, satisfied smile that beamed with pride. "You said her name in your sleep the last time I visited."

"You were watching me sleep?" He felt a bit creeped out.

"I had a dream and came to talk to you," she said. "But you were asleep on the couch, talking about Annie."

Outside, the drizzle slipped down Mike's arms and neck, making him shiver. His truck beeped as he unlocked it, and he winced, ready for the alarm to go ballistic again.

"What was I saying about Annie?" he asked, climbing in as Maria jumped into the passenger seat and buckled up.

"You sounded angry," she said, smiling again. She enjoyed this way too much. "No, not angry. Irritated, like she was teasing you and you didn't like it. Much."

Mike pulled out into traffic, choosing not to reply.

"Is she your girlfriend?"

Mike chuckled. "No, not my girlfriend. Just my friend, like I said. We went out once."

She stared at him, the mischievous grin still plastered on her face.

"What?" Mike asked. "Why are you staring at me?"

"Why do you smile so much when you talk about her?"

Mike guided his truck through an intersection, then looked at her. "I do not. My expression doesn't change at all when I talk about Annie."

She giggled and looked out her window at the falling rain, but said nothing.

Mike felt like he should fill the silence, should keep the momentum going, but he didn't know what he should say. His cellphone bailed him out.

Michelle, of course.

He answered it through the truck's stereo.

"Hi, Michelle."

"Hi, Mom," said Maria.

A pause made Mike smile. He'd caught his ex off-guard.

"Hi, baby," Michelle said to her daughter. "Mike, can we talk privately?"

"Can't do, Michelle. I'm driving. It would be unsafe."

Another pause. She hadn't expected that either. "You picked up Maria, then?"

She kept her voice almost neutral, but the slightest edge of irritation slipped in, audible through the phone line.

"I did. We're going to hang out with a friend and watch a movie."

"A friend?" She sounded disappointed. "I was hoping you'd come over here, to my place. Maybe we could watch a movie together, you know, like a family."

The hair on Mike's arm stood up. This sounded like another trap of hers.

"I'm not sure that's a good idea," he responded, choosing his words like a surgeon chooses instruments. "Besides, I made these plans a week ago. I can't cancel them now."

"So some friend is more important than your family?"

And the trap sprung.

"No offense, Michelle," he said, still walking through an emotional minefield, "you and I aren't family anymore. We're divorced."

"Maria, baby," Maria listened intently beside him as Michelle spoke, "would you rather come stay with me tonight? No need to be a third wheel on Daddy's date."

The bitch. Using Maria to manipulate him pissed Mike off.

"Stop it, Michelle," he snapped. He pulled over to make sure he could argue safely. "Tonight's my visitation night. She'll be staying with me."

Michelle started to answer, but Mike pushed the "End Call" button on his steering wheel and looked at Maria. To his surprise, she smiled even wider than before.

*

Annie steered her car down East Colfax, wipers beating an intermittent rhythm as drizzle coated the glass in between each swipe. Traffic didn't slow her much, as most people still slaved away at their desks. Annie had left early, telling Carol the truth: She had a migraine. She didn't get them often—not even enough for her to see a doctor—but when she had them, they debilitated her, crawling up her shoulders, tying her neck in knots, and making her head feel like it was slammed in a door. If they lasted long enough, her vision would blur and she'd eventually pass out.

Of course, the fact that Mike would be fixing her wiring that afternoon may have played into her decision to leave work, too. He might need help, after all.

She eased to a stop at a red light, rubbing her temples and breathing in slow, measured breaths. She tried not to stress, even though city traffic drove her nuts. It wouldn't happen in most cases if people weren't trying to cut in line or do something else stupid. Yet people continued to pass on the right, force their way into lines, and merge like idiots. No one in Colorado seemed to know how to merge. It wasn't rocket science, but for some reason, no one knew how to do it right.

Traffic moved again, and Annie let her own Fiesta drift forward with it. As she drove west, into the setting sun, her cellphone rang, the caller ID showing an unknown number. Before she could send the call to voicemail, her car's Bluetooth picked up, leaving her no choice.

"Hello?"

Silence.

"Hello, can I help you?"

"Annie, it's Frank."

He slurred the last two words together, making Annie roll her eyes.

"Frank, you're drunk."

"Fuck you, bitch," he said. "Don't sit there and judge me from your piece of shit Fiesta. You're not better than me."

Her neck muscles locked up even more, making her see stars. Was he watching her? Following her? She looked around frantically, but didn't see his car. "I'm hanging up now, Frank. Don't call me again or I'll get that restraining order."

"We will ruin you," he slurred. "We can take your life apart, make it hell."

"Who's *we*, Frank?" She didn't think there was anyone else with him. He just wanted to frighten her. "Who's with you?"

He stammered, stumbling over his words as he tried to backpedal. "There's no one else. No one. It's just me. Just me."

Something about his voice, a fear she hadn't heard before, made her throat tighten like her shoulder muscles. She croaked her words. "Where are you, Frank? And who's with you?"

"I'm alone," he said. "I like your paintings. The one of your mom, though—that one sucks. Oh wait, that's all you paint...your pathetic, dead mommy."

Her heart rate skyrocketed, crashing in her chest as if she were running at full speed. She gunned her motor, swerved around a pickup truck, and turned south on a side street.

"Get the hell out of my house you sick bastard! I'm hanging up and calling the cops right now!"

She ended the call and fishtailed left. A few blocks later, she turned left again, onto her street, her tires sloshing across the wet asphalt.

She plunged into the tunnel of her street, the large oaks, elms, and maples on both sides coming together to form a canopy that shrouded most of the street. Unlike Colfax, the drizzle hadn't pooled here yet, the pavement damp, but not drenched, so she didn't slosh or fishtail.

She saw it immediately, her migraine spiking as soon as she did. Mrs. Mudge stood on her porch, clipboard in her hand, scribbling manically. Her front door stood open. Annie screeched to a stop at the curb, threw open her door, and stormed out of her car.

"What the hell are you doing?" she yelled. "And where the hell is Frank?"

Mudge put her hands on her hips, holding the clipboard against her black skirt. "I'm conducting an inspection of your property, as authorized by the covenants. Who's Frank?"

Annie pushed past her and studied the front door. No sign of forced entry—did Frank have a key somehow? She wheeled on Mudge.

"Did you open this door? Did you go inside?"

Mudge looked insulted. "I did neither. My authority doesn't extend to your interior, so—"

"Did you see anyone else?"

Mudge seemed to soften a bit, her posture relaxing ever so little. "No, no one. Did you not leave the door open?"

"Of course not," Annie said. "I locked up before I left. You're sure you didn't see anyone? Maybe a bald guy with a goatee?"

"No one," Mudge said. "I will call the police."

Mudge pulled out an archaic flip phone and dialed. Annie nodded and slipped inside the door, tiptoeing to the stairs. She paused and listened, straining to hear even the slightest sound. She heard nothing.

She checked the downstairs—kitchen, living room, and dining room—and found only one thing out of order: The kitchen door stood open into her back yard.

As she mounted the stairs, Mudge poked her head in the front door.

"The police will send someone as soon as possible. I don't think exploring your house is a good idea. You should wait for the police."

"I appreciate your concern," Annie said, "but he's gone. I'm perfectly safe in here."

"Who's gone?"

"My ex. He called while I was driving home and described something inside the house to me, something he only could have seen from inside."

Mudge gasped and straightened. "I still think it would be best if you let them clear the house. Just in case."

Annie couldn't disagree with the old bat, so she joined her on the porch. Mudge studied her for a moment, looking unsure about what to say. "You still have a lot of repairs to make."

Annie rolled her eyes. "I've had some inside stuff to take care of. My dishwasher, an electrical fire. I'll get on the—"

"Your primary responsibility is to maintain the exterior of your home in accordance with Historical Society standards. If you cannot do so, you will leave us no choice but to force your compliance."

Annie spun toward her, jabbing her index finger into the taller woman's chest. "I'll get the exterior items fixed on time. I just hired a contractor who has agreed to do the work to your standards. He will start next week."

Mudge sniffed and looked at her checklist. "Shutters falling off. Yard un-mowed. Weeds everywhere. Paint peeling. Broken window. Sidewalk cracking." She looked Annie up and down, peering over her prudish spectacles. "That's a lot to fix in the time you have remaining. I'm not sure you can get it done, given your...lack of enthusiasm for our rules."

Rules. This was all about the rules, all about forcing compliance to make the point that Mudge had power. A conservative, snooty, stuffy old woman forcing her will on the young, rebellious, ungrateful girl with all the tattoos. Keeping the neighborhood's historical flavor alive was simply an excuse for her to push Annie around.

But forcing a confrontation wouldn't do Annie any good. She just wanted Mudge off her porch. A police car rounded the corner onto the block.

"Thank you, Mrs. Mudge," Annie told the older woman. "I give you my word that it will be done, as you say, and on time. I'm not arguing with you, but right now, I need to deal with this possible break-in. Frank's been stalking me for months now. I know the Historical Society wouldn't want anything to happen to a resident."

Mudge stared at her a moment, then nodded. "Very well. You're right. We will deal with this intrusion first. Safety is most important."

"We?"

Mudge tucked her clipboard under her arm. "Of course. The police will want my statement that the door was open when I got here, and no one was visible in or around the house. You and I can talk about the standards another time."

Annie thought for a single, fleeting moment about telling the police that Mudge had been leaving the house. They'd arrest her without hesitation, probably on Annie's word alone. It might get the woman off Annie's case for a week or two, but in the end, she'd be back, madder than ever. Besides, Annie hated liars and lying, so she rubbed her throbbing neck, swallowed her pride, and kept her voice pliant.

"Thank you."

Mudge nodded as the police car rolled to a stop at the curb.

The police searched her house and declared it clear. She told them about Frank's phone call, explaining how he'd been harassing her, but when they looked at her phone, they found only unknown numbers during the times he'd called. Most showed all zeroes as the calling number.

The responding officer—a muscular man who looked like he'd just left high school—told her they would talk to Frank, but would need more concrete proof of stalking before they could do anything else.

"You really should get a restraining order, ma'am," he told her. "Then we can haul him to jail anytime he gets close enough to you or your home to violate the order."

Annie told him she would look into it, and thanked him as he left. Mudge shot her an icy glare and walked back up the sidewalk as well, leaving Annie alone on her front porch.

She thought about going inside, but her home no longer felt like hers. It felt violated, like someone had robbed it of its safety. She wondered if Frank had planted cameras somewhere, designed to record her getting dressed, bathing, or sleeping.

Sighing, she moved toward the door. It would take most of the night for her to search the house, and her migraine had gotten worse. She doubted much sleep was in store for her night.

Chapter Thirteen

Mike pulled up to Annie's house as a cop car rounded the corner out of the neighborhood. He watched it go, easing his truck down the street. Annie hadn't seen him, and she closed the door behind her as she went inside.

"She's cute!" Maria said from the seat beside him. Her face lit up as she talked, and she rocked forward against her seatbelt. "And there's a lot to fix outside—that's perfect!"

Mike chuckled and looked at her sidelong. He'd given her a quick summary of his relationship with Annie, leaving out the part about her struggles at work and with her mother.

"How do you figure that's good?"

She rolled her eyes and pinched him on the arm. "Because it gives you plenty of reason to be here and make up for that blundered date!"

"Hey, now, she's already forgiven me for that," he said. "I don't need to make up for it anymore."

"Okay, how about making up for getting her in trouble at work?"

Mike pulled to a stop outside Annie's house. In the distance ahead, an old woman strode away down the sidewalk, her back military-straight.

"Yeah, you might have a point there," he said.

They piled out of the truck, with Mike grabbing his large toolbox and Maria grabbing his small tool bag. Together, they marched up the steps and Mike let Maria ring the doorbell.

A few seconds later, Annie answered the door. Her eyes glistened, puffy and pink, and she sniffled as she looked up. When she saw Mike, her eyes opened wide and she gasped.

"Oh, God, I forgot you were coming," she said, wheeling around and wiping at her eyes with her shirt sleeve. "I'm sorry, come in."

Mike closed the door after Maria slipped in behind him. She looked at the floor and shuffled her feet, obviously feeling awkward.

"Is everything all right?" Mike asked Annie.

She took a deep breath, straightened her shoulders, and looked at him.

"Yeah, I'm fine. Who is this, your apprentice?"

Before Mike could answer, Maria stepped around him and extended her hand. "I'm Maria, his daughter. You must be Annie?"

Annie smiled and shook her hand. "I must be, huh?" She leaned down close to Maria's ear. "I don't know what your dad has said about me, but it's all a lie."

Maria giggled and whispered back, loud enough for Mike to hear, "The same goes. I'm not nearly the demon he says I am."

The two of them shared a laugh that told Mike he was now outnumbered and should probably seek legal counsel.

"Well, I'll leave you two to get acquainted," he said, taking the tool bag from Maria. "I'll get started in the bathroom.

Should take about an hour, kiddo. Then we'll grab pizza and go see that movie."

Maria nodded and followed Annie to the kitchen, while Mike went upstairs.

Two hours later, he had cut through the drywall under the sink, following the wires all the way down to the base, where they turned left and headed out of the room. They looked like they'd been replaced during the renovation, and while not the newest materials, they weren't hazardous. So Mike decided to replace the wires to the floor, and the outlet, rather than all the wires. That would save Annie some material costs and him some time.

Knowing he was running late, he went downstairs to check on Maria. He found her with Annie in the living room, the two curled up on the couch in front of Annie's big screen. Annie sat on one end of the sectional, with Maria right next to her, leaving the other end open. Annie scrolled through a list of chick flicks while they discussed which one to watch. As he opened his mouth to ask how Maria was doing, the doorbell rang.

"Mike, can you get that?" Annie asked, not looking away from the television.

Maria smiled back over her shoulder. "Yeah, Dad, that should be the pizza guy. Annie already paid for it."

"How did you guys know I was here?"

"You think you're quiet, Dad, but you're not."

Mike shrugged and went to the front door. The pizza guy turned out to be a teenage girl with a face that looked like a pizza and thick glasses low on her nose. She handed him two pizzas, but when he took out a couple of bucks to tip her, she waved it off.

"Already handled, sir. Your wife's a great customer."

"She's not my—"

She turned and walked away, not even listening. Mike stood a moment, watching the drizzle fall from the iron-gray sky to the lighter gray concrete, wondering why he'd insisted on clarifying their relationship. But then the fresh scent of marinara, oregano, and garlic hit him and his stomach growled. He took the pizzas to the dining room table, where a stack of paper plates sat, and called through the opening into the living room.

"Chow's on, ladies!"

Maria moved cat-quick, bursting into the dining room and falling on the pizza like a starved bobcat. Annie followed at a more leisurely pace, standing next to Mike as they watched the nine-year-old load up a plate with three slices, then drop into a wooden chair to scarf them down.

"It's going to take me another hour or so," Mike told Annie. "Then we'll be out of your hair."

"You're not in my hair," she answered, keeping her voice low. "Maria's a great kid, Mike. And honestly, I'm glad for the company tonight."

Her voice quavered as she spoke.

"What happened today?" he asked her. "You seem really rattled."

She shook herself and ran her fingers through her curly, dark hair. She gave him a look of exhaustion.

"I'm all right. Just a rough day."

"Talk about it?"

She shook her head. "Another time. I want to get my mind off things right now. So I'm going to steal your movie date, if that's okay. We're going to watch something gooey and romantic."

"I'll try to keep the noise down upstairs, then." He gave her shoulder a quick squeeze. "When you're ready to talk, you know how to find me."

She nodded and motioned to the pizza. "Help yourself. You're the one doing work here."

She winked at him and he took her advice. The pizza hit the spot and he went back upstairs recharged.

When he finally finished up, he stood back and admired his handiwork. The scorch marks around the outlet were gone, and the color of the new faceplate matched that of the light switch and second plug almost perfectly. He'd been unable to replace the burned wallpaper, so he'd put a slightly larger plate, covering the singed portions. The sheetrock underneath had been painted, not papered, as it sat inside the sink vanity, so he'd patched the hole, then filled and sanded the seams. He'd paint it later, once the mud had dried.

Satisfied for the moment, he cleaned up and carried his tool kits downstairs, placing them by the front door. The sound of the television carried down the hallway, muffled and muted. The flickering silver light danced like a fairy on the wall outside the living room. He walked to the room and stood, reveling in what he saw.

Annie still sat at the end of the couch, head nodding to one side. Maria had curled on beside her, her blonde hair tumbling across Annie's lap while the girl slept. For a moment, Mike wanted nothing more than to stand there, drinking in the pure peacefulness of the scene, seeing his daughter's innocence and Annie's tender side like never before.

Annie seemed to sense his presence, though, and turned her head. "Hey. All done?"

Mike nodded, but didn't speak. Words escaped his grasp like butterflies slipping out of reach.

"What?" Annie asked. She twisted on the couch, making Maria squirm and breaking the spell over the room. "Is something wrong?"

"No, nothing at all," Mike said. "Just enjoying the peace and quiet."

Annie's smile crackled with warmth, telling him she understood. She motioned to the open spot on the couch, patting the cushion with her hand. On the screen, Ryan Gosling mentored Steve Carell on picking up a woman in a bar.

"You watched this with my nine-year-old?" He kept his tone light and grinned at her as he sat on the couch. He patted Maria's foot, making her stretch it out to rest in his lap. "You doing better?"

Annie nodded, looking at ease for the first time all night. "I am now. Thanks for letting me borrow her."

Mike nodded. "Well, your bathroom is almost done. I just need to paint under the sink."

"No problem," she told him with a wave of her hand. "As long as I can use the bathroom, we're good to go."

"It's useable," he told her. "If I can ask, why don't you use the master suite?"

She looked away, returning her attention to the movie. "It was my mother's."

She left it at that, as if Mike should understand what she meant.

"Don't you think she'd want you to use it?" he asked. "To be comfortable?"

She clicked the remote, turning down the movie, and turned her green-eyed gaze on him. For a moment, something lingered there he didn't recognize, a depth that made her eyes look like oceans. Then it was gone.

"You didn't know my mother," she said. "Growing up, we were forbidden access to her room. Going in there would buy us a spanking and grounding. She called it her domain, her kingdom. When we were little, she told us she kept a giant snake under the bed, and if we went in, it would eat us. Later, she just promised us punishment for going in. It's stupid, but I'm still terrified of that room.

"After Dad left—when I was six—Mom turned meaner. She drank a lot and turned into a control freak. We had to do exactly what she wanted or we'd pay the price. She controlled who we saw, what we read and watched, where we went. Even when we did most things. She used to order me to go to the bathroom. I told her once that I didn't have to. Know what she said?"

Mike shook his head.

"She told me I was lying, that I needed to pee but was too lazy to get off my butt and do it. She said I'd rather wet my pants than go to the bathroom. She scared me so much I went to the toilet and peed as much as I could, then sat there until I thought she'd be happy. I wasn't mothered, Mike—I was smothered."

"That's awful, but she's gone now, Annie. She can't punish you."

Annie sighed and her gaze slid outward, far away for a moment, like she was looking at something out the window.

"I don't know sometimes." Her voice sounded like she was dreaming. "Sometimes I think she's still here, watching me."

Mike stared at the TV, unsure how to respond. He'd known her mom drank a lot, but the rest was new information and he needed time to process it. Annie seemed to sense his discomfort.

"Anyway, enough of my depressing drama," she said, forcing life into her voice. "How's your life going?"

Mike laughed. "Well, as long as I have Pipsqueak here, my life is great. I screwed up today, though. Picked her up late. Job ran long and I got to the school late—first time all year. There are only two days of school left, but I couldn't do it. Couldn't pull off the perfect year without being late. Needless to say, Michelle was not happy."

On the television, Steve Carell argued with his ex-wife over his new-found love-life.

"The school called her?" Annie asked. Mike nodded. "Bummer. What about Maria?"

"She was pretty upset until she found out we were coming here."

That made Annie grin, and her eyes lit up. She combed Maria's hair with her fingers.

"I like her," she said. "She has a good heart, something you don't find often these days. You've done well with her, Mike. Don't kick yourself for every mistake. If you're feeling like a bad parent, come ask me about my mother and you'll feel better."

The volume jumped up, Gosling's voice slicing through the softness of the moment. Annie fumbled with the remote, but managed to get it turned back down after a moment. In her lap, Maria stirred.

Annie stroked her hair again and the girl calmed.

Mike decided to take a chance. "So, you want to take another shot at that dinner? Maybe someplace more reasonable this time? And I'll bring cash, just in case."

Annie pursed her lips in thought, making a show of tapping her chin with her forefinger. Mike rolled his eyes in mock indignation.

"Oh, come on," he said. "How long will you punish me for one bad date?"

"Well, mandatory sentence would be at least six months." An impish grin played on her lips. "But I suppose you could get time off for good behavior."

"So is that a yes?"

She nodded, but before she could say anything, the television went to static, the hissing sound exploding through the room. Mike's heart rate jumped, his neck muscles bunching. Annie patted his arm, and her touch soothed him.

Maria, though, sat bolt upright, her eyes wide.

"Stop that!" she snapped, looking at the TV.

Annie clicked the power button on the remote, but the TV stayed on. She tried again with the same result. Finally, Mike stood and turned it off on the set, surprised to find his heart pounding the instant he broke contact with Annie.

"What the hell was that about?" he asked.

Annie looked at her hands. "Things like that keep happening. Remember the disposal the first night you came here?'

Mike nodded. Maria looked Annie in the eye and said, "The lady changed it."

Mike and Annie both gaped at her.

"Annie didn't do anything, sweetie," Mike told her.

"Not Annie," his daughter explained. "The older lady. She changed it. She turned it up, too."

Mike and Annie exchanged a look of confusion.

"What did this lady look like?" she asked Maria. "Can you describe her?"

"Of course," Maria said. "She's old, has black hair, and is wearing a blue dress. It's pretty."

Annie's hands flew to her mouth, stifling a gasp. Even Mike's gut twisted itself into a knot. As far as he knew, she'd never been to the painting room, and hadn't seen the portrait of Annie's mother. Neither had he told her about the woman. She must have overheard their discussion, but they hadn't discussed what Annie's mother looked like.

"Can you see her now?" Annie asked. "Is she here with us?"

Maria shook her head, the adults' fear reflecting in her downcast gaze.

Annie rose, brushed her hands on her jeans, and sighed.

"Well, it's late," she said to Mike. "You'd probably better get her home to bed."

Mike could see the discomfort on her face. This really bothered her, but she didn't want them to see it.

He nodded and took Maria's hand. Annie walked them to the front door.

"So, Friday night, Applebee's?" Mike asked.

That put a smile back on her face, if fleetingly. "Friday night it is."

In the living room, the television came back on, volume blasting static through the home.

"Thank you!" Maria yelled.

Annie paled and dashed for the living room while Mike led his daughter to the truck, wondering what he'd gotten himself into.

Chapter Fourteen

Annie put her head in her hands and yawned. Just closing her eyes helped her feel better. She wished she could put her head down on her desk and sleep.

The antiseptic fluorescent lights burned her eyes and their incessant buzzing echoed at the base of her skull, giving her the beginnings of another migraine. Maybe here, in the mind-numbing din of the cubicle farm, she'd be able to fall asleep. Since Wednesday night—when Mike and Maria had been at her place—she'd gotten exactly three hours of sleep, two of them that night. She intentionally didn't look in anything reflective, not wanting to see the dark circles under her eyes or the rat's nest of hair on her head.

"Hey, Annie, you all right?"

She pried her eyes open, lifted her head from her hands, and found Veronica there looking at her, forehead creased.

"Peachy," she grumbled, putting her head back down.

"Do you need an aspirin? Caffeine?"

"I need sleep." She didn't even care if her words were muffled by her palms. "About three days of it."

Veronica's hand found her shoulder for a quick squeeze, a move that surprised Annie. She'd always assumed Veronica talked to her for gossip, to gather things to tell other coworkers. It never occurred to her she might actually care.

"Well, you'll get two days of it starting tomorrow!" The blonde was entirely too chipper. Annie wanted to puke.

Instead, she lifted her head, rubbed the sleep out of her eyes, and ran her hand through her hair. A couple of strands fell to the wood-grain surface of her desk.

"Yeah, but I need to get through tonight first." She regretted it as soon as she said it. This was the gossip the blonde wanted.

"What's tonight that's so..." Her hand jumped to her mouth. "You have a date, don't you?"

Annie plopped her head back into her hands. No use denying it now.

"I'm seeing Mike again," she mumbled. "Call it a pity date."

To be honest, Annie didn't know how she felt about the date. Part of her looked forward to it, causing the slightest excitement. But part of her dreaded it, fearing she'd see Mike's anger and rage again. She couldn't handle that.

But Veronica bounced up and down, clapping like a middle-schooler. "That's so awesome!" the hapless, virtual teenager said in a sing-song voice. "I'm happy you're giving him another chance."

Yeah, it gives you something to talk about behind my back, Annie thought. She kicked herself for her negativity. She couldn't let herself be this jaded at twenty-eight.

"Yeah, lucky him. He gets to date a zombie woman. That'll be thrilling for both of us."

Veronica turned to go. "Well, you know one thing that helps you relax and sleep, Annie." She winked and nudged Annie. "A little mattress workout at bedtime does the trick. Think about it. Two birds with one stone."

Once she'd gone, Annie pulled a bottle of Diet Pepsi from her desk drawer, unscrewed the top, and took a deep pull. Bubbles up her nose perked her up a bit.

Maybe Veronica had a point. Seeing Mike with Maria, and getting to know the girl herself, had changed things for Annie. She didn't see herself as mommy material—her own mother had been a rotten example—but she liked the dynamic between the two, and if Maria reflected even a little of Mike, Annie loved what she saw. The girl was smart and polite, but with a sassy side that spoke to her self-confidence. Annie saw a lot of her father in her, and that was most definitely a point in Mike's favor. It was hard enough to raise a kid, but to do so in a split family with the issues he had told her about reflected how capable he was.

And he certainly passed her physical requirements for a potential bed-mate. Good looking, fit, and apparently at least somewhat clean for a handyman. Those blue eyes could lock her up in a room and his roguish smile—tilted ever so slightly up on the right—just about melted her knees into wiggly blobs of gelatin.

So maybe Veronica had a point.

But where? She hadn't been in a guy's place since Frank's attempted assault, and wasn't sure she was ready to trust Mike that much. In her place she had more control, more safety.

But her house was completely out of the question. She hadn't slept for a reason, and she didn't think she could focus on being romantic with Mike given the odd goings-on in her home.

Wednesday night's TV happenings had been just part of it. She'd heard a woman's voice. Seen things moving in the corner of her eye, felt someone watching her. And there were the cold spots, pockets of icy air that either passed over her or that she passed through. And they smelled, reeked of rotten meat or dead things, like a cat's corpse left too long under the porch.

She'd gotten two hours' sleep that night, waking up to knocks, creaks, groans, and bumps, most of them probably normal for an old house. Or so she'd rationalized.

The next night, last night, she'd tried sleeping in the living room, curled up on the couch with the lights on and her flat screen unplugged. She'd just nodded off when she heard footsteps upstairs, right over her, coming from the master bedroom above. She thought about going to her bedroom, to the relative safety of her blankets, but that meant passing the master. Her hands shaking, she'd plugged the TV in and watched old movies all night. It had been a long night, and Annie had started doubting her decision to keep the house.

Her cell phone ringing shook her back to reality. She glanced at caller ID and saw Daniel's number. She thought about not answering—talking to her half-brother would only make her migraine worse. In the end, her sense of family won out and she picked up.

"Hi, Daniel," she said. "I hope your day is going better than mine."

"Today just started. How can it be going wrong already?" His voice was deep as the ocean and dripping with the salt of spite.

"Your day just started," she corrected him. "I've been here two hours already."

"You spend too much time at work," he told her. "Especially at a job that has so little future for you. How much can you make as a minor advertising specialist, anyway?"

"I make enough to get by. Did you call just to insult my job?"

"I drove by the house yesterday," he said. Annie rolled her eyes. She'd known this was coming sooner or later. "I noticed you still haven't managed to fix up the exterior. You know they have a lien on the house, right? They could take you back to court."

"I realize that, Danny." She used his nickname because she knew it irked him. He preferred Daniel. "I'll get it done on time, don't worry."

"I knew you couldn't handle the responsibility." The anger oozed from his voice. "I told the judge that. If I owned it, I'd have it fixed by now, and be selling it for a profit."

She leaned forward, almost down to her desk, hoping no one in the office would hear her.

"Danny, you stayed there a couple of weeks after Mom died, right?"

Her question must have surprised him, for his response took a moment. "Yes, three weeks, almost a month. Just one more reason the house should have gone to me. You never cared—"

She cut him off. "Listen for a minute, Danny. Did you notice anything unusual in the house during that time?'

"Like what?"

"I don't know. Noises. Lights going on or off. Cold spots. That kind of thing."

He paused again before replying. "What's going on here, Annie?"

She told him about the last two nights, and all the strange things before, too. She laid it all out, hoping he'd know what was going on or at least verify that he'd seen similar things.

"It sounds like maybe some of Mom's addiction might have gotten ahold of you, because you're saying you think the house is haunted. And that's either nuts or the product of too much booze."

"So nothing like that happened while you lived there?"

"Look, it's an old house, Annie. They're drafty. They creak and groan. The wiring is old—as you found out—and sometimes they even smell funny. That's one of the reasons you gut them and renovate, which I would have done. I'd be turning a profit by now!"

"Oh my God, Danny, is profit all you care about? We grew up in that house. It has memories for us."

"Yeah, shitty ones. Memories of Mom drinking, Dad leaving. Control. Yelling and screaming and spanking and... nothing I want to remember, that's for sure."

She understood now why he wanted so bad to sell the place—it was his way of purging the demons, of making the past disappear. Her annoyance at him changed to pity.

"Come on, Daniel," she said, leaning back, "I know our childhood wasn't the greatest there, but we both deal with it differently. I do it by living there, by proving to myself that I can be me without letting that past determine who I am. It's my way of beating her, I guess."

Daniel said nothing, so she went on.

"Anyway, I hired a handyman to make all those repairs, and he says he can get them done on time. Then we can talk about interior renovations."

If she'd hoped for a positive response, she got none.

"What does it matter?" he asked. "You'll still own it, and I'll still drive by, knowing it's still in the family. The house isn't haunted, we are. As long as it's in the family, she still has control. You think you're beating her, but you're letting her control you." His voice was getting louder, fraught with tension. "Can't you see? That's why she left it to you, because she knew you'd live there. She wanted that house to stay in the family forever."

"Daniel, relax," she urged. "Don't forget your heart. The doctor told you to keep calm. I know we disagree on this, but it's not worth risking your health."

"Don't patronize me! You know damned well I'm right, you just want me to calm down so you don't have to hear about it."

"Maybe you're right, Daniel," she said. "Maybe I'm playing right into her hands a year after she died, but I don't want to lose you, no matter what. So please, please relax."

He took a deep breath. "Fine. Don't say I didn't warn you. Get the house fixed before you wind up in court or lose the house. Then we make nothing off it. Nothing at all."

He hung up without saying goodbye.

Annie slapped her phone on her desk and rubbed the back of her neck.

"Ahem."

Annie jumped up out of her chair, spinning around and finding Carol standing there, arms crossed over her tiny, flat chest.

"Sounds like a personal call on company time," she said. "Do I need to remind you of our policy?"

More like your policy, Annie thought. "No," she said, looking at the floor. "I'm sorry, my brother called. I'll mark it as personal time on my timesheet."

"I expect you to produce while you're here, Annie. We're still short someone in Frank's position, thanks to his firing, and the rest of you need to pick up that load."

Inside, Annie fumed at the remark, but she kept her face stolid. "I understand. It won't happen again."

Her cellphone rang again, making Carol's eyebrows arch. Annie looked at the phone—it was Mike. She sent it to voice mail with a swipe of her index finger then turned her phone off.

"I'll do better," she promised.

"I should hope so." Her boss marched off, no doubt reveling in her victory. Annie stood, watching her tiny back, wishing for a drink.

Chapter Fifteen

Mike pulled out the chair for Annie to sit, but she didn't even see his act of chivalry, for she was engrossed in a yawn that brought tears to her eyes.

"Oh, geez, I'm sorry," she said, slipping off her knee-length raincoat and hanging it on the back of the chair. She sat, allowing him to at least push her in a bit. "I'm not used to a guy who knows table manners."

"Seriously?" Mike asked. "Frank never—"

"Not even once," she interrupted him. "But we're not going to talk about him tonight. You already know that sob story."

Mike had chosen the chair that put his back against the wall, and now he sat, his gaze darting around the room before settling on Annie. He flashed his disarming smile and seemed to relax.

So far, so good.

Around them, the Friday night Applebee's crowd went about their business to the muffled sounds of silverware clinking through polite conversation. Even the crowd at the bar—mostly middle-aged businessmen watching a Rockies game—were subdued. Outside the windows, rain pattered down on South Colorado Boulevard, turning the evening commute into a swishing mess. He'd waited in his truck for her to arrive, then rushed to the door of her Fiesta, holding an umbrella over her while she got out. She smiled, remembering how soaked his jeans had been when they finally got to the restaurant door. He'd sacrificed his comfort for hers, something Frank never would have done.

"How was work?" he asked, looking her in the eye.

"Oh, just as wonderful and rewarding as ever. Carol's such a dynamic leader. She counseled me today on having personal phone conversations during company hours."

"Ah, so that's why I went to voicemail."

She nodded and yawned again, covering her mouth with the back of her hand. She rubbed her eyes, too, but it did little to ease their fatigue. She felt—and probably looked—like she'd been crying for an hour. She needed sleep.

"Hey, do you want to do this another night?" he asked. "I think you could use some rest tonight."

She shook her head. "It's not like I'll get any sleep."

"What do you mean?"

Their server arrived, a perky college student whose bouncing ponytail and chipper demeanor only made Annie feel even more haggard and worn out.

"I'd like a screwdriver," Annie said. Mike's eyes narrowed. She'd surprised him, but he recovered quickly and ordered a beer.

"I thought you didn't drink the hard stuff," he said. "You sure you're all right?"

"I'm fine, Dad." She grinned after saying it, but knew she left a little too much edge on her words. She caught herself and looked down at her lap. "I'm sorry, that was uncalled for."

"No harm, no foul," he replied.

"I know, this is my mother's old drink. But I really need to sleep tonight, so maybe this will help."

For a moment, he looked like he might dig deep, ask her a difficult question. Instead, he gave her a break.

"So why aren't you sleeping? Stress from work?"

Another point in his favor. He knew when not to pry. Maybe his anger on their first date had been a fluke.

She locked eyes with him until it almost seemed awkward, then nodded and sat back. She didn't know why, but she knew she could trust him. It was completely illogical to think so, but she knew in the very core of her being that she could talk to Mike. He'd never tell anyone.

"I'm going to put my faith in you, Mike Tolbert," she said. "I'm going to trust that you'll take me seriously here, and not laugh. I've been yelled at by one man already today, and I don't think I could bear it from another. So promise me none of that will come from you."

"Absolutely not," he promised. "I heard some pretty outlandish things in the PTSD support group I used to attend, so I doubt anything you have to say will faze me much."

She studied him a moment longer, then launched into her story. "Remember the weird stuff that happened when you and Maria were at my house?"

He nodded, but kept his mouth shut.

"Well, that kind of stuff keeps happening," she said. "And it has been since I moved in."

She went on to tell Mike about every out-of-place occurrence that had happened to her, from the incident on moving day to her reasons for losing sleep just last night. The server brought their drinks, and Annie downed hers in one gulp then ordered another. When she finished, he sat back, his hands behind his head, and thought.

"You probably think I'm crazy, don't you?" she asked, as the server delivered her second drink.

"No, not at all," Mike said. "And I think you have two separate things going on in your house. Some things—like the rock through our window and the person you saw outside—appear to be external to the house. Those, I think, are being caused by someone who wants you to be afraid. Very afraid."

Her gut twisted with fear. He'd cut right to the chase, slicing through her distraction to the matter she'd been trying to avoid.

"Frank," she said. "He's been coming around, almost stalking me."

She took it slower with her second drink, telling Mike about Frank's appearances at her house. Before Mike could reply, the server took their food order. When she left, Mike narrowed his eyes at Annie.

"That's not 'almost stalking,'" he told her. "That *is* stalking. I've seen it before. That man is dangerous."

"I know, but—"

"Annie, he was in your house without your permission. He has a way in, a key or something. Where would he have gotten that?"

"I don't know. He could have copied it when we were together, but I didn't live there then. I just had a copy of Mom's key."

Mike leaned in and touched the back of her hand. Her heart skipped a beat. "Doesn't that worry you at all? He's been planning this for some time now."

She smiled and downed the rest of her drink, waving to the server for another.

"No, I mean, he's smart enough not to, you know..."

"Then why have you downed two screwdrivers before our food's even here?"

As if on cue, the server appeared with a tray of food. She set Mike's club sandwich in front of him, then Annie's Cobb salad.

"I'll be right back with your drink, ma'am," she told Annie. Then she looked at Mike, as if asking for his approval. He nodded and she scampered off. It'd been a simple look, one Annie probably would have made if she were the server, but it cut her like a red-hot blade. Had she become that much like her mother that servers would question her sobriety?

"I told you, I need to sleep tonight." She looked at him over the top of her glass. "I will do whatever it takes to finally get a full night's rest." She broke eye contact just as she finished.

"Anyhow," he returned to their original subject as Annie poured ranch dressing on her salad, "you have that stuff going on, and then you have stuff internal to the house happening, like the TV, the voices, and so on. Those could be more Frank bullshit—he could have a universal remote, recording equipment, and so on—but they don't seem his style."

"I agree. So what do you think is going on? Am I imagining all this?"

He shook his head. "Not at all. You live in an old house. Things like this happen. I've seen some of them before. Old lead pipes make noises that sound like voices. Old wiring—like you had in the bathroom—cause things to turn on and off. Things die and rot and smell in the walls or floors and you never find out what they are until you gut the place and renovate.

"With the stress you're under, it's easy to let things like that get in your head, especially with the feelings you have over your mom. Your mind is jumping to conclusions based on pain, fatigue, and stress, not logic."

Annie crossed her arms over her chest, her defenses coming up. "So it's my mind playing tricks on me?"

"I'm not saying that, really. Just that the filters through which you experience things right now are foggy to say the least. You know how the glass in those old windows has distorted and warped, making things look weird sometimes?"

She nodded, the sound of his voice massaging her stress away.

"It's like that, only with a layer of grime and scratches to make things look even worse."

"So you're saying I'm not crazy, just old, warped, dirty, and damaged?"

Mike paused, sandwich just short of his mouth. He grinned back. "Yeah, exactly."

She kicked him in the shin under the table, making him grunt. Then she took a deep breath, sipped her third drink, and leaned back with a sigh.

*

Mike still nursed his first bottle of beer as Annie put her third screwdriver back on the table. Her green eyes were turning glassy, and her words slurred enough to tell him the vodka had kicked in. But at least she was there, talking to him. He hadn't realized how much he'd missed her until he'd seen her little blue car pull into the parking lot in the pouring rain. He hadn't even noticed how wet his own pants were until ten minutes into their meal.

"I suppose that all makes sense," she said. "I'm definitely tired. Work is stressing me out. Frank won't leave me alone. And I have sixty days left to get my house up to standards or Mrs. Mudge and the Historical Society will fine me and take me to court. Could be some stress issues there."

Finally she was thinking straight after just two and a half drinks.

"You let me worry about the house," he said. "That's the easy part of your problems to fix. You need to go get a restraining order against that insane ex of yours before he does something that can't be fixed."

She nodded and re-attacked her salad. "How did you get so good at this?" she asked.

He felt some color rushing to his cheeks, so he shrugged and took a bite of his sandwich, talking and chewing at the same time.

"What you're going through is pretty similar to my PTSD. You've been traumatized, but instead of one huge event causing it, a bunch of little things did. I think your way might be harder to handle than mine. At least I have one root cause too address. You have several."

"I suppose," she said, "but I'd take my mom, Frank, Carol, *and* the house over being in a war zone anytime."

"You keep mentioning your mother, but you have yet to tell me much about her. What did she do that hurt you so much?"

"Oh come on, you don't want to know about my childhood. We have much more exciting things to talk about, like paint colors, construction timelines, and who you'll bring in for landscaping."

"You're not getting out of it that easy," he said, shaking a finger at her. "If you want to continue to have movie nights with my little girl—which will be helpful if I'm working on your house a lot this summer—I need to know a lot more about you. Consider this your background check."

She laughed for the first time that night, a loud, barking sound that caught him so off-guard he jumped. An older couple in a booth a few feet away looked over, then returned to their discussion.

Annie adjusted her chair, pulling in closer to the table, and put down her fork.

"Well, since you put it that way, Mr. Marine sir, I suppose I have no choice." Her eyes glittered, the glow of amusement replacing the fatigue. "Once my stepdad left, Mom changed. She went from protective to over-protective in a flash. I was seven at the time, so I remember a little what she'd been like before.

"She always had plenty of money. It was never about that, since my dad kept paying the mortgage even after he left. Plus, she had alimony and child support coming in from my dad and stepdad, and she had a trust fund my grandfather had left her. So she didn't need to work, though I wish she had."

"What do you mean?" Mike asked. He hadn't talked this in-depth to someone since Michelle had left.

"Once Stepdad left, she had nothing to do but sit around and dwell on it. Eventually it made her paranoid that Daniel and I were going to leave her completely alone. So she did everything she could to keep us dependent on her.

"She restricted how much time we spent with friends. She'd have teachers spy on us, reporting to her about who we hung out with at school. We couldn't go anywhere alone unless we snuck out, and that risked a beating if we got caught."

"She beat you?"

Annie nodded. "She was harder on Daniel, I think because he was a boy and reminded her of my stepdad. His biological dad. But yes, I took a brush across my bottom, a belt on my legs, a yardstick on my thighs, and even a ruler across my knuckles many times. More than I care to think about.

"Daniel's lucky he lived through it. He was born with a faulty heart valve, which leaves him susceptible to heart attacks. He had one when he was fourteen and it almost killed him."

Mike polished off his beer at the same time Annie downed the last of her screwdriver. Her cheeks were turning red now, and she seemed to think carefully before ordering another from the server.

"So did your dad never do anything to stop all this?" Mike asked. "I know I'd never let someone—anyone—do those things to Maria."

"I've never met him." She looked out the window. "He divorced Mom before I was born. Didn't even leave me a note."

"I'm sorry to hear that."

"Don't be," Annie replied, her gaze returning to the restaurant. "My stepdad made up for it at first. He treated me just like his own, and I always thought of him as my dad. Never wanted to see the other guy as long as Chuck was around. But once they left, neither of them ever so much as looked back, which hurt. I blamed myself for a long time, but now I think they were afraid of my mother. She treated them very much the way she'd treated us—controlling, manipulating, and even punishing if they didn't live up to her expectations. I'm surprised neither of them turned to drugs or drinking."

She shifted in her seat and looked him in the eye. "Now...I think it's only fair if you do some sharing, too."

Mike started to protest, but she cut him off with a sharp look from her jade eyes.

"Okay, okay," he said, raising his hands in surrender. "My life story is pretty boring. Only child from Philly. My dad was a cop, Mom was a school teacher, so I learned early on how to get by on little money. And with both of them working full time, I learned to be independent by the time I was ten.

"As soon as I graduated I joined the Marines. A few weeks later, 9/11 happened and I shipped out for Iraq. The rest is history."

He didn't want to talk about the war, didn't want to open those wounds in front of Annie. She wasn't letting him off that easy.

"Come on, the rest is history for you, but not for me. I gave you intimate, personal details, so at least give me something to go on. Something to get to know you better, since I'm trusting you with my home."

Mike leaned back, took a deep breath, and looked into Annie's eyes. She stared back without any hesitation, locking her green eyes on him and refusing to look away.

So he told her about Kyle. She sat silently the entire time, not speaking or judging or trying to intervene when the telling got tough. Even when he started to tear up and had to sit in silence for several minutes to regain his composure, Annie sat patiently, letting him get through the story on his own. Even Collins couldn't show that kind of restraint, and Mike respected her for it.

He moved into his post-war life as they polished off their food, talking about his marriage, about Maria's birth, and finally about his PTSD and the symptoms that came with it.

"Lately, the symptoms have started coming back," he said. "Nightmares, flashbacks, jumping at loud noises. They started getting worse after Michelle and I split up."

When he finished, Annie looked at him over a forkful of rice and raised her eyebrows.

"Are you going back to counseling?" she asked.

"I'm trying," Mike said. "But running your own business doesn't leave you much time for that kind of thing. If I want to make Michelle's payments on time, and not get thrown out of my apartment, I need to work as much as possible."

"Aren't you worried about getting worse?"

He shrugged. "What can I do? Maslow's hierarchy says I have to feed myself before I take care of my psyche."

"Well, don't let it get too bad," she said. "At least not until you get my house fixed up."

They both laughed loud enough to draw disparaging looks from their neighbors, but Mike didn't care. He just wanted to keep talking with her.

The server set down Annie's drink and picked up the empty food plates. She looked at Mike, concern in her eyes. He'd seen that look more than once during his active duty years—a server who knows someone's had enough to drink, but is afraid to cut them off and lose a tip.

"We'll take the check now," he told her with a reassuring smile.

The girl looked relieved as she moved off to tally up their bill. Annie started to reach for her wallet, but Mike cut her off.

"You got the last one," he said. "Let me redeem myself at least a little tonight, though this bill won't be as steep as the one I stuck you with."

"I don't know," Annie replied. "These mixed drinks are pretty expensive. Might add up."

Mike waved it off, covering up his concern with a chuckle. He'd brought a hundred dollars in cash, so that Michelle couldn't ruin this date too, but now he worried it wasn't enough.

He wasn't ready for their talk to end, but the server brought the check, in a hurry to get patrons cycled through. Mike sighed as he realized he had enough to pay and still leave a good tip. He put the little black plastic tray with his payment on the table between them and looked at Annie. Their eyes met, and for a time-stopping moment, they locked that way, neither one looking away. Then she shifted in her seat and glanced down at her empty glass.

"I had fun tonight," she said. Her words slurred just enough for him to notice. "I've never met a guy who opened up like that before, but I still feel like we focused on just me. I want to know more about Mike Tolbert, More Than Handy Man."

"Well," he said, pushing his chair back from the table, "we could head somewhere else and talk about me there. I've always been a fan of the downtown area. Want to head over to LoDo's and continue this discussion there?"

She smiled and stood, but wavered and plopped back down in her chair, rattling their table with her knee. She gripped the table's edge as she tried to steady herself. The same older couple gave her a dirty look, the woman looking Mike over from head to toe, as if appraising his intentions with this very drunk young woman.

After putting her head down and closing her eyes, Annie seemed to gather herself. She rose, slower this time, and steadied herself on her chair.

"Whoa, those hit me harder than I expected."

Mike helped her into her jacket, then held out her purse. She took it, but swayed again as she slung it over her shoulder.

"I think maybe a bar is a bad idea," she told him, plucking her keys from her purse. "I need to go home."

"You're not driving anywhere," he said. "I'll give you a ride."

They walked out to the parking lot, Annie hanging onto Mike's arm for dear life.

"I can't leave my car in an Applebee's parking lot," she said, pointing to her sparkling blue Fiesta. With rain beading on its paint, it looked like an automotive Liberace, glittering in nature's sequins right next to the uncouth Sly Stallone of his truck.

Mike looked up. The restaurant huddled in the shadow of the multi-story Wells Fargo building just to the west. He had an idea.

He led Annie to the passenger door to his truck, opening the door and easing her up onto the seat.

"Give me your keys," he said.

She eyed him, and he couldn't tell if she was suspicious or just couldn't focus on him.

"Are you trying to steal my car?" she slurred. "I mean, you could just drive off in my very expensive Fiesta and leave me here in your dumpy work truck."

Mike tucked her feet into the cab and took the keys as she offered them. "Trust me, Annie, if I were going to steal a car, it would not be a sparkly blue Fiesta."

He eased the passenger door closed and folded himself into her Fiesta's front seat. He had to move the seat back, but once he did, the fit wasn't all that bad. He drove her car about ten yards into a slot under a lamp post in the Wells Fargo building's parking lot, locked it, and returned to the truck.

Climbing into the driver's seat, he could feel Annie's eyes on him.

"No one will touch it in the bank building parking lot," he explained. "There are at least three security cameras looking at it and the lot's well-lit."

She glanced at the car, then back at Mike. She looked confused for a moment, like she couldn't decide what to do. Then she nodded and put her head against the window.

"I'm going to rest a bit," she said.

Mike patted her forearm and backed out of the slot. "You're safe with me."

"I hope so," she said. "I'm kind of betting on it. Just drop me at home and I'll be fine."

Twenty minutes later, as Mike pulled to the curb outside her house, the sound of the rain disappeared under the thick blanket of Annie's snoring. He turned the truck off and nudged her shoulder. She groaned, but didn't wake up. He tried again with the same result. Sighing, he went around, opened the passenger door, and caught her as she slipped out.

She woke then, just enough for Mike to half-carry her to the front porch, where she pointed to the lantern outside the door. Mike found a spare key hidden there and opened the door. As soon as they crossed the threshold, she passed out again, and Mike had to carry her up the stairs.

He pushed open the door to the master bedroom, pulled back the blanket on the bed, and put Annie down, her dark hair splaying out across the white pillow case like ink spilled on a piece of paper. Gently he tugged off her ankle-high leather boots and eased her out of her jacket, then covered her up, fully dressed.

He stood there, looking down on her, unable to take his eyes off her face. Her long eyelashes twitched, telling him she had found the deep sleep she needed. Her lips, still covered in maroon lipstick, turned up at the corners, as if she were smiling. It was the same look of peace he'd seen when she'd curled up with Maria, only this time she'd found it with him.

Her right shoulder peeked out from under the blanket, the swirling purple and blue ink of her tattoo stark against the pale perfection of her skin. The tattoo was a rose bush, twisting around to form the word "MOM," the thorns drawn as if they pierced her skin in several places, each drawing a single drop of red blood.

Mike smiled. A little dramatic for his taste, but he understood the reasoning now. His only tattoo took up most of his right shoulder and upper arm, spelling out the names of everyone his unit had lost in Fallujah, with "USMC" underneath and the Marine Corps emblem beside it.

He leaned down to kiss her forehead when someone cleared their throat behind him. Mike spun, hands coming up instinctively, but no one was there. He looked around the room, even out into the hallway—no one.

"Now you've got me hearing things. Sleep tight, Annie." He planted a quick peck on her forehead and left the room, standing for a moment in the doorway to watch her sleep. He could have remained that way all night, as peaceful as she looked, but he knew he had to go.

Back downstairs, he thought about snagging a pillow and crashing on her couch. On the one hand, he'd know Annie was safe, and his would be the first face she saw in the morning. On the other hand, his would be the first face she saw in the morning, and she might not like that. She'd never invited him to spend the night, and her experiences with men were just bad enough that she might feel violated or threatened finding him there in the morning.

In the end, he decided to leave. He'd sleep better in his own bed, once he got there, especially if he didn't spend the rest of the night worrying she'd be mad.

He took a deep breath and looked at his cellphone. Almost ten o'clock. Plenty of time for one last errand.

He locked her door with her own keys on the way out.

Chapter Sixteen

Annie opened her eyes cautiously, like a child dipping one toe in the water at a pool to see if it was cold. Sunlight streamed in through the windows on either side of her mother's bed, illuminating the room with dusty shafts of white gold.

She sat bolt upright, throwing the blanket from her and jumping to the floor. The action made her head throb and her vision blur. She thought something moved in her peripheral vision, but she looked and saw only herself in the mirror over her mother's dresser.

Her heart pounded in her chest, and her breath came in raspy gulps. She could almost feel her mother's baleful eyes on her, scrutinizing her for being in the off-limits room. She smoothed the blanket back into some semblance of order, snatched up her boots and coat, and tiptoed out of the room.

In the hallway, she leaned against the wall, almost panting, and thought things through. She remembered being out with Mike. Drinking. Drinking a lot.

Oh, God!

A quick inventory of herself found she still wore her jeans and t-shirt, even her socks. The only things removed had been her boots and her jacket.

She let out a sigh of relief. Mike had been a gentleman.

A flood of memories rushed over her. The drinks. The talk—she'd told him so much more than she'd intended. He probably thought she was crazy, but he'd opened up to her, too. She remembered more than she should have, given her level of intoxication, and it brought a smile to her face remembering how he teared up talking about Kyle. It took bravery to show that on a second date, trust. And she smiled thinking about how he'd caught her as she stumbled from his truck.

Her car! They'd left her car at the Wells Fargo building. She'd need to call Mike to go back and get it, which meant swallowing her embarrassment at her drunken condition and riding across town with him. He'd wear that lopsided, shit-eating grin the whole way, too.

Maybe she'd take a cab or the bus. The added time would help clear her head. Or she could call Jason. Anything would be better than facing Mike.

She wobbled down the stairs, a death grip on the railing, and worked her way to the kitchen. Her mouth felt like it was filled with sand, and her eyes kept trying to drift closed on her. She started a pot of coffee and dropped onto the living room sectional. The sunlight streaming through the huge picture window burned her eyes and drove itself like a spike into her brain, so she rose, shielding her eyes with one hand, and walked to the window. She reached for the curtains and paused. The sunlight reflected off her windshield as her little Fiesta sat in her driveway, waiting for her.

She went to the stand table near the front door and found her keys in the bowl where she always left them, her front door somehow locked, deadbolt and all. The spare. She didn't even look—she knew he wouldn't have put it back in the lantern, not after Frank's nonsense. Mike would have put her safety first.

She leaned against the door, closed her eyes, and pictured Mike's face, with its mischievous smile and stunning blue eyes. She thought about what could have happened, and what probably would have if it had been Frank. He'd have taken advantage of her without so much as a thought. As far as Frank was concerned, she was his property, free for the using whenever he wanted. How had she stayed with him so long?

Simple: She hadn't met Mike yet.

Thinking of him made her close her eyes and smile, a kind of warmth spreading from her chest throughout the rest of her body until she wiggled her fingertips with its comforting glow.

Somewhere in the back of her mind, she wondered if she was falling for him. Or if her feelings were simply exaggerated because he was so much the opposite of Frank.

The smooth scent of coffee tickled her nose, drawing her back to the kitchen. She sipped at her first cup while two slices of toast crisped in the archaic toaster oven her mom had refused to get rid of. Annie nibbled at the toast, but when her stomach rebelled, she dropped the rest in the trash and refilled her coffee cup. She felt gross, and probably smelled it too. Alcohol did that to her, made her feel like she hadn't showered in days. She started up the stairs, to the tiny guest bathroom, but paused at the top.

Mike was right. Old houses did weird things, and all the things she'd seen had plausible, realistic causes that made a lot more sense than her mother's ghost haunting the old place. She needed to face her obsessive fear of her mother and move on. It was time to grow up.

She passed the guest bathroom and pushed open the door to the master suite. It made a sucking sound, like a sealed tomb being opened, and Annie almost closed it again. Instead, she stood tall, stuck her chin out, and walked into the bathroom.

The master bath had been redone in the nineties, and thus was a bit more modern than other rooms in the house. It had been her mother's hideaway, her retreat from the world. Many times she'd warned the children, "If my bathroom door is closed, you'd better not knock unless it's an emergency."

They'd never knocked on it, not even when Daniel had slammed his finger in the front door and needed stitches, nor when Annie had set fire to grease on the stove and had to put it out using baking soda. Those things were less frightening than disturbing their mother in her sanctuary.

The bathroom was small by modern standards, but her mother's redesign had been nothing short of brilliant. The old claw-foot tub had been retained and a showerhead option mounted high on the wall. The tub stood alone under a glazed window, with no curtain, since her mother never used the shower. An archaic elm tree clawed at the frosted glass, as if trying to get in, its branches like witch-fingers, knotted and crooked. Twin sinks stood against the back wall—odd, since her mother had been divorced and very anti-man at the time of the renovation—with tall mirrors over each, and gleaming black marble counter tops. The commode sat in its own, separate room, adjoining a small walk-in closet.

Annie took off her socks and let her feet enjoy the cool, smooth surface of the gray tile floors, wiggling her toes as the cool radiated up into her calves. She walked to the tub and turned the brushed nickel handle until hot water steamed from the faucet. Then she plugged the drain and undressed.

She looked at her disheveled self in the mirror. Her hair looked like a squirrel family had built a summer home there, and her mascara had run partway down her cheeks. She must have cried in her sleep. A least she hoped it was in her sleep and not with Mike. Men saw weakness as a sign of a "typical woman," one who needed a man to fix her life. Annie hated the thought of needing a man almost as much as she hated the thought of turning into her mother.

Strands of her hair tumbled to her shoulders, becoming hard to distinguish from the dark lines in her tattoos, but stark against her skin like a raven in a field of snow. One of her tattoos, the stem of a rose, wound its way down her right breast, stopping just short of the nipple. That one had hurt, but it had been worth it. In the right low-cut shirts, she could completely disarm most men, as they found it impossible not to wonder how far down the ink went. Then she'd make a show of catching them staring and the ensuing embarrassment would give her an edge.

She thought back, though, and couldn't remember Mike doing that, even though her shirt had been a V-neck. Again the gentleman.

Steam had started to fog the mirror, so Annie dipped herself into the tub and felt the hot water drawing the grunge and pain and even the alcohol itself right out of her. She let the water run, filling the room with steam until the water lapped at the rim of the tub. Then she turned it off, leaned back, and closed her eyes.

She let her mind wander back to Mike, tried to picture him laying her down in her mother's bed. She wondered if he'd kissed her, and absently touched her forehead, somehow certain he had. It would have been an innocent kiss, gentle and warm, an expression of tenderness and caring. Not a rough demand for gratification or an expression of ownership.

She pictured him in her mind, his eyes piercing and clear. He had no shirt on, and his abdomen rippled with muscle, his arms lean and strong. She slid down under the water, holding her breath while she let thoughts of Mike make her bath feel even better than it already did. She felt each muscle in her back relax, followed by those in her shoulders and neck. She floated, her arms rising in the water while her hair fanned out around her head.

Her muscles tensed again, starting at the base of her skull, then spreading down to her shoulders. Something felt wrong, and it took her a moment to recognize the feeling: Someone was watching her.

She opened her eyes under the water and saw a shape in the glazed window over the tub, the fuzzy, nondescript form of a face. She splashed up, propelling her body completely out of the water. Her feet slipped on the wet tile floor, forcing her to hold the edge of the tub. When she looked at the window again, the shape was gone. She wiped water from her eyes and looked again—nothing. Her heart thudded in her chest, and she had to force her breathing to slow. Had she imagined it?

She stared for what seemed like minutes at the window, but the shape did not return. Finally, as the steam in the room started to clear, Annie found herself shivering. Convinced she'd imagined it all, she grabbed a white towel, wrapped it around herself, and turned to the vanity.

Her heartbeat leapt again, and she felt her throat constricting even as a muffled scream escaped her lips. There, in the steam on the mirror, someone had written two words: "HURT YOU."

Screaming, she ran through the master bedroom, across the hall, and into her tiny room, slamming the door behind her. Chest heaving, she made sure her drapes didn't allow even the slightest crack where someone could peer in, and she got dressed.

Then she sat on the edge of her bed in jeans, a white t-shirt, and bare feet, staring at her hands.

"I'm going crazy," she said out loud. "This kind of stuff can't be real. Oh, Jesus, I really am losing my mind."

She stood up and froze, arms out as if testing her own balance, then took a step toward her door. There was no way this had really happened. She needed to face reality and go clean up the mess she'd left in the master bath. At least wipe up the water on the floor before it turned to mold in the grout.

Steeling herself, she opened her door and took a cautious step into the hallway. She'd gone halfway across when a car engine roared to life outside and tires peeled out on the pavement behind her house. She recognized the thunder of a V-8 and knew in an instant who it was.

"Damn you, Frank!" She ran down the stairs, sliding on the throw rug at the bottom, and burst out onto her front porch. The car had shot around a corner to her right, its throaty engine fading away into the distance, out of sight. "You son of a bitch!"

She stormed down her front steps and looked right, but still couldn't see the car. She stomped her foot, feeling the rough heat of the sidewalk on her heel. Ready to scream again, she heard heels clacking on the concrete behind her. Turning, she saw Mrs. Mudge striding down the sidewalk, her glasses already riding low on her nose, so she could look over them, even from a distance.

Annie bowed her head. At least she'd gotten a bath and no longer smelled like alcohol.

"Good morning, Mrs. Mudge," she said, hiding her spite behind a sugary tone of voice. "How are you—"

Mudge pointed at her house, saying nothing.

"I know, it's not fixed yet, but my contractor will start soon, and—"

"No, Miss Brown, look," Mudge said, still pointing.

Annie looked, and immediately wished she hadn't. Her fists bunched at her sides, and she felt herself trembling with rage.

Someone—and her money was on Frank—had spray-painted in bold, red paint, the word "SLUT" across the front of her porch.

"I'm going to kill him," she muttered, wandering closer to the house without willing herself to do so. "That chicken-shit bastard is going to pay for this."

She felt a presence behind her and whirled to find Mudge there, clipboard in hand, writing something on paper.

"Seriously?" Annie cried. "You're going to write this up as a covenant violation?"

Mudge locked her dark eyes on Annie's and shook her head. "I was noting that your home had been vandalized so you would not get complaints from other Society officials."

Annie felt like a fool and could feel herself blushing. "I-I'm sorry," she said. "It's been a long couple of days."

Mudge looked over her glasses again. She looked ready to turn away, but then her expression changed, her features going from neutral to angry. Her eyes seemed far away, like she was focused on something behind Annie, and she took a step closer.

"You should get your emotions under control, Annie. An emotional woman is too easily victimized. Don't be his victim."

The she shook her head and stepped back as if surprised she stood so close. She seemed to gather herself for a moment, then turned and stalked back the way she'd come.

Annie stood, watching her ruler-straight spine move away.

"What was that all about?"

Looking again at the graffiti on her porch, Annie took out her cellphone and called the police again. She had their number in speed dial.

*

Mary peered through the bedroom window, sunlight streaming in and hiding her from her daughter below. Annie spoke with the black policeman, her arms crossed under her breasts, as if to boost them for the officer to see. Her daughter wore no bra, and even from her room, Mary could see her nipples. Even though the officer's back was to her, she was positive he is eyeing them.

Annie had slept in the off-limits room last night, and even though Mary had tried to wake her, tried to warn her that the bearded man had come, Annie was too drunk to wake up. Mary had tried to frighten him, tried to make him run off before he could do any damage, but he did not believe and therefore did not see.

Foolish girl! Not only had she violated Mary's sanctuary, destroyed her private place, but Annie—passed out the whole time—had let the man do his damage with no one to witness but Mary. And no one listened to Mary, not even her daughter.

Her frustration rose like steam in a kettle, threatening to blow off the lid and scald anyone nearby. If the man continued, he would either hurt Annie or drive her from the home. Either way, Mary would be alone again, would lose Annie forever. She couldn't bear that.

If Annie left, Mary would be unable to protect her, unable to help her make the right decisions. She had to find a way to keep Annie there, safe from both men. From the one that would break her body, and the one that would break her heart. If Annie left, Mary could never fulfill her purpose.

She'd have no one to mother, and if not a mother, Mary was nothing.

She moved from the window and stared down on the rumpled bed. Her ethereal fingers could not make it, could not erase the evidence of the man and his invasion of her private space. He'd shown more sense than Annie, leaving the room and the house while she slept, but he'd still come in, had soiled the purity of Mary's sanctuary.

As she stared at the messy bed, something felt wrong. She couldn't put her finger on it, but it nagged at the back of her mind, its muffled voice unintelligible but urgent, insistent. She'd felt it before, recognized the feeling that she was making some sort of mistake. She didn't know why, but it made her feel ashamed, as if she was a horrible mother.

She chased the feeling away, stashed it in a dark corner in the back of her being where she could no longer hear it. She knew what she had to do. She had to make Annie understand, had to communicate with her. Tell her the men were bad. All men. Both men.

She would make Annie understand, even if it hurt.

Chapter Seventeen

Mike stepped out of his truck and into the oppressive heat and smothering humidity. He looked at the house in front of him. Sitting on a cul-de-sac, it looked exactly like the ones on either side of it, just with different paint and facings. Even the grass, with mosquitoes floating up from it to greet him, had been cut to the same length.

Mike saw the damage right away. The front gutter had ripped from the roof over the garage and now hung from one end, blocking the door. The homeowner—a twenty-something woman with her blonde hair in a ponytail—stood inside her garage, talking on her cellphone, gesturing wildly for Mike to come closer. Mike left the truck unlocked and strolled up the driveway, mopping at his brow while she chatted.

Denver technically sat on a high plains desert, so humid days were a rarity, but today he could have sliced the air with his packing knife and eaten it like pizza. With the heat came the mosquitoes, another rarity at 5,280-feet elevation. It made him love Denver even more: the lack of mosquitoes and cockroaches. They were around, but not nearly like they were in other places he'd lived.

Still, on this day, with leftover rain pocketing in low spots and still dripping from trees, the city had turned "muggy and buggy," according to one local meteorologist. And this neighborhood in Centennial had taken the brunt of both.

"Oh, thank you for coming so quickly," the blonde said, said, stuffing her phone in her back pocket. "My husband is deployed and I need to get to work. My boss is already pissed. I've had to take so much time off since Brad deployed. I think they might fire me. I'm Christine Stanley."

Mike looked around the garage. Posters of F-22 Raptors, B-2 bombers, and other aircraft plastered the wall. Hanging by the door into the house, a dark blue jacket gathered dust. A tricycle sat in one corner next to a two-seat stroller.

"Your husband's in the Air Force?"

"Air National Guard," she told him. "F-16 pilot at Greeley. They sent him to the desert again, covering for some active guys to come home. Of course, like every deployment, they botched up his pay. I hope you take credit cards."

"Well, to thank him for his service," Mike told her, "I'll get this fixed and you won't owe me until he comes home."

The relief on her face transformed her. Gone was the stressed-out woman trying to make ends meet while her husband was gone, and in her place stood a woman who seemed, for that instant, to have everything together.

"Thank you," she said.

"From one veteran to another," he said, "it's no problem. Now let me get this out of the way so you can get your kids to daycare and yourself to work."

Mike held up the gutter while she backed out under it, her kids waving. When she was gone, he surveyed the damage while cars whooshed by outside and birds sang in the trees. It looked like someone had jumped up and hung on the front lip of the gutter, pulling it down. The gutter was bent in the middle, forming a "V," and all the nails holding it had torn loose from the roof edge except for two at one end where the downspout held it up.

Mike set up his folding ladder and had climbed three steps when his cellphone rang. Normally, he'd have ignored it, but the ringtone was assigned to Maria. He never ignored her calls.

"Hey, munchkin," he began. The sound of sobbing stopped him.

"Daddy, can you come pick me up?" she asked through choked-off sobs.

"I'm on a jobsite right now, sweetie, what's wrong?"

She said nothing, which by itself put Mike's senses on high alert. In the background he heard Michelle's shrill voice yelling, the same shrill voice that had been directed at him more times than he could count.

"Maria, what happened? Where are you?"

"We're at Pitt's house." Now Pitt was yelling, presumably back at Michelle. Mike couldn't make out the words, but he knew rage when he heard it. "Daddy, he hit me."

Mike's world stopped. He no longer heard cars passing by, birds in the trees, or anything. His mind filled with the sound of Maria's voice and nothing else.

"He did what?" He kept his voice as even as he could, but his hands were shaking and he had somehow stepped down off the ladder without knowing it.

"He slapped me."

"Where?"

"On my butt. There's a hand print, Daddy. I took a—"

The sound of a scuffle reached Mike over the phone, and he held his breath until he heard Maria yell, "That's mine! You can't take it!"

She sounded distant, so Mike knew she didn't have her phone.

"Who pays for this phone, you ungrateful brat?" Pitt's voice still quivered with rage. "I do, so I will take it anytime I want, you understand?"

"That's my dad on the phone." Her voice was quieter this time. Confident. She knew Pitt stood on thin ice. Too bad Pitt didn't.

"Oh, so that's how it is? You go running off to your daddy every time things go wrong here?"

"At least he doesn't hit me."

Mike had heard enough. He raised his voice enough to be sure Pitt could hear him. "Pitt, don't hit my daughter." He smiled. He'd managed to keep it civil and to leave out violent threats. Quite an accomplishment, since he wanted nothing more than to break Pitt's arm at that moment.

"Mike, if I need your help I'll ask for it."

"That's my daughter you slapped," Mike said, the tension in his voice ratcheting up a notch. "If you do it again—"

"What, soldier-boy? You'll kick my ass? You'll have me arrested? I'm a lawyer, you stupid jarhead, I'd make you look like a fool in court."

"Then we'd have to settle out of court, and I guarantee you'd look like an ass then, Pitt."

"This is my home, Mike. Your daughter mouthed off to me, and corporal punishment is legal in Colorado. So mind your own damned business."

And the call ended.

Mike nearly threw his phone against the driveway. The only thing that stopped him was the possibility of Maria calling him again.

He pictured her, locked in her fancy bedroom at Pitt's place, her eyes red-rimmed and glistening, hoping for him to come and save her. His little angel needed him.

He took one look at the gutter, dragged it out of the way, and jumped in his truck. His heart pounded in his chest, the blood pulsing in his temples. He looked in the mirror and saw a ghoulish version of himself staring back. His face had turned purple, veins bulging in his neck. His eyes had a wild look, like he'd seen on men in combat, fighting for their lives or the lives of those they cared about. He knew Maria should not have to see him like that, that Michelle could take care of her. He also knew that going to Pitt's would be a huge mistake, but the part of him that knew it was in the chokehold of something else. The part of him that was in control wanted one thing only—Pitt's blood.

He peeled out of the court, dodging a dog that ran from a neighbor's driveway. As he dashed out of the neighborhood, he mustered enough presence of mind to make one phone call.

*

Annie's cellphone buzzed in her purse under her desk, the faint light of the touchscreen shining on her ankle. She could also see Carol three cubicles down, chatting with

Veronica about a client. Every few minutes, she'd glance at Annie—like she was doing right then—and Annie would pretend to not hear her phone. In reality, Carol probably couldn't hear it buzzing, but every look from her boss made her suspicious.

The phone kept buzzing until Annie couldn't bear it any longer. She ducked her head under her desk and pretended to scratch her ankle, while stealing a glance at her phone.

Mike's picture showed up on the screen, and while she longed to pick up, when she popped her head topside again, Carol was stalking toward her. Annie went back to pretending to type a proposal letter until she heard Carol's office door close behind her. By then, the phone had stopped buzzing. She'd missed the call.

A moment later her phone chimed.

Voice message.

She took her phone, checked the time, and headed for the break room. She smiled at Veronica as she passed.

"I'm going to take five," she said. "Need to stretch my legs and get some caffeine."

She didn't have her coffee cup, of course, but ditzy Veronica didn't notice. She smiled in return.

At the tiny kitchenette they called a break room, she listened to Mike's message, her stomach tightening with every word.

Annie, You're the only person I could think to call. Damn it, that son-of-a-bitch Pitt hit Maria. She's a mess and he's still raging. I heard him yelling, and calling her names. I can't let him touch her. She's all I have. I'm going over there to put an end to this and save my little girl. Highlands Ranch area.

He rambled off an address that Annie jotted on her wrist for lack of paper, then hung up without saying goodbye.

She couldn't let him do this. He thought he was doing the right thing, but he'd be making a huge mistake, possibly the biggest of his life. After he'd taken care of her on their date, she owed him one. She had to try and stop him.

She dialed his number, but the call went straight to voice mail. She left him a hasty message urging caution and restraint, telling him to call her before he did anything. His message was only ten minutes old, meaning he probably wasn't to Pitt's yet. If she hurried, she could intercept him.

She glanced at Carol's office—the door stayed closed. She thought only a moment before dashing back to her desk and grabbing her purse. Then she sprinted for the door, slowing by Veronica's desk.

"Emergency," she told the brunette. "Tell Carol I'll take personal time!" And with that, she was out the door.

She took Lincoln to the interstate, traffic sparse for a Monday afternoon. The humid air seemed to slow her more than the lunch crowd, squeezing in on the Fiesta. She rolled down the windows and disengaged the air conditioning, needing every ounce of power she could coax out of the tiny motor.

As she whipped onto I25 south, she wondered what had made Pitt smack Maria. She'd been nothing but respectful to Annie, who couldn't imagine her giving anyone reason to hurt her. And she wondered how Michelle had allowed it to happen. For as poorly as she treated Mike, she seemed to care for their daughter.

Their daughter. What was she driving herself into? She'd dated a cop once, long ago, and remembered how he'd hated responding to domestic disturbance calls. Anytime that kind of emotion came into play, people turned unpredictable, often violent.

That made her think of Mike. The anger in his voice shocked her. He'd never shown her that side of himself, though she knew PTSD meant it was there, lurking under the surface, waiting for the right trigger to set it off. And she knew how much Maria meant to him, how his life orbited around the little girl. If she didn't get to him first, he'd do something to lose his visitation rights. And that would destroy him.

She swerved off the interstate, dodging a huge pickup coughing diesel fumes, and a few minutes later she was in Highlands Ranch. She'd always been good with directions, but in this case, her car's GPS guided her right to the address. She pulled up as Mike was slamming the door to his truck.

"Mike, wait!" she yelled. He either didn't hear or ignored her.

Pitt's front door banged open and the lawyer came out, his cellphone to his ear. He and Mike marched toward one another, bent on confrontation.

"Come on, tough guy!" Mike yelled. His fists bunched at his sides as he stopped a few feet short of Pitt. So he still had some judgment left. "Hit me like you did her. I fucking dare you!"

Pitt stopped too, but ignored Mike. "Yes, operator, I'd like to report an intruder on my property. He's behaving violently, and I fear for my family's safety."

Mike stepped closer, almost into Pitt's face. "Yeah, good idea, Pitt. Call the cops. We can tell them how you abused my daughter. You know what happens to child abusers in prison, dickhead?"

"Yes, operator, that's him." Pitt moved a half-step away, half-turning his back on Mike. "No, I didn't abuse anyone. I'd like a police officer to respond, please. Maybe two. This man is a known nut-job and has a history of violence."

The door opened again and Michelle stormed out, still in a bathrobe, striding toward the men. But Annie got there first, just as Mike started to reach out his hand for the lawyer.

"Mike, don't," she told him. "That's exactly what he wants you to do."

Mike's gaze bored into her like twin blue lasers. She almost stepped back, frightened of the hatred she saw inside him. But he hadn't abandoned her when she'd been drunk. She couldn't leave him now.

She put her hands on his elbow and felt his arm relax. "Think about your daughter, Mike. Think about Maria."

His glare softened and his shoulders sagged as she kept her hands on his arm, gentle pressure to tell him she was with him. She felt the tension drain from his body like sand.

"Yes, Mike, think of our daughter!" Michelle snapped, stepping between the two men. "Don't do anything stupid."

Mike winced like she'd slapped him on the cheek. That put Annie's hackles up. "Stupid? You mean like letting some psycho lawyer hit your kid?"

Everyone froze, their jaws open, and stared at Annie. She looked for a rock to crawl under.

"I'm sorry," Michelle said, planting her hands on her hips, "but who the hell are you?"

"Mommy, that's Annie." Annie hadn't seen the nine-year-old come up. No one had. They all stopped and stared at her instead of Annie. "She's nice."

Michelle snapped at the girl. "Go back in the house!"

Pitt opened his mouth to say something, but looked at Mike and thought better of it. He'd lowered his phone from his ear and Annie noticed it was off. So he'd been bluffing—good to know.

Michelle turned back to Annie, pushing her way around Pitt to stab a finger at Annie's chest. She stopped short of touching her. "So you're the crazy bitch who convinced my daughter ghosts exist?"

The b-word grated on Annie's nerves almost as bad as the one starting with "c," since Frank had used both the night he'd assaulted her. She forced herself to remain calm.

"She drew her own conclusions."

"So you admit to believing your house is haunted?"

Annie hesitated a moment and the other woman seized it like a wolf on a piece of meat.

"See, she won't deny it," she barked, her eyes taking on a wild look as she turned to Mike. "This is the kind of loony you expose our daughter to? Nice, Mike. Really good influence. Maybe we should rethink visitations."

"At least I provide my own income," Annie said, "instead of mooching off my divorce attorney and sucking some ex-husband's bank account dry every month."

Michelle drew herself up with a stifled gasp, but Mike took ahold of Annie's elbow and led her away.

"Good, get off my property and don't come back," Pitt said to their retreating backs.

Mike froze, and Annie locked her grip on his forearm. He turned like a tank turret and placed his right index finger almost gently on Pitt's breast bone. Then he told the lawyer, in a voice as cold as death, "The next time you want to hit someone, call me. You can hit me instead, but don't put your hands on my daughter again. Ever."

Pitt paled and muttered something under his breath, but Mike rolled his eyes and walked Annie to her car. Opening the door, he looked at her, his smile touching the corners of his bright blue eyes.

"Brilliant strategy."

"Which strategy was that?" She felt herself melting under the heat of his stare, her knees turning to jelly.

"The one where you distracted me from kicking Pitt's ass by starting a fight with my crazy ex."

"Oh, that one," Annie laughed. "Whatever works. You want to do dinner tonight? My place?"

"Can your mother's ghost come, too?"

"Nope, she's not invited."

"Then I'll be there at seven."

She paused, looking in his eyes, until he smiled.

"I'll be fine," he assured her. "I promise."

Still, she sat in her car until he pulled out of the neighborhood, then drove back to work.

Chapter Eighteen

Annie watched Mike walking to her living room, her eyes drawn to the curve of his butt in his tattered blue jeans. He'd left his work boots at the front door and now walked in his socks, a pair of frayed once-white tube socks that had seen better days. He still wore the gray t-shirt with the black Marine Corps emblem over the heart, and his chestnut hair looked like a mini-tornado had struck his head.

"You want something to drink?" she called, heading for the kitchen. She dropped the remnants of their Chinese takeout in the trash.

"Got any beer?"

She peeked in the old green fridge. "Couple of Corona Lights."

Silence for a moment, then he answered, "I'll have whatever you're having."

In truth, she'd been thinking of having water. Or soda. Milk. Anything without alcohol, since her last time drinking with Mike had ended badly.

"One Shirley Temple coming up!" she yelled.

Mike laughed in the other room, and Annie settled on coffee for both of them. It would keep her awake in case things got interesting, and would not get her drunk.

When she joined him in the living room, he'd taken a seat on one end of her sectional. He didn't see her at first, so she stood and watched him from behind as he ran his fingers through his thick hair. The action accented the lean muscle in his forearm. He caught sight of her and turned around.

"Spying on me's no fair. You have a stalker to learn from. I don't."

That's when she noticed the exhaustion in his eyes and the stubble on his jaw.

"When's the last time you slept a full eight hours?" she asked him.

"Is it that obvious? I sleep well when I try, but there have been a ton of after-hours calls lately, so I get about four hours a night."

She handed him a cup of coffee and joined him on the couch, leaving just a few inches' space between them.

"Then I'm glad I went with coffee," she told him.

"Sorry you had to see that today." He looked away as he spoke. "I wanted to keep you out of my domestic strife, if possible."

"It's no big deal, really. Now that you're not ready to rip someone's arms off, why don't you tell me what happened?"

Mike told her the story, glossing over anything having to do with his emotions. He kept talking about saving Maria from Pitt, but never once spoke about how it made him feel.

"You must have been pissed," she prompted.

"That doesn't even begin to describe it." He stared out the window beside her television, into the yard of her next door neighbor. "The problem when you have PTSD is that you don't know when it's real and when it's your illness making things worse than they should be.

"I probably shouldn't have driven over there. I've spanked Maria before, so I don't really have the grounds to get pissed at him for doing the same. Even worse, I knew in the back of my mind that I was playing right into his hands, doing exactly what he'd hoped I'd do. I let my anger—my rage—rule my decision-making, and that's when I get in trouble."

"That's not just you, Mike. When any of us let anger drive us, we generally make bad decisions. For what it's worth, I thought you handled things pretty well. How's Maria? Have you talked to her?"

Mike nodded. "Pitt finally gave back her cellphone right before I came over here. She texted me and said she was fine, and that Michelle had taken her back to their place. So for tonight, at least, I know that jackass won't touch her."

"It might not be my place," she let her words out like a fisherman feeding out line, "but you might want to talk this over with the VA counselor."

"I will," he said. He shifted in his seat, his discomfort obvious. "He wants to do some long-term therapy, and I suppose this kind of proves I need it.

"Still, most days I manage it. I'm better than I was when I first got back from Iraq. I fell into severe depression, started thinking about suicide. It hit Michelle hardest, and drove her into the arms of another soldier. Which of course worsened my depression, and one day I found myself sitting in my bathroom, a gun in my hand, ready to blow my brains out."

"What stopped you?"

He thought about that, and a wan smile crossed his lips. "Maria was little back then, and she'd drawn on the tiles of the tub wall a picture of our family. In the picture, I looked angry and Maria was crying. I knew right then I could never kill myself. She needed me too much."

"She still does," Annie said. "You guys have a really cool dynamic. I love watching you together."

This time, his smile brightened. "She's the reason I go on every day."

"How did you get into being a handyman?"

He leaned back on the couch, reaching his arm across the back, resting his fingers close to her shoulder, but not quite touching it.

"I started out trying to be a teacher," he said. "After realizing Maria had saved my life, I thought being around kids would help me stay out of depression. I got my bachelor's, earned my teaching certification, and got hired on to teach high school shop. My dad had always taken me with him when he went to do construction jobs, so I'd been exposed to it my whole life. I knew a lot more than I thought I did. But then during class one day a kid fired off a nail gun by accident and I kind of lost it. Dressed him down Marine-style, including some colorful metaphors. I had no tenure, so they fired me the next day. Said my PTSD made me unpredictable around children, so I was blacklisted. Couldn't land another teaching job in the state."

"That's terrible. I thought they couldn't discriminate like that." She patted his fingertips on the back of the couch, letting her touch linger a moment. "You've been nothing but amazing with Maria from what I've seen. You're not dangerous to kids."

"Damage was already done," he replied. "And looking back, I don't think I could have handled the politics of the teaching career, anyway. Too much political correctness for an old leatherneck like me. So I used my GI bill to get certified in electrical work. I got hired by a company here in town. Good money, steady, predictable pay, but the foreman was a dick. Eventually, once I earned my plumbing certification and my MBA, I got a small business loan and started my current gig."

She stared at him a moment, not sure what to say. On the one hand, he had a mental illness that made him unpredictable, especially in situations of high emotion or anger. On the other, he'd taken a bad situation and made something positive from it. He'd shown he could run his own business and lead a pretty normal life.

"What is it?" he asked, pulling back his arm and sitting up. "I can see a question or two bouncing around in there, so ask away. I'll be as open as I can."

She didn't know how much he would answer, or how much she wanted to know.

"Your PTSD...how is it now?"

He shrugged and seemed to relax, as if he'd expected a tougher question. "It has its ups and downs. The more stress I'm under, the more I show symptoms. Like today. I was tired, stressed over work, missing Maria, even wondering about you and me. You know, where we were headed, kind of feeling uncertain. So when she called me, my PTSD responses kicked in and I overreacted. I could have lost visitations today if he'd really called the cops. They'd have done a report and Michelle would have had evidence to use against me."

"You knew he wasn't really calling them?"

Mike nodded, a wolf's grin spreading across his face. "I could see his phone's touchscreen was blank, and couldn't hear anyone on the other end. And he wasn't answering the questions a 9-1-1 operator would be asking during that situation. I knew he was bluffing."

Before she could say anything, her cellphone rang. She looked at the screen and rolled her eyes.

Mike arched his eyebrows. "Not someone you want to talk to right now?"

"Frank. I'm done playing his games."

In an instant the rogue was back in his smile. He held out his hand.

Annie shook her head. This seemed like a horrible idea, but Mike pressed her.

"Come on, I promise to be good. I want to gauge how dangerous he is."

Annie still didn't like the idea, but she pushed the speaker button and handed Mike the phone.

"Is this Frank?"

Silence.

"Hello, Frank?" Mike went on. "You there, buddy?"

"Who is this?"

"Oh, there you are, Frank. My name's Mike, Annie's date for the night. How are you?"

"Uh, can I speak to Annie, please?"

She'd never, not in the five years she'd known Frank, heard him say "please" for anything from anyone. She grinned.

"She doesn't want to talk to you right now, Frank. In fact, she asked me to tell you to stop calling."

"I don't believe you." Frank's pitch rose at least an octave. "Let me talk to Annie."

"I don't think so, Franky." Mike was pushing all the right buttons. "You're going to stop calling Annie now. And you're going to stay away from her, stay out of her house, and leave her alone."

"Why should I do that?"

She pictured him, his goatee twisted in rage, his face turning the shade of purple it always turned when he got angry.

"Because she's not with you anymore, you sniveling little sicko. She's with me, and I'm one person you don't want to piss off. I'm unstable, or so they tell me. I'd hate to think what would happen if you showed up at her house while I was visiting. I might lose control."

Frank mumbled something unintelligible, making Mike wink at her.

"Do we understand one another, Franky-boy?"

"Don't call me that," Frank growled. She could sense his rage now, an almost tangible thing crossing the lines. "My name is Frank."

"Fine, Frank. I'll stop calling you that if you promise me you won't bother Annie anymore."

Again Frank hesitated, and she could hear him clicking his teeth, grinding them in frustration. He hated being outdone in front of her. She hoped there were no small animals around for him to maim.

"Well, Frank? How about it? Deal?" Mike's tone stayed calmer this time, almost respectable.

"Fuck you!" Frank yelled. "Annie won't love you, not the way she did me. You go to hell!"

And the line went dead.

Annie looked at Mike for a long moment, then laughed.

"Did I do okay?" he asked. "I didn't let my PTSD win this time, right?"

"No, you owned it. And you know, some PTSD might be just what I need in my life."

Mike's half-hearted laugh told her she'd crossed the line, so she decided to try something.

"Follow me," she said, standing.

She led him up the creaky stairs, blushed as she pulled closed the door to her very messy hallway bathroom, and stopped outside the closed door to her art room.

"Close your eyes," she told him.

"I don't know," he said. "I hear this house has a ghost or two."

She gave him a playful slug in the arm. He winced and closed his eyes. Annie opened the door, flipped on the light, and led him inside. She fussed with the canvas on a portrait of a man that looked a bit too much like him for her comfort, then stood beside him. Her current work sat on the easel, a landscape of the Denver skyline, done from a hill just south of Pitt's house. She'd gone surrealistic with it, using bright oranges and deep blues and purples to show the skyline at night. It was her favorite so far.

"All right," she said. "Open your eyes and see my latest stress relief projects."

His eyes opened wide, and he moved right to the easel. He leaned in close, examining the canvas from a couple inches away, like he knew what he was looking at. He looked at it from different angles, even peeking behind the canvas. He did the same quickly for two other paintings, then stopped dead at a half-finished painting of the house which leaned against her mother's portrait, hiding the face. He glanced at it, then at Annie, then back again. His finger trailed along a pencil line of the front porch, stopping short of where the paint began.

"I started that one before my mother died," Annie told him. "Maybe four years ago. When she died, I couldn't bring myself to finish it."

"You should," Mike told her. "I love the way the bright colors of the house stand out against the dark of the background and in the windows. Very creepy."

"Thanks," she said, her voice suddenly awkward and tinny. "Maybe I will."

"Could I use it as a pattern for when the painters do your exterior?"

"I hadn't thought of that," she answered, "but those are the original colors, so you'd probably make Mrs. Mudge and the historical society very happy."

Mike took out his phone and took a picture of that painting and several more, then stood facing Annie, close enough that his breath caressed her face.

"You're very good," he said. "You should do a showing in one of the smaller galleries downtown. I know a lady who owns one—"

She cut him off. "No, Mike. Thanks, but I learned long ago that my art is for me and me alone. It's therapeutic, but only if I know no one else will ever see it. Then I can paint it the way I truly want to."

Mike considered her a moment, then shrugged. "Well, okay, but this stuff is really good. Seems a shame not to share it with the world."

She looked up into his eyes and felt herself being pulled in to twin azure whirlpools. They stared into each other's eyes, and Mike took her hands in his. "Thank you for coming to stop me today," he said. "You didn't have to do that."

"It was my thanks to you for taking such good care of me the other night." She broke the iron grip of his gaze and looked at their hands. "You were a perfect gentleman, which is rare these days. Frank would have...behaved differently."

He lifted her chin with a forefinger, tilting her head back. "To hell with Frank," he whispered. His breath brushed hot across her lips, and she opened herself to him. She wanted this. Needed it.

Mike's kiss conveyed a soft kind of hunger, a delicate urgency to which her body responded. She kissed him back, her left hand sliding up his muscular arm and shoulder to the back of his neck. He put his hand on the small of her back, pulling her toward him.

A sudden gust of frigid wind buffeted the room through the open window, tossing the sheer white drapes in the air. The painting of the house took the brunt of the gust, tipping forward and falling face-down. Mike moved to catch it, but wasn't fast enough. Standing where the painting had been was Annie's mother, or the portrait of her at least. For a moment, Annie thought the painting's eyes burned a cold blue, like they had the day the movers had carried it into the house. Then the wind died, the eyes went back to normal, and the room fell into calm again.

Mike glanced at the portrait, then at Annie, then back again.

"Your mother, I presume?"

She nodded, afraid to open her mouth in case her heart might jump out through her throat. It crashed like cymbals in her chest.

"Must have been a microburst," Mike said. He stood the house painting back up, hiding her mother's fierce-eyed stare, and closed the window. "Just in case we get a storm. I'd hate for these masterpieces to get wet."

He returned to her, put his hands on her shoulders, and looked down at her. "Now, where were we?"

That didn't help Annie's heart stop pounding, so she took a step back. "Did you feel how cold that air was?" she asked. She still had goose bumps on her arms from it. "Weird."

"Don't read too much into it," Mike said, easing her out of the room. "I've been in storms that cold before. It's Colorado weather—we've seen snow in June."

Annie nodded. He obviously hadn't seen the eyes flare to life, glowing with her mother's ire. Had she actually seen it, or had she imagined it?

She tried to shrug it off, moving closer to Mike. Even if it was her mother somehow, she was not going to let her ruin this night, not with all the promise it held. She took his right hand, gave him her most demure look, and pulled him down the hall.

Mike misunderstood and tried edging toward the master bedroom, but she redirected him toward her room, pushing the door open with her butt. She left the light off—partly so he wouldn't see her mess, partly for ambience—and tugged him toward her bed.

Standing there beside her twin bed, the one she'd slept in as a child, Annie pulled Mike close, put her hand in his hair, and pulled his lips to hers. This time his hunger was ravenous, his hand sliding up under her t-shirt in the back, fumbling with her bra clasp. She slid her hands down to his butt, pulling him in so his hardness pressed against her.

She moaned as her bra opened and he ran a thumb over her nipple. Her blood coursed through her veins, and she felt more alive than she had in years. Her body responded to his every touch as if programmed to do so, like they'd been engineered for this, created solely for the passion that flooded them.

Annie slipped his t-shirt over his head, tossed it on the floor, and let her hands wander the length of his torso, from his chest down to his carved abs, stopping on the button for his jeans.

Something flew at her, wrapping around her head. She stumbled backward, ripping Mike's t-shirt from her and holding it out.

"Oh, you want to be playful?" She grinned at him, showing fangs, but Mike didn't return the emotion. He stood, shirtless in the dark, gaping at her. "What's wrong?"

"I didn't throw that," he said.

She went numb from her toes to her fingers, her throat constricting.

"Sure you did," she said, a tremor in her voice. "You caught it and flung it back at me."

She flipped on the light as Mike shook his head. "No. I didn't."

She felt eyes on her then, like someone watched her through the window, but when she looked, only darkness met her. She swallowed hard, her throat dry. The muscles of her neck bunched.

"If you were having second thoughts," Mike said, "you could have just said something. I'm not Frank. I would have stopped."

"I didn't want you to stop. Jesus, Mike, did it *feel* like I had second thoughts?"

He studied her, then the t-shirt on the floor. She could almost see the wheels turning in his head.

"This is the kind of thing I've been talking about," she said. "It's been going on since I moved in. Now you've seen it. Twice."

He shook his head, grabbed his shirt, and slipped it back on.

"Maybe it isn't meant to be tonight," he said. "Maybe we're moving too fast for you, and that's fine. We'll take things slower."

She tried to argue, but he kissed her on the mouth, a tender gesture that melted away like a snowflake on her lips.

"You're worth it to me to take things slow," he said, stepping around her for the door. "Call me tomorrow. We'll get together."

With that, he was gone, and Annie stood alone in her room, wondering what the hell just happened.

*

Mike got behind the wheel of his truck and gripped it with both hands while he wrapped his mind around what had just happened.

Annie had seemed willing enough at first, even initiating their kiss. She'd been as hot and heavy as he'd been, groping and kissing and even taking his shirt off. So why had she changed her mind? What had made her decide to slam on the brakes of their passion train?

He started the truck and pulled away from the curb, driving north, letting the lights and the steady pattering of the rain cleanse his mind. He turned west on Colfax, merging with traffic and letting himself drive on autopilot while he sorted things out in his mind.

He had to ask himself some serious questions, the most pressing of which bounced around in his mind like lottery balls. Was Annie long-term material? Could he make her a permanent part of his life? More importantly, could she be a long-term part of Maria's life?

He went over what he knew about her so far, his military mind breaking things down for analysis.

She was gorgeous. No, not traditionally gorgeous, but a cool, quirky kind of beauty. Annie possessed something most women would never understand, much less desire: individuality. Her face stood in contrast to her tattoos like her dark hair stood against her ghostly white skin. And those eyes! Her eyes were like gems, shining as much at midnight as they did when the sun was out. She was definitely smart, something every bit as sexy as any physical trait, and she had a sense of humor as quirky as her looks. And he couldn't overlook her job—she had a good job, her own money, and a solid career.

But his mind wouldn't let him ignore the things that nagged him. She had some definite mommy issues, and showed some typical signs of an adult child of an alcoholic. He'd read through a book Larry had given him on the topic, so he knew the issues it caused, especially with intimacy. She had a completely insane ex, though Mike couldn't exactly hold that against her given Michelle's ability to ruin his life, and she struggled to trust since Frank had hurt her. And that great job? She seemed to be in trouble there, too, running up against her manager and treading on very thin ice. Maybe it wasn't as secure as he thought.

Then there was her house and the odd things happening in it. Mike's logical, analytic brain told him she was losing her mind, that being back in the home where she'd suffered so much as a child made her see things that weren't happening, or interpret things through a warped filter. But his gut told him something else was going on, that Annie was too smart to not see how crazy things looked. His gut told him to trust her, to put faith in her instincts.

He usually listened to his mind in these situations, since his gut fell victim to the scars of war, but something felt wrong about it this time. He couldn't bring himself to ignore his gut, couldn't write off things his mind told him were likely nonsense.

He sighed and pulled into the parking lot for his apartment. He parked, cut the engine, and put his forehead on the hard surface of the wheel.

He tried to think straight, struggled to keep his logical mind engaged on the subject, but one image kept invading his thoughts, brushing aside all others: Annie's smile. He couldn't get it out of his mind's eye. Whenever he closed his eyes, her face hovered in his thoughts.

He sighed and leaned back in the seat. Like it or not, he couldn't reason this girl away. She'd captured his heart, and against the heart, the mind doesn't stand a chance.

She needed a shot of self-confidence, though. Something to show her the magic he saw in her. She needed something to go her way, then maybe she'd start to overcome the demons haunting her.

Then it hit him. He had the perfect way to show her how special she was, to break the pattern of things going wrong. She just needed one thing to go very publicly right: her art.

Grinning like a thief in a jewelry store, Mike got out of the truck, formulating a plan in his head.

Chapter Nineteen

Annie poured the orange juice into her tumbler, watching the golden liquid flow over the ice cubes, making them pop and crackle. She added a shot of vodka.

She'd done her best to cover up the dark bags under her eyes before work that morning, but that didn't stop Veronica from seeing them.

"Oh, Mike must have kept you up *late* last night," the airhead had cooed, and of course Carol had been one cube over, listening to the whole thing.

She had to do something about sleep. After Mike had left, Annie'd tried going to sleep, but her adrenaline still roared, making her jittery and nervous. She'd thrown that t-shirt on the floor, so either Mike had thrown it back—which seemed unlikely—or something else had. After he'd left, Annie was left alone to deal with her fear. Sleep had fled like a rabbit from a fox. So she'd spent another work day nodding off at her computer, hoping Carol wouldn't catch her during an impromptu nap. In fact, sleep had eluded her for three days now.

She picked up her drink and sipped it as she trudged back to the dining room, where Jason sat at the table, holding a dice cup, ready to throw. His golden eyes studied her as she entered the room, his brow furrowing.

"You look like a zombie, honey, just without the ripped clothing and blood. Why don't you go to bed? I'll stay here all night if you want—I've slept on couches before."

"You'll do no such thing," Annie told him. "It's Tuesday night, and we both need to be at work tomorrow."

"Then why are you drinking?" he asked.

Annie dropped into the hard-backed wooden chair across from him, setting her drink on a coaster and regarding it like it was a venomous spider.

"My nerves are shot, Jason," she explained. "I can't do another night like last night. This house is driving me mad—I think my mother is still here, and I don't think she likes Mike."

Jason clucked his tongue and shook his head. "I don't really think your insomnia's about the house, even if your mother is still here, trying to control your life. I think the real haunting is the one Mike's doing to your heart."

She had to admit, when she wasn't scared silly by the house, the only thing on her mind was Mike.

"I just don't know what to do, Jason. I mean, I'm happy when I'm with him, and we always seem to have a great time until we get back here. Then things fall apart."

"So don't come back here."

Annie blinked. "It isn't that simple," she said.

Jason put the dice cup on the table, wove his fingers together, and rested his chin on them.

"Why not?"

She wiggled in her chair, suddenly uncomfortable, but she knew she needed to get this out in the open. She needed to work her way through her feelings for Mike, and Jason was her best sounding board.

"I'm not sure how much of a long-term prospect he is," she said. "The man has a serious mental illness that can result in violence. His ex is a complete bitch—"

"Now, hold on," Jason interrupted, "so is yours, in all fairness."

"Exactly," Annie replied, lifting her glass, but not drinking from it. "Do I really stand a chance if I'm adding someone else's madness to my own? I need to find someone who can be a foundation for me. A rock."

"So rather than ground yourself, you want to find someone else to ground you? You know what that's called, right?"

Annie shook her head.

"Codependency," Jason said. "Exactly what the adult child of an alcoholic doesn't need in her life."

Annie put the glass down without drinking. "So you think it's better for me to go to bed with a potentially violent man than to find a more stable guy who helps me figure things out? Besides, I'm not too keen on going to a guy's apartment, especially after what Frank did."

Jason patted her hand and took her glass, downing its contents in one gulp.

"I think you can trust Mike," he said. "If he was going to take advantage of you, he'd have done it when you were drunk. You struggle to trust people, Annie, and Mike's already gone a long way toward proving he's worthy of your trust.

And even more important than his PTSD or his ex-wife or his daughter, is something Mike has that none of your previous guys even knew existed—class.

"Mike's a classy guy. Maybe not in how he dresses or where he eats or what kind of car he drives, but he's classy where it matters." He tapped his own chest with two fingers. "In here. You can't buy that, Annie. Frank had money. He drove a nice car, or he used to, when you were dating him. His family situation seemed stable on the outside. And he turned out to be a psychotic freak.

"So you need to ask yourself just how important all that stuff really is to making you happy with a guy. So far, it doesn't seem to have helped even one little bit."

Annie stared at Jason, her eyes welling up, until he looked at the ceiling. "How did you get so smart?" she asked him. "You always seem to know what to do."

"Oh baby, that's not smart. That's just knowing your best friend better than they know themselves. You've done the same for me, or did you forget my nightmare with Ian?"

Annie laughed louder than she had in days, the sound echoing off the dining room walls and into the hallway. "Oh yes, Ian and his fetishes. I do remember warning you about him. But you didn't listen."

"And you got to say, 'I told you so,'" Jason said. "I own up to my mistakes. But you need to ask yourself one question: Do you love Mike?"

Annie looked at the floor and shook her head. "I don't know. I'm not sure what love looks like anymore."

"Love looks like a person that makes you smile," he said. "One who makes you happy." He bounced to his feet, yawned, and stretched.

"Time to go?" she asked, pouting to try and pressure him into staying longer.

"Oh, tuck that bottom lip back in," he said, starting for the hallway. Annie rose to follow him. "It's eight and we both need to be up early tomorrow. You need to take a shower and get some sleep."

He reached into his pocket and pulled out a plastic bag with one round, blue pill in it. He handed it to Annie.

"Try this," he told her. "I'll bet you nod right off without a single thought about your mother or Mike. Just make sure your alarm is set and ready to go or you'll miss work completely."

Annie eyed the pill like it was a coiled snake. She disliked the idea of using pills to get to sleep, especially ones she wasn't prescribed, but she couldn't do another sleepless night. Reluctantly, she took the bag.

"Just take it about thirty minutes before bed," Jason instructed. "And don't drive for at least eight hours after you take it. It's given me some wonderfully realistic dreams. Very...detailed."

She didn't really want to know the details, so she ushered him to the door.

"You sure you don't want me to stay?" he asked, his back to the muggy darkness outside. He hated hot weather, and he didn't have air conditioning, so her couch probably sounded like a luxury hotel.

"No, Jason, the last time you slept on my sectional, your back hurt for days. If you can't stand, you sure as hell can't cut someone's hair, now can you?"

"You're right about that," he said, stepping out onto her front porch, making a show of fanning himself with his manicured hand. "Now you get some sleep, missy. No staying up fantasizing about your handyman. And no second-guessing yourself on him, either. I've never steered you wrong, have I?"

"Not even once," she said. "Now go home. Love you!"

He made a kissy-face and headed for his Mini-Cooper, still fanning himself. Annie laughed and closed the door behind him.

Inside, she bounced the baggy with the sleeping pill up and down on her palm. It was only eight o'clock. Taking it now would mean a full eight hours of sleep. She trudged upstairs, brushed her teeth, and swallowed the pill.

"Thirty minutes, huh? I guess I can paint until it kicks in."

She plopped down in front of her easel, picked up a brush, and looked at the canvas before her. She'd sketched out the rough shape of an old man she'd seen in a park the day before. She closed her eyes for a moment, then got to work. She fell right into her painting trance, losing herself in the stroke of her brush, the melding of colors, and the rhythm of her work.

A photo of him hung beside her easel, the late afternoon sun forming spots across his face, hiding it from view. So she painted it mostly from memory, recreating the lined cheeks, bushy brows, and sagging jowls. She could see him, like he was sitting there with her, the photo only a key to unlock her mind's eye so she could see every line, every eyelash, every pore.

She yawned and realized the sleeping pill was kicking in, so she set down her brush and admired her work. She'd gotten much of the old man's face filled in, his features drawn out in the texture of her oil colors, so he looked even older than he had, even wiser.

But something was off, not quite right. She stood back a step and studied it, tilting her head sideways, as if that would make everything clearer.

Then she saw it. She'd done the eyes wrong. The old man had brown eyes, but she'd given him blue ones, and while she'd given him crow's feet at the corners of those eyes, they weren't nearly lined enough. It took her another moment to realize what she'd done: She'd given him Mike's eyes.

She smiled. She would add some lines, make the eyes older, but she'd leave them blue. Maybe Mike wouldn't notice. Or maybe, if she was lucky, he would, and then maybe they'd pick up where they'd left off the other night, with his shirt off and hers on its way.

She closed her eyes and thought back to their kiss. The feel of his hands, strong but delicate as he touched her, came flooding back to her, and she let the memory come, washing over her like a healing river.

But another feeling intruded, one that crept up her spine and made her scalp tingle.

She was being watched again.

Snapped out of her fantasy, Annie looked around the room, her head jerking from side to side, eyes searching. Something moved near the doorway, but when she looked right at it, the shape disappeared.

She jumped to her feet, ran into the hallway in time to catch a glimpse of something dark going down the steps.

Heart pounding, Annie followed on cat's feet, measuring each step to avoid creaky spots in the floor. Her mind screamed at her to go back, to hide in her bedroom with her head under the covers, praying she'd be invisible. But that was stupid, child's crap that somehow followed her to adulthood.

She needed to face this head-on, to see for herself if she was really seeing these things or going insane.

She reached the top of the stairs, holding the railing like it was all that kept her from plunging head-first over a thousand-foot drop. Each step came with deliberateness and caution, her feet moving in slow motion.

Halfway down, her head swam and she gripped the rail even tighter to keep upright. She held on as the room spun for a moment, nausea sweeping her until she thought she might throw up.

Then it lessened enough for her vision to steady itself. The room stopped turning and her stomach's churning slowed enough that she thought she could hold its contents in.

She drew in a deep breath, trying to cleanse herself. The sleeping pill. Some of the side effects were dizziness and nausea. That explained it. She wracked her brain, trying to recall side effects of sleeping pills. She was pretty sure hallucinations were among them. Great.

Again from the corner of her eye she saw something, roughly like a large ink stain, slip into the downstairs hallway, then into the kitchen. Her heart still thundering in her chest, she descended the rest of the way down, then tiptoed to the kitchen. She stepped inside the narrow room, and at first she saw nothing out of the ordinary. As she turned her head, though, the ink stain appeared again in her peripheral vision, hovering near the back door.

Annie turned to look at it and it disappeared. When she turned away again, it reappeared.

"Okay," she muttered to herself, "looking right at you doesn't work. That's not at all weird."

The shape seemed to swirl and eddy, as if stirred by some great storm. Roughly Annie's size, it began to coalesce, forming itself into something while she tried not to watch. When it finished, Annie wanted to run, screaming, from the room.

There, in the corner of her vision, as if existing on the edge of her world, stood Annie's mother. Careful not to look at her head-on, Annie took in her mother's appearance. Although she was little more than an inky fog the shape of a woman, Annie didn't doubt the apparition's identity. Her hair piled atop of her head, the stern, accusatory stance, hands on hips, the flare of the blue velvet dress from the painting. It was her! The face grew clearer, and her mother's icy blue eyes bored a hole into her daughter's heart.

Her mother's lips moved, and Annie heard something, like a voice muffled by water. Her mother's hands waved, but Annie couldn't understand what she said. Heart racing, Annie raised her hands helplessly in front of her.

"I can't understand you," she said. Her gut twisted and she thought she might pee herself, but she held it together through sheer strength of will.

Her mother looked frustrated, eyes going ten degrees cooler, hands pulling at her ethereal hair. She glanced around the kitchen, then saw the glass door of the oven and seemed to have an idea, her eyes widening.

Annie braced herself on the counter as her mother's ghost leaned down close to the oven, writing something with her finger on the glass. When finished, she waved Annie over for a look. As soon as Annie turned, her mother disappeared, but she went to the oven anyway.

Nothing. The glass was clean.

She looked away and her mother appeared in her peripheral again, her face close to the oven glass, lips pursed.

Annie got the hint. Her heart thundered now, but the edge of her fear had dulled. Her mother had done nothing to hurt her so far. Annie wasn't even sure she *could* hurt her.

She leaned close to the oven and felt a shiver run down her body. The air seemed frigid, like a winter draft passed through at knee level.

Annie breathed on the glass, gasping as letters appeared, mere smudges in the fog of her breath, but letters nonetheless.

Men dangerous.

Annie's fear retreated as her rage took over. Her mother couldn't even leave her alone after death, still meddling in Annie's life.

She wheeled on the ghost...and it disappeared. She angled away until her mother's shape reappeared in the corner of her eye.

"Damn it, Mom!" she snapped. "Leave me alone! I'm not a little girl. I make my own decisions, and I like Mike. He's a good guy. Butt out!"

Her mother shook her head, misty hair swirling as she did. She jabbed her ghostly finger at her daughter, her lips moving so fast Annie was glad she couldn't hear her.

"Mom, no! Just stop. I won't talk about this anymore!"

Her mother's eyes went from ice-blue to graveyard-black in a heartbeat, which Annie counted because her own heartbeats pounded in her temples. She floated closer to her daughter, the air around Annie thickening and cooling until she could see her breath before her face. The ghost stopped, considered for a moment, and then backed off.

Annie screamed, a high-pitched screech that she thought might shatter glass or attract the neighborhood dogs. Her mother covered her ears, eyes going black again. Annie's stomach felt like she'd swallowed a swarm of hornets, but she managed to turn her back on her mother and storm out of the kitchen. She threw herself onto her couch, picked up the remote, and pointed it at the TV while pushing the power button.

Of course. Nothing happened.

"Mom, knock it off!"

The TV came on to static, the volume blasting her ears with white noise. She frantically pushed the power button over and over, to no effect. The snow screen on the TV shifted, pulsing in an almost three-dimensional manner, seeming to bulge from the console until the shape of her mother stuck out, hands reaching for her daughter with black-and-white fingers.

Books flew from the shelves, crashing on the floor, while pictures rattled in their frames. The lights flickered on and off, even Annie's cellphone blinking in time with it all.

The noise grew louder and more frantic in a giant crescendo of her mother's fury. A ceramic figurine fell to the floor, shattering into a hundred pieces. The window shook, and Annie felt certain the glass would shatter.

The noises collided inside her head, creating an earthquake of panic. She trembled, a violent shaking that made her teeth chatter and her neck muscles bunch. Desperate, she shoved couch pillows against her ears and squeezed her eyes closed, but nothing helped. The tempest of rage still found its way into her mind, threatening to drive her mad.

Flinging the pillows to the floor, Annie jumped up and ran for the door, snatching her keys up off the stand on her way. She threw open the front door and ran outside, still wearing her sweat pants and t-shirt, with not even a bra underneath.

As soon as she reached the porch, it all stopped. Silence dropped like a shroud and she found herself listening to the crickets chirp in time with the distant rush of traffic on Colfax, a few blocks away.

She stepped back inside, and immediately, the cacophony started again, so she retreated to the silence of her porch. Dizziness swept her and she held onto the porch rail for support.

The sleeping pills had a firm grip on her now, just as Jason had warned her.

Still, the thought of going back inside made her heart stop cold. She needed a night away. She looked at her cellphone: dead battery. She locked the front door and went to the garage where her Fiesta waited.

She knew she shouldn't drive, not with the drug in her system, but what choice did she have? She couldn't sleep here, not tonight.

Jason lived halfway across town, though. She'd probably crash or get arrested between her house and his. She couldn't sleep on the porch, or even in her car.

That left her only one logical choice.

Sighing, she got in her car, plugged in her phone, and turned the key.

From the south came a muffled, warning peal of thunder.

*

Mary watched through the master bedroom window as Annie drove off, her taillights disappearing into the night like a retreating storm. No doubt she'd flee into the arms of the new man, the one with the icy blue eyes and thief's smile. He *was* a thief, looking to steal Annie's heart and rob Mary of her only daughter. And somehow her daughter fled to him for comfort, not to Mary. Never to her mother, always to men, no matter how much they hurt her.

She put her hand on the window, its cold arcing up her arm and into her chest, and when she pushed her palm into the glass, it stung like a million little needles piercing her hand.

She'd failed again, failed to make Annie understand her. To help her daughter hear her warning and protect herself. The girl had closed herself to the one person trying to care for her, the one being in the entire world who wouldn't hurt her. Annie was stubborn and foolish, a girl in a woman's body. She still needed her mother.

Anger coursed through Mary and she shoved her entire arm through the glass, crying out as the pain lanced through her like fire. She held her arm there as long as she could, then jerked it back and fell to her knees, sobbing.

She and Annie hadn't communicated well when she was alive, and now that Mary was dead, their communications were even worse. It was if Annie was a teenager again, stubborn and riding a wave of teen hormones, lacking in reason or judgment. She was blinded by her own pain and her own fear. She thought herself scarred by her childhood, broken somehow, and needed to defy her mother to heal the wounds.

But Annie didn't know pain, didn't understand it the way Mary did. Pain was Mary's oldest friend, the one she knew best, the one still with her after all that time.

She looked down at her arm, half-hoping to see blood, but knowing she would not. Could not. She had no corporeal form, no substance. She was all energy and no matter, and thus couldn't reach Annie easily. Mary had been able to use pain and punishment to make her listen when she'd been alive, but now she had to find new methods to motivate her wayward girl.

She thought for a moment, searching for anything that might help. Some way to create enough pain or fear for her daughter to listen.

One image appeared in her mind, crystal clear and bright as the sun: Mike. The thief of hearts, seeking to steal Annie away and hurt her.

That's how she'd get through to Annie, how she'd break down the walls and make Annie see the truth. Without Mike, Annie wouldn't have a choice—she'd come back to Mary like she always had as a child.

And then Mary would be able to protect her again. She would not fail. She would protect her daughter forever. No matter what it took.

Chapter Twenty

Mike tipped back the bottle of Coors, took a long pull, and focused on the ballgame on TV. The Rockies were down two runs in the bottom of the seventh, with the meat of their lineup coming up to bat against the weakest finisher on the Phillies' roster. Mike liked their odds.

He put the beer down and grabbed a handful of greasy potato chips, shoving them into his mouth. He tried not to eat things this junky, but sometimes he had to break his own rules. This was one of those times.

Outside his window, lightning flashed far to the south, followed a few seconds later by a warning roll of thunder that set his nerves on edge. The storms had stayed to the south so far, pounding Castle Rock and Monument, but moving east without bothering Denver, leaving the city with a muggy drizzle, mosquitoes, and vague, distant threats of more.

His tiny apartment needed to be cleaned. Or maybe burned out, fumigated, and disinfected were better terms. He'd been so busy between work, Annie, and Maria that he hadn't kept up with it like he normally did. A load of laundry sat in a heap on his kitchen island, the tiny pendant lamps highlighting it for anyone to see. Muddy work boots, caked with much of Mrs. Delaney's back yard, sat in the doorway, and his soft-sided tool bag occupied one of the two stools at the island.

The door to his bedroom was closed, but that room was actually clean, since he hadn't had the time to use it much. He even thought he could smell something rotting in the overflowing kitchen trash.

None of it mattered, though. Not tonight. He'd had a successful date with Annie the night before, Michelle was for some reason being nice to him, and the Rockies were on TV. Three great reasons to celebrate.

He was reaching for another handful of grease when his doorbell rang, making him jump. He paused the game, marveling for the dozenth time on how the digital video recorder, or DVR, was the greatest invention since duct tape. He rose and peeked through the peep hole. Two young men in white shirts and ties stood outside, clean-cut and handsome. All-American types, with a hint of nerdiness to each of them.

Mike opened the door.

"Good evening, sir," said the dark-haired one on the left. "We were just wondering if we could serve you in some way tonight."

"Uh, what?"

"We're on mission, sir," said the one on the left, brushing his blond hair from his eyes. "Our mission is to help anyone who needs it tonight."

"So tell us," said the first, "do you need us to do anything? Laundry? Wash your car?"

The blond one peeked past Mike, eyeing the apartment. "Uh...cleaning, maybe?"

Mike narrowed his eyes at them. "So what's the catch, boys?"

"Oh, there's no catch at all," the blond proclaimed, beaming with pride. "We'd just like to talk to you about the Church of Jesus Christ of Latter Day—"

Mike slammed the door in their faces, plopped back on his couch and re-started the game. He felt a pang of guilt, but not enough to change his mind. He'd watched two pitches when the bell rang again. Irritated, he turned up the volume on the game.

The doorbell rang again, followed by more thunder rolling up from the south. Now his temper started to take over, bubbling up from deep inside, from that secret, dark place where he tried to hide it. He swallowed it back down, reminding himself that he'd been a young man on a different kind of mission once, a mission for freedom. Serving his country rather than God, and he'd carried the gospel of liberty as proudly as these young men carried their faith. He couldn't fault them for doing their best.

Still, manners and common courtesy had to stand for something, so when the bell rang a third time, he vaulted off the couch, stomped to the door, and flung it open.

"Damn it! Can't you two take a—"

His words froze in his throat. Standing in the hallway, wearing sweats, a t-shirt, and no makeup, was Annie. She looked like she'd been drinking and crying, from the moist glaze over her emerald eyes, and her skin seemed even paler than normal.

"Oh, uh, Annie," he stammered, "What are you doing here? I mean, I wasn't expecting you tonight. Did we have a, uhm...did I forget a date?"

Despite the obvious haze surrounding her mind, she grinned at his fumbling and mumbling.

She barked her ruffian's laugh, which echoed down the hall. "No, not at all. I'm having a rough night, that's all."

"I'm sorry to hear that," he responded. "Have you been drinking?"

As the words tumbled out, he realized how gruff and rude they sounded, but Annie didn't seem to mind. She shook her head, then swayed on her feet. Mike caught her hand to steady her.

"Sleeping pill," she said. "Uh, can I come in, or do we have to do this in the hallway so your neighbors can hear?"

"Of course," he said, stepping aside. He caught a glimpse of the trash and his laundry and kicked himself for not cleaning up. "Sorry. It doesn't normally look like this, I swear."

She wrinkled her nose. "Does it normally smell like this?"

He kicked himself again as blood rushed to his cheeks. He closed the door behind her.

"No, it's normally worse," he joked, hoping it would convince her. "I've been so busy I haven't had a.."

Her lip quivered and her eyes brimmed. She ran a pale hand through her hair as if the motion would strengthen her, but the next thing Mike knew, she flew into his arms, sobbing, her tears soaking through his shirt to his chest.

He forgot about the mess and the smell and the game—none of them mattered anymore. The moment she'd started to cry, Mike's instincts took over. He stroked her hair, holding her tight with the other arm, whispering to her.

"Hey, it's okay. You're here now, with me. You're safe. What's wrong, what happened? Was it Frank again, because so help me, I'll beat his ass."

Annie shook her head, wiped her nose, and sat on one of the chairs at the island. If she saw the underwear peeking out of the laundry pile, she said nothing about it.

"No, Mike, it wasn't Frank. It was...you'll think I'm crazy."

She turned away, staring at the game on TV. Mike paused the game again and took the other chair, turning Annie to face him.

"Nothing you say is going to make me think you're crazy," he said. "And since I'm actually mentally ill, I'm kind of an expert on the matter."

She smiled, but it held no strength, and betrayed her disbelief in him and in herself. Mike realized she believed herself crazy, at least a little bit. And if she didn't believe in herself, she probably thought he couldn't either.

"Tell you what," he offered, taking her hand and tugging her to the couch. "Why don't you just tell me what's wrong, and if anything starts to sound like you're at all insane, I'll stop you and let you know. Okay?"

Annie eyed him for a moment, then nodded. She took a deep breath, gathered herself, and looked him in the eye.

"I saw my mother in my kitchen tonight." Mike held her gaze, but said nothing, allowing her to continue. "And I talked to her."

"Did she talk back?" He tried to not sound mocking, but it did no good. Annie threw her hands up and started to get up off the couch. Mike grabbed her forearm and stopped her, not quite pulling her down, as that would be too forceful. "I'm serious. Did your mother talk to you?"

Her defenses stayed up, as she leaned back from him like he might hit her, but she answered.

"She didn't talk, but she communicated. At first she tried mouthing things, but I couldn't look at her straight enough to make out her words. So then she wrote them on the front of the oven."

Mike covered the worried expression that tried to jump onto his face, the one he made anytime Maria was sick or hurt. Annie needed him to believe in her, not act like a father.

"What did she write?"

Again Annie hesitated. "That you were dangerous."

Mike sighed and leaned back against the couch. "Well, she's right about that. I have been known to screw up dinner dates pretty badly."

He flashed her a teasing smile, making her chuckle. It turned into a yawn.

"All right," he said, "before you fall asleep, why don't you tell me from the beginning?"

Annie went through the whole night, and if she left out any details, Mike couldn't see how, since she talked for twenty minutes about something that took about five when it happened. When she finished, the explanation seemed clear to him. He just had to word it in a way that wouldn't raise her defenses.

"Look, I think there is a perfectly logical, non-crazy explanation for what happened tonight, but I'm not sure you're in a spot to see it right now. Not clearly anyway.

You're exhausted, on a powerful sleep drug, emotional, and distracted by a really hot guy right in front of you."

She barked her quirky laugh, making him jump a bit.

"Maybe you're right," she said. "I might be able to sort through things better in the morning, but there's only one problem."

"What's that?"

"I can't sleep in that house and I'm not getting back in my car to drive to Jason's tonight."

"Well, either I can drive you to his place or you are welcome to crash here. I promise to be a gentleman."

She nudged him with her elbow. "Darn."

Mike grinned seeing the relief on her face. Her entire demeanor relaxed, shoulders slumping, head nodding forward. It was like he'd lifted the weight of the house off her shoulders. She was completely terrified to sleep in her own home.

"So grab some chips. Beer's in the fridge, right under my dirty socks. And settle in here to watch some baseball with me. It'll take your mind off things."

"I think I'll skip the beer," she said.

Mike feigned offense, his hand over his heart. "My beer's not good enough for you? I may have to reconsider letting you spend the night here. I'm not a fan of elitists."

She slugged him in the arm, moved the bag of chips out of the way, and slid over next to him, hooking her hand through the crook of his elbow. Her hair tumbled down across his chest as she rested her head on his shoulder.

"Thanks, Mike."

He planted a kiss on the top of her head and hit play on the remote.

Thanks to the miracle of fast forwarding through commercials, the game ended twenty minutes later and Mike killed the TV. They sat a moment in silence, neither one moving. Mike thought she was asleep until she slid her hand across his chest and up to his chin. She turned his face to hers, leaned up, and kissed him.

Mike had never seen fireworks during a kiss before. Not with Michelle, not in the Marines. Not even the first time he'd kissed Annie. But this time he did. Her lips touched so lightly on his, with such tenderness and care, that it caught him off-guard. That kiss told him everything he needed to know. Annie needed him, needed his presence, his strength. Not his money or his reputation or his handyman skills. She was frightened, and she needed him to help her through. Her kiss told him all this and more.

He kissed her back, and her kisses turned hungry, longing. She straddled his lap, so she could look down at him, staring into his eyes. He felt himself harden, his hands roaming up her thighs, stopping on her hips.

"Are you sure about this?" he asked, straining to hold back.

She stood, pulled him up, and unbuttoned his jeans, letting them slide to the floor. Then she teased him with her hand and walked toward the bedroom, tugging on his boxer waistband.

"Oh yes," she said. "And this time, no one will interfere."

Chapter Twenty-One

Mike popped the collar on his short work coat, wishing he'd remembered the old green poncho he'd been issued in the service to ward off the steady drizzle. At least then his pants would only be soaked from the knees down, not all the way up to his crotch like they were.

His hair, even short as he kept it, stuck to his skull like plaster, making his head cold, despite the eighty-degree temperature. Only his feet, tucked inside his snug, waterproof boots, stayed dry, a fact for which he had to grudgingly thank Michelle, who'd bought him the boots right before their split. At least he'd gotten something of use from the marriage.

He trudged down Santa Fe, his boots splashing on the wet sidewalk, searching for his turn. Even in the cold afternoon drizzle, Denver's Santa Fe Art District looked like an art district. Two- and three-story buildings sided in tan and brown stucco huddled against the rain, their north sides darkened with moisture and wind.

He took a left on Ninth Street, then stopped outside a small, glass door with a display window beside it. Paintings and sculptures filled the open space of the window, positioned against black felt. A prairie landscape as big as Mike's TV dominated the display, surrounded by paintings of cougars, rams, and other wildlife. Sculptures of similar subjects shared the space, done in ceramic, acrylic, wood and even iron.

As he looked, the front door opened and a wispy woman with long, graying hair stepped out, wrapped in a knitted shawl and wearing sandals despite the rain.

"Hello, Mike," she said, her smile highlighting the crow's feet at the corners of her eyes. "How can we help you?"

Mike gave her a quick hug, admiring the timeless features of her face. She'd looked the same the whole ten years he'd known her, since he'd first fixed a broken ceiling light in her tiny cottage across town. Same number of gray hairs, same crow's feet, same pale green eyes. Her beauty defied time, he thought, and she would probably be just as lovely in a decade or longer.

"I need a favor, Liz," he told her. "I need to use your gallery for a showing."

She eyed him a moment, her lips curling upward. She patted his arm. "You'd better come inside and tell me about her. She must be pretty special for you to call in favors."

Inside, the tiny gallery looked like an expansion of the display case, with paintings on the wall and on easels, while sculptures sat in bunches, all with a familiar pattern Mike couldn't quite make out. He found himself staring at the displays, feeling like he was surrounded by wildlife. Mountains on the left, plains on the right. To the north, cold weather displays, to the south, a desert.

"You arranged it geographically," he said as she led him through a door in the back of the studio. "Mountains west, plains east, and so on."

She paused in the doorway, reviewing the displays, then smiled.

"Not me," she said. "The artist, Paolo. I make the artists arrange their own work in a way that's meaningful to them. Paolo paints and sculpts things and places and animals from around Colorado, and while it took him a whole day to figure it out, he arranged them much as our state is laid out. I think it worked perfectly."

Mike had to agree. That's why it had seemed familiar to him—he recognized Colorado when he saw it.

She guided him into a small back room, where a floral-patterned couch that had seen better days lined one wall. A coffee table with a landscape oil painting under the glass top sat before the couch, while a small curved-screen TV sat on a stand across from it.

Liz pointed Mike to the couch and pulled out an old-fashioned glass bottle of Coke from an equally old-fashioned refrigerator.

"Can I get you anything?" she asked him.

Mike shook his head, knowing it wouldn't matter, as she handed him a Coke anyway, then took the spot on the couch beside him.

"Now tell me about this girl for whom you're willing to step way outside your comfort zone, Mike Tolbert."

Mike told her everything, from the day he'd met Annie to the night before, leaving out the juicier details, even though he was pretty sure Liz filled them in on her own. He made sure to mention Annie's painting, and how it was the one thing that took her away from the dark spots in her mind. When he finished, she tilted her head back and took a long swig of the soda. She giggled, rubbing at her nose.

"Sorry," she said, "tickled my nose, but it's not that different than what you're feeling. I love seeing you with that bubbly, new-love look in your eye, Mike. So how can I help you with this new love?"

"Display her art," Mike said. "Just for a week. I think it would give her so much self-confidence that it might help her break out of the funk she's been in."

"Not to mention scoring points for you."

Mike grinned, but said nothing. He'd considered that, but not in the manner Liz thought. He'd thought of the possibility that Annie might think he was trying to score points, or just plain score, by doing this, but in the end, he'd decided it didn't matter. She needed something to give her a boost, some morsel of "you're worth it" stew to carry her through the rough spot she was in. Seeing her art displayed seemed like just that boost.

Until Liz spoke again.

"What has Annie said about showing her work?"

"She doesn't want to," he said, "but that's just her lack of self-confidence holding her back. She doesn't believe her art is worth displaying, so she avoids the issue altogether. She hides behind some excuse about it being private, something she does for herself."

Liz leaned forward with a sigh and tapped on the glass of the coffee table.

"You see this painting?" she asked. Mike nodded. "Well that was done by an old friend of mine, Elle. She painted some of the most beautiful things I've ever seen, and I've seen a lot. She wouldn't let me display any of it in the gallery while she was alive. She said much the same thing your girlfriend has said about her painting, but like you, I didn't think she knew what she was talking about. So when she gave me this painting to put on my wall, I turned it into this table instead. I put it out in the gallery, spread out some magazines on it, and left it there for people to see or not see.

"One day, Elle came in and saw what I'd done and got so angry she made me drag it into the back room right there in front of my customers. She didn't speak to me for months, but when she did again, she told me she hadn't painted a thing since she'd seen her painting in my table. Told me that painting was her quiet place, the one place in all the world where she could find serenity, where no one could follow her unless she wanted them there.

"By putting that one painting on display, she said, I had allowed everyone in my gallery to traipse through her private, secret place, dragging their muddy feet across her clean floor, and robbing her of the privacy she needed to be creative."

Mike considered her story, doubt nagging at his mind. "Did she ever paint again?"

"Oh, of course she did," Liz said, taking another swig from her Coke bottle and putting it on a coaster on the coffee table. "And before she died, she painted dozens more things. But my point is that painting for Annie may be very much like it was for my Elle. Artists are a strange lot. They create beautiful things that they often want no one else to ever see, because to create something beautiful, they had to tap into something ugly in themselves.

"Annie might well get the ego boost you think she needs, but she might also resent you for a very long time."

"Do you think it will make her stop painting?"

Liz shook her head. "Not permanently. Artists also create because they need to do it. It's something inside them clawing its way out, fighting to make them open their veins and bleed onto the canvas or the paper or the stone. It's a kind of spiritual cleansing for them. So if she's kept painting through all you've told me, she'll keep painting the rest of her life. She just might live that life without you. She could see this act of kindness as betrayal."

Mike put his head in his hands and rubbed his temples with his fingers. Of course, Liz was right. She almost always was. He knew he was taking a huge chance with this. He'd known it when he first had the idea, but something in him told him it was the right thing to do. Would Annie push him out of her life? Possibly, but he could handle that if it gave her some measure of strength, rebuilt some of her shattered confidence. No one—not Frank, not her brother, not her boss, or even her mom—believed in Annie, and that lack of belief had woven itself into her being. She put on a fine confident mask, but he knew what lurked behind it, knew the self-doubt that reared its ugly head anytime things went wrong.

And he remained convinced seeing her art displayed would help her understand the good he saw in her, even if it meant she'd kick him to the curb.

With a sigh, he made up his mind.

"I still want to do it."

She stared at him, her sea green eyes measuring every inch of him, weighing his intent as if it were the key to her whole decision. Then she nodded.

"Show me her work," she demanded.

Mike showed her the pictures he'd taken with his phone, and with every one, she leaned closer, her eyes narrowing more and more. When he finished, she let out a breath he hadn't know she was holding in.

"Extraordinary," she said. "Annie is talented. Very talented. I have an opening next month. It's only for a couple of days, but I can have some people here that I think will be very interested in her work."

Mike kissed her on the cheek and stood. "Thank, Liz," he said. "This means the world to me."

Liz shook her head. "No, Annie means the world to you. That's the only reason I'm going along with this, but you're to blame if she dumps you on your butt."

Mike smiled over his shoulder as he left the room, into the gallery. "I know, I know. I will deal with that. Thanks!"

As he exited the gallery, the drizzle had stopped, though water still shone on the sidewalk. He stood, staring up at the sky, watching as the sun struggled to break through the clouds and dreariness, and he felt like his life looked much the same as the Denver sky at that moment. He'd spent all his spare time the last week with Annie, either fixing up her place or just hanging out, talking and having fun. She seemed to get along great with Maria, meaning his daughter had a positive female role model. Mike's anxiety had lessened, his symptoms dropping off to almost nothing. He hadn't had a nightmare all week. He was even getting along better with Michelle, his ex-wife becoming less demanding, almost seeming friendly.

His personal storm clouds appeared to be breaking up.

And now he had the gallery showing to plan for, something that he hoped would bring Annie's self-esteem up, making things even better between them.

That reminded him—he needed some way to sneak her art out of her house and to the gallery, a time when he knew she wouldn't be home, and had access to her house. She'd trusted him with a lot, but he didn't think she'd be ready to give him a key without being there herself, especially since all his work was on the outside. He needed a conspirator, and he knew just the guy, assuming he could get Jason to help.

He pulled out his phone to call Annie's friend—Jason had slipped Mike his number when Annie wasn't looking one day—and noticed he'd missed a call. His phone had been on silent during his meeting with Liz and for a moment, his stomach tightened on the possibility he'd missed a call from Maria. When he saw Michelle's number in the call list, he cursed himself. He didn't owe her money until Friday, two full days away, but she'd probably bitch at him to pay. Still, if he didn't return her call, she'd make things more miserable for him. Stopping a half-block from the gallery, he dialed her number.

She answered on the first ring. "Mike? Oh thank God!"

His heartbeat jumped, his throat tightening. "What's wrong, Michelle? Is Maria ..."

"Oh, Maria's fine," she said. Her voice sounded strained, as if she were holding back a flood of emotion. "It's just... well, she needs a place to stay. We both do."

Mike's defenses went up. The only thing she ever asked for was money, so this was highly unusual.

"What happened?"

At first she said nothing, fighting to hold back the flood, but it didn't last long. When the dam broke, her tears rushed out, pouring over him in a torrent that tore at his heart.

"Pitt and I fought," she said between sniffles. "About him spanking Maria. He said some awful things to me, Mike, things you never said. Then he threw us out. We have nowhere to go."

"What about your place?"

She sucked in her breath and Mike braced himself. This had to be bad news.

"I missed some payments there, Mike. The landlord booted us. All our things are either at Pitt's or in storage."

He took a deep breath and calmed himself. "I pay you all that child support so you won't miss those payments, Michelle."

"I know," she said. "We were planning on moving out completely and moving in with Pitt, so I used the money on other things. We're in my car right now, with everything we could fit inside it."

In the background, Maria sniffled just like her mom.

"What are you going to do?" Mike asked, fearing her reply.

"Mike, could we stay with you? Just for a couple of nights until I'm back on my feet?"

Mike growled under his breath. Her plea tugged at his heart strings. No matter that they were divorced, her need strummed the strings of his instincts and he longed to take care of her, to make everything all right. Divorced or not, she was the mother of his child. She deserved a place to sleep. For Maria's sake.

He took a deep breath, fought down his instincts, and answered her. "Maria has a place, you know that. Bring her over now. She can stay as long as needed."

Silence told him she didn't like that answer. When she spoke, the helpless sorrow had fled her voice, leaving behind a tense, coiled sound.

"Just Maria? You can't open your home to me, even for a few nights?"

Mike knew this would go nowhere fast if he played into her trap. She knew what buttons to push to set him off, too. He wasn't about to let her do it, so he kept his voice as loose and unemotional as he could.

"Michelle, that's not a good idea right now. Can you stay with your parents?"

"They're in the Bahamas right now, Mike," she replied, her voice tightening further. "You know that. They go every summer."

"So that means you have their house to yourself," he said. "Five bedrooms, four baths, a theater room. All for you."

More silence. He was digging his hole deeper, not filling it in.

"You don't care, do you? You really must hate me. Well nice job, Mike. Way to show our daughter we can get along for her benefit!"

"Says the woman chewing me out with her in the back seat."

He cursed himself silently for letting her goad him, but it was too late now. The words were out and Michelle changed tactics. The tears resumed, and the fear returned to her voice.

"Please, Mike," she begged, adding the note of pathetic need she expected to further play a tune on his sympathies. And it did, but his anger overruled it as she went on. "Just for a couple of nights. I don't want Mom and Dad to know about Pitt and I yet. You know how they are. I'll never hear the end of it. Just give me a chance."

Mike decided to play his trump card. "Michelle, I have a girlfriend now, and it wouldn't work having you in the apartment. Too awkward."

"You mean that tattooed tramp who came to Pitt's place?" she snapped. "You're still seeing her? You can do better, Mike. I thought you and I were really reconnecting lately."

"Whatever, Michelle. My answer remains. Maria is welcome anytime, but you'll need to stay somewhere else."

This time her reply was quick and sharp as a dagger. "Fine! Maria and I will stay at Mom and Dad's. Way to be there for your daughter, Mike. And for me."

The line went dead. Mike swore, then sent Maria a text.

You can stay with me anytime, but only you.

Her reply came just seconds later.

I know, Dad. It's OK. We're going to Grandma and Grandpa's.

She signed it with a heart made from symbols. Mike patted himself on the back for not giving in, then walked back to his truck.

Chapter Twenty-Two

Annie caught herself daydreaming again, glancing over her right shoulder at Carol's office. The door stood closed. Annie let out a sigh.

She sat at her desk, hands poised over her keyboard, staring at her monitor, but doing nothing else. The flyer for the company Independence Day picnic gazed back at her, done in patriotic red, white, and blue, with fireworks and flags in the background and all sorts of picnic food in the fore. It looked the way it had thirty minutes ago, when she sat down to finish it up.

She punched in the prices for hot dogs, burgers, sodas, and chips, then looked at her work. Her crowning achievement for the week, hell for the month, thanks to Carol's realignment. Maybe after this, she could start working on a flyer for the Thanksgiving pot luck, followed by the employee holiday party.

She had to admit, for the first time ever she was looking forward to the Fourth of July party. In part because she'd set it up, so she knew the music and food would be good, but even more because she knew she'd be going with Mike. No one at the office had met her man in person yet, not even the gossipy Veronica. Annie had kept him hidden to keep him out of the office water cooler discussions, and to keep anyone like Veronica from moving in on him. They'd been together a month now, seeing each other almost every day, with Sundays being the exception; that's when he spent quality time with Maria. Seeing him with his daughter rang in her like a bell, a clarion call that told her he was the kind of guy long-term relationships were made of.

Mike had taken her to a Rockies game, just as promised. They'd gone to the Denver Fine Arts Museum, seen a concert at the Pepsi Center, gone to plays, and seen more movies than she'd seen the entire year before. He'd even given her a key to his place. For once, her romantic life seemed to be coming together.

They'd even fallen into a cute kind of couple's routine. He'd be in her front yard when she got home, working on one thing or another for the house. They'd go inside and eat dinner, then adjourn to his place for extracurricular activities two or three nights a week. Mike had tried to initiate intimacy twice at Annie's house, and both times she'd stopped him before anything weird could happen. She seemed to have reached a peace treaty with her mother, keeping things with Mike rated G at her house and saving R-rated activities for his place. Granted, she was pretty sure from the way the people downstairs from him looked at her that they could hear everything going on upstairs, but performing for strangers appealed to her more than doing so for her mother, dead or not.

She couldn't wait for the look on Carol's face when she showed up to the party with him. Even better would be watching Mike respond to her attempts to undermine Annie, which would no doubt start as soon as he showed up.

It made her grin just thinking about it.

"Is *that* the flyer for the party?"

Annie whirled around in her chair and jumped up, suddenly towering over her boss. She took a step back so she could see Carol's dark face, not just the midnight black of her perfect, unmoving hair.

"Oh, Carol," she breathed, her hand coming to her heart out of reflex. "You startled me. Yes, this is the flyer."

Carol leaned in and studied it a moment, then stood and wrinkled her nose.

"Not very imaginative," she complained. "Looks like last year's flyer, and we had no one at that party. See if you can come up with something catchier, something that screams 'fun!' This one whispers 'nap time,' at least to me."

Annie swallowed the retort that sprang to her tongue and nodded. "I was just thinking the same thing."

Carol raised an eyebrow. "So that's why you were so lost in thought that you didn't see me. And I thought you were just daydreaming."

She turned and stalked away, trailing drops of sarcastic dislike on the carpet behind her.

Yes, Annie looked forward to the company picnic this year.

She had just sat back down when her cellphone chimed with a text message from Mike. Her frown did a flip.

Need access to breaker box in the house to fix outdoor lantern. Can I get your key?

He added a winky-face symbol, making her laugh. The sound brought several of her coworkers' attention for a moment, but she no longer cared. She texted him back.

Sure, come and get it if you're man enough. ;)

We're already in your parking lot, came his reply.

That seemed odd. He'd never come to her work before, hadn't even asked about it. And who was with him?

Gathering her keys, Annie locked her computer and walked out to the front parking lot. Heat buffeted her, rising in waves from the asphalt, and the air seemed thick as wet cotton. The humidity was odd, and made her wonder if storms were due for Denver. Their air was normally dry, something she'd learned to appreciate during trips out east for work. New York and Washington both made her feel like she was breathing through a sponge.

Mike's truck sat there idling, with Mike's big blue eyes slicing through the thick air like blue scimitars. Sitting beside him was Jason, teeth glittering like jewels as he smiled.

"You two together?" she asked. "Have I lost you to the dark side, Mike?"

Mike laughed as she kissed him on the cheek. "Nah, he just wants to help me with your lamp."

She rolled her eyes at the two of them and handed Mike her house key.

"Well, he's about the least handy guy around, so he'll probably slow you down, but whatever hammers your nail."

"Speaking of hammering, let's go out tonight."

She rolled her eyes. "You're such a romantic, Mike. How could I resist that offer?"

"Ha, you date a contractor and you get contractor pickup lines. Six o'clock at your place. We're going downtown, so we should probably take your car. Easier to park."

"Oh, we're going out and parking are we? That's so high school."

Mike smiled, while Jason made a pained expression. "Could you two lovebirds get a room later so Mike and I can get going, please?"

Mike turned to Annie with a helpless look on his face. "You heard the man. Gotta go. See you at six?"

She gave him a sly, promising smile, pecked him on the cheek, and waved as he pulled away.

Annie watched the truck turn out of the parking lot and disappear into traffic. She stood a moment, not quite sure why, watching the exit, as if Mike might turn around and pull back in. Instead, a red Monte Carlo pulled up, stopped, and then exited onto the street, disappearing the same direction Mike had. There had to be a dozen of those cars in Denver, given the large population of NASCAR enthusiasts in the city, but Annie knew in her gut she'd seen this one before. Cruising past her house on moving day, and peeling out the night someone had thrown a rock through her window.

Frank.

Was he following Mike? She didn't think so—he'd been at least a half-minute behind him in leaving the lot. But she decided not to take a chance. She called Mike.

"Miss me already?" he answered, his cockiness making her smile. She did, in fact, miss him already, but she wouldn't let him know that.

"Mike, be careful. Frank's car just left the parking lot. I think he could be up to something."

"We'll come back to you, but go inside where it's safe, and tell Security."

"No, he's gone, Mike. I think he might be following you. Red Monte Carlo. Peeling paint, ugly white dude driving it."

Mike said something unintelligible to Jason, then replied, "Okay, Jason's here, so he'll keep an eye out for your ex. But please, go inside just in case."

"I will. Mike, maybe you shouldn't go to the house. He knows where I live."

"Sweetie, if he shows up at your house while I'm there, he'll be getting to know some police and paramedics in a hurry. Don't worry about me."

She hung up, unconvinced, shaking her head and trudging back toward the door. What if Frank's presence at the building had nothing to do with Mike? What if he'd been there for some other reason, like stalking Annie or slashing her tires?

She made a quick pass by her car, but it all seemed in order. No flats, no scratches, no shattered glass. She went back to her desk, knowing she should be looking forward to their date, but wondering what Mike was up to.

And what Frank was doing following him.

*

For once, Mike showed up for a date on time, arriving at her house a little before six. She was surprised to see him in a polo shirt, jeans, and boots—truly dressed up for him.

"Okay, now I'm really suspicious. What are you up to, Mike Tolbert?"

His exaggerated look of innocence confirmed to her he was hiding something.

"Hey, now, can't a guy dress up a little for a date with a gorgeous woman?"

"Hmmm, flattery, too. Now I know something's wrong."

Mike only smiled.

He had her drive to the Santa Fe Art District, one of her favorite stomping grounds. Her heart rate kicked up a notch—she didn't recall telling him about this place, so he must have figured it out on his own. It was very romantic that he knew her that well.

The minute they stepped out of the Fiesta, though, the rain started slashing down from the leaden sky. The drops themselves were almost as hot as the air, making her wonder if the clouds hadn't boiled, making the rain bubble over the edge and fall to earth. Mike took her hand and they jogged down to Ninth, then swung a left.

Annie stopped cold when she saw the sign sitting outside the tiny studio. Her name was splayed across the top in black letters on a white background, much like an old gas station marquee. Underneath it read, "Wed-Thur-Fri Only!"

"What did you do?" she asked, pulling away from Mike and moving toward the door. Now her abdomen clenched, her knees turned soft as whipped cream.

Sure enough, when she reached the display window, her painting—the one of the Denver skyline—stared out at her like a command to go inside.

She obeyed, slipping into the gallery, Mike on her heels. A few people milled around, looking at paintings on the wall or on easels. Her paintings. Her private expressions, the things she'd never shown anyone but Mike and Jason. Not even Frank had seen most of them.

A thin, graying woman strode toward them from the back of the room, her smile comforting and soft, hair trailing behind her. She took Annie's hand and studied her with eyes the color of a tropical bay.

"Hi, Annie, my name is Liz," woman said. "I just want you know your paintings can stay on display here until Friday night. And if you happen to sell any, we've waived our commission fees since you're a new artist."

Annie's mouth opened, but the words stuck in her throat, clambering over one another to get out. So she stood, mouth open, staring at the older woman.

Mike bailed her out. "I told Liz about your paintings," he said, grinning like a dog who'd cornered a cat. "She took one look at the pictures on my phone, and she's agreed that you are an artist worth showing. Between her and I, we invited a number of people to come to the showing. As long as you're open through Friday, you should see some interest in your work."

"How did you … when … I mean, you should've asked me."

Mike's smile faded in a heartbeat, shoulders slumped, and a light seem to go out in his eyes. "If I'd asked permission," he replied, "you wouldn't have done it."

"Exactly the point, Mike! These aren't yours to display. They're my private thoughts and feelings, my blood spilled on the canvas, not yours. I might have said yes to some, but it should have been my choice."

Mike looked at his shoes, kicking at the carpet like a teenager in trouble with his parents. "Then there wouldn't have been a surprise."

Annie took a deep breath. Mike meant well, and she was being oversensitive. All she had to do was get through three days of her most intimate thoughts and feelings being on display for the public, then she could take all the art back to her home and hide it there.

"You're right," she said, putting her hand on Mike's forearm. "I know you meant well, and I need to be more open to this. What good is art if no one sees it?"

That put a little bit of a smile back on his face. He patted her hand and moved it up to his elbow, leading her around the gallery so she could see the people looking at her art. Against the back wall, a young hipster couple looked at the painting she'd done of the old man at the park. They bowed their heads close together, whispering to one another as if the painting held a secret they could only share with each other.

By the display window, an elderly woman with white hair and a long fur coat examined a grayscale chalk drawing Annie had done years ago of a man scalping tickets outside Coors Field. She tilted her head to the left, then back to the right, and leaned in close to examine the work, as if looking at each individual stroke.

"What do you suppose she's looking at?" Annie asked Mike in a whisper.

The woman must have overheard, for she turned her head just enough to see Annie, and smiled in a way that crinkled the corners of her eyes.

"I was trying to read the sign on the stadium," she said. "I've been to almost every Rockies game in the last ten years, so I was probably here for this game."

"Oh, well I'm sorry," Annie said. "I don't remember what game that was when I drew it. But if you look on the back of the canvas, you might find a date."

"You're the artist?" she asked.

Annie nodded. "Yes, I drew that about five years ago."

"Well you have a wonderful talent," the old woman said. "Do you happen to know how much they're asking for this drawing?"

Annie looked at Mike. He shrugged and waved Liz over.

"Annie was wondering what you think a fair price is for this chalk piece," Mike said.

Liz gave Annie a reassuring look, and turned her away from the old woman.

"Why don't you go mingle with the other patrons?" she said. "When the business questions come up, just come and get me."

Without waiting for an answer, she turned and pulled the old woman to the side to talk price.

Mike led Annie around the shop a little more. The largest crowd, consisting of seven people, stood facing the left-hand wall, gathered around a large, framed portrait that Annie hadn't noticed before. It sat on the floor, leaning back against the wall, so the patrons' bodies blocked the majority of it. Annie squinted, looked closer, and felt her stomach tie itself in a knot.

Letting go of Mike's arm, she hurried to the back of the crowd, put her head between two people, and gasped when she saw the portrait of her mother staring back at her. Her mother's ice blue eyes seemed to stare straight into Annie's soul, accusing, condemning, and punishing her, all with a look.

Annie's head swam, and fought down the bile rising in her throat.

It hadn't occurred to her that this portrait, this one part of her insides she didn't want anybody to see, would be here tonight. If she'd thought of it earlier, she would've canceled the whole show. She wheeled on Mike, her finger jabbing him in the chest.

"Not that one!" she hissed. "Why did you have to bring that one?"

Mike's hands came up defensively in front of him, he and he took a step back. "I'm sorry, Annie," he whispered. "I'll have Liz take this one to the back."

But it was too late. Annie watched the people, their heads close to one another, whisper about her mother. About her. They knew! They could tell just by looking at the painting that Annie still feared her mother. From that painting alone, Annie knew they could tell everything about her. They could see into her soul, and tell everything she never wanted anyone else to know.

As if to confirm her suspicion, the young hipster couple joined the crowd, took one look at the painting, then glanced at Annie. Even the youngsters knew.

Heat rushed to her face, making Annie spin around so no one could see her blush. The tiny gallery seemed to shrink around her, its walls pressing in, its ceiling pushing down. People's faces loomed in her vision. Mike. Liz. The hipsters.

As sweat broke out on her brow, she bolted and ran from the gallery.

Chapter Twenty-Three

Mike stood in the door to the gallery, staring out into the dim light of the street as the sun set behind the mountains to the west. Humidity clung to his face and chest, a second shirt that made him sweat. Fat drops of rain splattered on the sidewalk, hitting the tips of his boots before disappearing into the thick air.

As angry as she was, Annie didn't go far. She wandered about ten yards down the sidewalk, stopped by a light post, and squatted down. She put her elbows on her knees and rubbed her eyes.

Mike decided to give her minute. He'd sprung this on her as a complete surprise, opening some of her most private thoughts and feelings to group of complete strangers. Behind him, the murmurs of gallery patrons thrummed like rhythmic guitars. Liz's voice danced across them like a nymph on water as she worked the business end of running an art gallery. If Mike knew Liz, she'd have at least one painting sold by the time the shop closed.

The rain picked up, the space between the fat drops decreasing and the sound of their patters on the sidewalk coming faster and faster. Mike grabbed an umbrella—he didn't know whose—from a barrel just inside the door, opened it, and jogged down to Annie's side. Squatting down, he held the umbrella over her, shielding her from the rain.

"I know you like watercolors," he said, "but I don't think the rain is a kind of water you need."

She turned her head just enough to glare at him over her shoulder. Then she put her face back in her hands. Wet spots glistened on her cheeks, but Mike didn't know if they were tears or raindrops.

"Okay, I'm sorry," he said.

"You should be," she snapped. "You should've asked my permission before doing this. This is an invasion of privacy."

"I'm not sorry for that," he said. "I'm apologizing for the corny joke I just made. It really sucked and was insensitive. I know this is hard for you, but I just wanted to show you how special your art is."

She lifted her head, ran her fingers through her hair, and shook the rain droplets out of it.

"I understand you meant well, Mike," she said. "And I do appreciate it. Really. I just wasn't...ready, I guess. Especially for the one of my mom. With everything going on, I wish you had left that one home. I haven't slept the night in my house in almost a month now. And it's all because of her. What made you think bringing that painting here would be okay?"

"I should've thought of that. I know that one's personal, especially with everything that's happened in the last couple of days. But you have a chance right now, Annie. There are people in there wanting to buy your paintings. People like your art enough to display it in their homes, or even better in their businesses. They feel the emotion you put in your paintings, they appreciate the craft as well.

"So you can get hung up on a painting of your mom, or you can go in there and make some money off your art. Liz's already working the floor for you. You could clear a couple hundred dollars or more tonight if you tried. That'll pay that handyman you have working for you."

He flashed his most roguish smile and even gave her little wink.

For her part, she tried to look angry, but her glare carried no heat this time. Maybe it was cooled by the rain, or maybe he'd gotten through to her. Either way, she only held her glare for a second before looking down and laughing. It started small, like a stream trickling from a mountain pass. But it grew as her mood lifted and she relaxed. She put her hand on Mike's wrist. A moment later she tilted her head back and laughed her loud, gaudy laugh.

"This was really uncool," she said. "You lied to me, basically stole my key, broke into my house, subverted my friend, and displayed my art without my permission. I really should kick your butt."

"Guilty as charged," he said, winking again. "But you'd much rather kiss me than kick me, wouldn't you?"

In response, she leaned over and kissed him on the cheek. "That's all you get for now," she said. She levered herself to her feet dragging Mike and his umbrella with her. "Now I have a deal for you."

Mike raised his eyebrows, but said nothing.

"I'll go in there and try to sell some paintings," she promised. "But you have to promise to spend the night in my house. I don't want to spend the night alone there. Oh, and we need to hide my mother's painting."

Mike nodded. "Your terms appear to be acceptable."

She grinned up at him, put one hand in the center of his chest, then turned and walked toward the studio. "Okay, let's go sell some paintings."

The rest of the night, Mike circulated among the customers that came to the gallery. He answered questions, pointed them toward art he thought they'd like, and when anybody asked about money, he got Liz to answer their question. Liz worked her patrons like she always did, a savvy art connoisseur with a nose for business. By the time the night was done, they'd only sold one painting, but they'd sold it for enough to cover Mike's work for two days.

When the gallery closed, and Liz locked the door with Mike and Annie watching, the rain had intensified. The steady downpour did not, however, dampen Annie's mood. She stood outside the gallery, arms crossed under her breasts, and smiled at her paintings displayed in the window.

"Thank you, Mike," she said. She leaned up and kissed him, this time on the mouth. Mike kissed her back, pulling her tight against him as he held the umbrella with one hand.

"You're welcome," he said. Then he went back to kissing her.

Neither of them noticed when Liz strolled away.

*

"You still want to come in?" Annie asked. "I cook a mean omelet in the morning."

Mike flashed his lopsided smile and moved closer. "I keep my promises," he said.

Laughing, she opened the door and shoved him inside.

As soon as the door closed, he jumped her. No romance, no music, no candlelight. He just pushed her against the door and kissed her hard, tongue groping for hers. The heat of his body swept over her, catching parts of her on fire as well.

It caught her by surprise, but his hand on the back of her neck made her body respond. She ran her fingers down the muscles of his back and grabbed his hips, pulling them against her so even through their clothes she felt him going hard. She wrapped one leg around him, wanting to pull him inside her.

Annie, said a woman's voice. Her mother's voice.

Mike stopped. "Did you hear that?"

"I said, 'fuck me,'" she whispered, holding back curses. She needed this too much to let her late mother ruin it. Still, the butterflies in her stomach were not all due to arousal.

Mike laughed and kissed her again. His hand slipped under her shirt, cupping her breast, his thumb sliding over her nipple. She arched her back against the door, fumbling with the button on his jeans. She wrapped her other leg around him, and by the time he'd carried her to the living room, she'd unbuttoned his shirt, too.

He dumped her on the couch, covering her with his body. He lifted her t-shirt over her head and enveloped her mouth in a kiss. She felt herself rising on a wave of passion and heat, a swell of desire that moved with such power she couldn't resist it even if she wanted to. Her control slipped with every kiss.

A loud crash scared them both off the couch and set her already rising heartbeat to racing. The two of them scanned the room frantically, trying to find what had made the noise. Her mother's Bible lay on the floor near the end table where it had sat just a moment earlier. Or at least she thought it had. She bent and picked it up. It had opened to 1 Corinthians 7:8.

Flee fornication. Every sin that a man doeth is without the body; but he that committeth fornication sinneth against his own body.

"Damn it, Mom," Annie muttered.

"What?" Mike asked.

"Nothing." She closed the Bible and set it on the table.

Mike swept her up in his arms and carried her upstairs, making her desire flare from a candle to a bonfire. So consumed in her own lust was she, that she didn't protest when he carried her into the master bedroom. It didn't even put a dent in her desire. Somewhere deep inside her, stubbornness flared. She wasn't about to let a figment of her imagination end this almost perfect night.

He tossed her on the four-poster bed, tugged her jeans off, and removed his own before crawling back on top of her. His kisses started on her forehead, swept down across her mouth and neck, then settled on her nipple. His hand slipped down to her ass, then moved to the front. She felt herself go slick, the muscles of her body tensing as she went rigid under him.

She moaned and closed her eyes as he slid into her. She grabbed his buttocks and controlled the rhythm of his strokes. Ecstasy consumed her more and more with each movement as she rocked her hips in unison with his thrusts.

"Look in my eyes," he whispered.

She opened her eyes and gasped. Her mother's ghost stood, translucent, at the foot of the bed. She wore the same blue velvet dress she always wore, and her gray-streaked hair stayed up in a bun, except for a few locks that fell around her face. She crossed her arms over her ethereal chest and frowned.

Annie froze, and Mike paused with her.

"Am I hurting you?"

Her mother scowled at her, but Annie flipped her off behind Mike's back. "No. Now come with me."

He grinned and moved his hips again. His thrusts became faster, almost frenzied. She kept her eyes closed and moved in perfect sync with him. She felt herself rising on the massive wave again, higher with every stroke. It had been so long. She moaned and dug her nails into Mike's back.

"Annie," he moaned. "Yes, Annie!"

She felt him tense, and felt herself moving closer and closer to the crest. She grabbed the sheets, holding on so they could come together.

His back went rigid and his hips thrust harder. "Annie!"

Then he screamed and jumped off her, scrambling back until he fell off the end of her bed. His head hit the back wall with a whump.

"Holy shit!" he cried, jumping up. He rubbed his head with one hand and, with the other, pointed to the painting over the headboard.

Annie looked at the painting just as her mother's grin faded from the glass. She forced herself to stay calm.

"What?" she asked. "My God, was I that bad?"

"No, Annie, you were great." His cheeks flushed. "You didn't see that?"

"See what?"

"Seriously?" Mike shook his head and tugged on his jeans. "Christ, now you've got me seeing things. There really is something weird about this place."

He plopped on the end of the bed, making it creak in protest.

Annie wasn't about to give up that easily. "Okay, let's go to your place," she sighed. "At least we can be alone there. I don't intend to let this end this way. You owe me an orgasm."

Mike shook his head and grinned at her joke. "Well, I hate being in debt, so you'll need to collect tonight."

They dressed like it was a game, and to her surprise the act of covering up each other's nakedness was almost as arousing as exposing it. Her mother might have won a small battle, but Annie was going to win the war. More than once tonight.

As they walked out of the bedroom, Annie thought she heard a cackle from the painting.

*

Mary couldn't stop herself from laughing. It bubbled from her like soda from a shaken can, frothy and out of control. She hated being out of control, but laughter was all that came to her, mirth the only reaction she could muster to the situation.

She laughed because if she stopped, the screaming would begin. Her pain was immeasurable, a shredding feeling, like her very being tore in half, ripped between the world of the living and that of the dead. She'd known speaking to Annie would cause her great pain, but she hadn't known how great until the force of crossing the barrier sliced through her. Now she laughed to hide the wailing that would ensue should she stop.

As soon as Annie and Mike left her house, the gap in the barrier slammed closed and the pain winked out as if someone had thrown a switch. She quieted herself and moved to the window, watching them climb into his truck and rumble off into the darkness.

Inside her, satisfaction glowed like a fire, crackling and warm and comfortable against the otherwise cold state of her existence. She'd stopped them from defiling her room, drove them from her quiet place and into the night. More importantly, she'd planted a sapling of doubt, one that would root in Mike's heart and grow like a weed until its canopy cast a shadow over their relationship. If Mary couldn't make Annie see Mike's danger, she could at least drive a wedge between them. It would hurt Annie, but would also save her far greater pain later on.

Still, they were headed to his place, still together and not fighting like she'd hoped they'd be. Her daughter still refused to see what lay before her, refused to listen to her mother's warnings.

A thought occurred to her then that sent a wave of cold from one end of her to the other. What if Annie left forever? She might choose to obey her fear and move in with Mike, selling the old house, leaving Mary alone, her purpose unfulfilled. She could not bear that thought, its pain almost as great as the pain of speaking across the barrier. If Annie grew frightened, she'd run to Mike's arms, possibly forever.

Mary found she'd planted her own doubt tree, one whose roots already undermined the ground on which she stood. She'd saved her sanctuary and driven their filthy behavior from the house, but had she driven them closer together?

She sighed and leaned her head against the cold, sharp window glass, letting its pain cut into her again, hoping it would clear her mind.

It did not. Mary wondered once again if she was doing the wrong thing. If her mothering was misdirected, or if somehow she'd miscalculated. Doubt crept in, now, like fog into a graveyard. Was her purpose really to protect her daughter, or was she doomed to roam the old house forever as payment for the debt of her past mistakes?

That thought wrapped her in a black cloak of sorrow, shrouding her with despair, a suffocating, restricting restraint from which many never emerged.

Yet Mary shook it off and straightened. She would not give up, not yet. Her daughter was stubborn, nothing more. And stubbornness was something Mary could overcome.

Something she would overcome. She had to.

Chapter Twenty-Four

Annie didn't budge her head from Mike's chest, letting her fingers run up and down the terrain of his abs. She didn't want to move, as if the slightest motion would disturb this little slice of heaven she'd found in Mike's apartment. His rhythmic breathing, steady and slow, lulled her to a state of drowsiness, and she almost fell back to sleep, wrapped in the warmth of love and trust. But Thursday was not a day to sleep in. She guessed it was about six o'clock, meaning she had to be at work in a little over an hour. She still had to run home, take a shower, get dressed, and try to eat something on the way in.

Or she could lie here, wrapped around her man, watching the warm golden sunshine stream in through the south-facing window of Mike's bedroom until eight o'clock rolled around and Carol made it into the office. Then Annie could call in, fake a cough, and take a sick day. Technically that was against the rules, and if anybody would enforce that stupid rule Carol would. But Annie was beginning to care less and less what Carol thought.

She reached back for her cell phone, stretching without moving her head, her hand flopping around on the nightstand behind her until she found it. She opened it quietly and gasped at the time. It was already six forty-five. So much for making it to work. It looked like she was taking a sick day after all.

She snuggled in closer to Mike, making him stir. He took in a deep breath, let it out slowly, and then his breathing returned to the rhythm of sleep. Her mind drifted back to the night before. She skipped over the whole part about her mother's house in what she supposed was her own private kind of denial. She didn't want to think about that right now, couldn't let it ruin the paradise in which she lay.

They'd left her house right away, but stopped on the way to his apartment to pick up ice cream at a convenience store. They sat on his living room couch, eating chocolate chip cookie dough, until almost midnight. They talked about everything. From her mother, to his PTSD. Nothing seemed to make them uncomfortable. Thinking of how Mike had listened made Annie think of all the times she'd tried talking to Frank, just to realize he'd tuned her out. Mike hadn't said a single word as she talked about her mother. Nor when she talked about the court fight, Frank's work, or anything else.

When they'd run out of things to talk about, he'd stood, taking her hand, and led her to his bedroom with the grace and quiet of a dancer. He'd undressed her caringly and had stopped several times to look her in the eye and make sure it was okay to keep going. His tenderness both surprised and aroused her. As always, he read her feelings, knew what she needed, and gave it to her.

Their lovemaking was unlike anything she'd ever experienced. As at her house, they just seem to fit and be in sync with one another. They moved as one, moaned as one, and climaxed as one every time. All three times.

She grinned. Three times. Something Frank wouldn't even have attempted. As long as he got his, he didn't care what Annie got or didn't get. Once he was done, they were both done.

The thought made her turn her head slightly and kiss Mike on his bare shoulder. He stirred again, this time harder. He rolled away from her and muttered something in his sleep that sounded stressed.

Annie leaned on one elbow and looked at him. His forehead was scrunched down, his eyes squeezed closed tight, and he shook his head from side to side as if vigorously telling someone "no." His legs spasmed, each one punching down toward the end of the bed, tearing the covers from them. It took Annie a moment to realize he was running, much like she'd seen dogs do when they dreamed about chasing a rabbit. Only Mike wasn't chasing anything. He was fleeing.

His movements became violent, and Annie had to get out of the bed to avoid being kicked or elbowed. She stood over him, her stomach knotted in worry. His fists smashed at the lamp on his nightstand, knocking it to the floor with a loud crash. But he didn't wake up. He stayed in his nightmare, pursued by whatever terrifying enemy gave chase.

He thrashed again and this time his headboard crashed into the wall, leaving a dent in the sheet rock. She had to stop him. He was going to hurt himself.

She moved beside the bed, kneeled on the edge of the mattress, and put her hands on his shoulders.

"Mike," she said, her voice a hoarse whisper. She knew waking someone up from a nightmare could be dangerous, both for the waker and the dreamer. "Mike, wake up. You're in a nightmare."

He continued to thrash, his pillows sliding up under him and his head striking the headboard. He yelled, shouting things she couldn't understand, Arabic perhaps. She tried again.

"Mike!" She raised her voice and shook him by the shoulders. "Michael, wake up!"

His eyes shot open, and in them she saw a terror so primal that it made her catch her breath. He lashed out, his hand moving too quickly for her to dodge. It struck her in the left eye. Pain exploded through her head as it snapped back, making something in her neck crunch. She fell backwards, grabbing wildly at the mattress but finding only air. When she hit, the back of her head bounced off the cold tile of his floor.

Her vision swam. The room spun. An iris of dark began to close, and she knew she was passing out.

Then Mike was there. His face hovered over hers, and his arms scooped her up as if she weighed nothing. As tenderly as he had undressed her, he laid her in his bed, positioning a pillow under her head and staring into her eyes.

Annie felt cold clammy hands of panic clawing at her insides. When she looked at Mike's face, for an instant she saw Frank's superimposed over it. Her mind fled back to that night, back to the terror of his attack. Her instinct was to get up and run. Get out of the apartment, get into her car, and lock herself in. Then to drive as fast as her little Fiesta would go.

But when she rose to her elbows, the room spun and Mike eased her back down in the bed.

"Don't try to get up," he said. His voice cracked, held a nervous edge like a blade against a throat. "Your head hit the floor pretty hard. You probably have a concussion."

When she opened her eyes this time, the room didn't spin. Mike was right. She probably had a concussion, but she was alert enough to know what happened. Mike had hit her. Hard.

Her emotions screamed at her, yelling that she should run as far from Mike as possible. Yet her logical mind spoke calmly, reassuring her that all would be okay. He hadn't meant to hit her. He'd been dreaming. He didn't know what he was doing.

Yet somehow that did nothing to calm her.

Seeing her distress, Mike rose quickly from the bed and ran his fingers through his tousled hair. She wondered when he'd put his jeans on. He paced the room, his bare feet silent on the tile floor. His breathing came in short gasps and she was sure that if she felt his wrist, his pulse would be beating like a marching band drum.

She eased herself to her elbows again, and this time stayed that way.

"Mike, I think I need to go."

That seemed to panic him more. He threw both hands up in the air, then seized the hair on either side of his head as if he might tear it out. "Great, just great! Now you'd rather face your haunted old house then be with me. I've blown it again."

"Why are you making this all about you?"

"Because I'm the one who did this," he yelled. "I'm the dumbass who punched his girlfriend. This is what I do, I mess up relationships. This is why Michelle left me."

"Wait, you hit Michelle too?"

Mike whirled on her then, his face red and clenched with anger. Even though she knew most of the anger was at himself, she feared a tiny bit might be directed at her and she shrank back against the headboard.

"No!" he snapped. "I never laid a hand on her, or Maria. But I couldn't keep control of my emotions, of my disease. She couldn't handle it."

Annie pulled the blankets up to her chin and her knees up to her chest. She wanted to pull the covers over her head and hide, but she knew that would do no good.

"Well I'm not Michelle," she whispered. "I don't run at the first sign of trouble. But I do need some space now."

Mike went back to staring out the window, his arms crossed over his chest. The muscles in his back formed an impenetrable wall, a shield she knew she could not penetrate and a barrier she could not climb. It was as if his back was made of ice.

"That's what Michelle said when she left." He didn't even turn around.

Annie rolled her eyes, lowering the blankets enough to talk to him, but not enough to show her nakedness. She wasn't ready to show him that vulnerability again so soon.

"You really need to get over Michelle. I think she caused your PTSD as much as the war did."

She regretted it as soon as it was out of her mouth, but the damage was already done. Mike spun and pointed an accusing finger at her.

"And you need to get over your goddamn mother! I've never seen somebody resist growing up quite as much as you have. Your mom's not in your house. She's in your head. She got in your head when you were little, and you're too weak to kick her out of it now. Maybe she's causing you have your own kind of PTSD."

This time Annie did pull the blankets over her head. She couldn't stand the thought of him seeing the tears in her eyes, of him knowing that he'd hurt her. It was another vulnerability she had to hide.

"Yeah, maybe she did. Maybe my mom messed me up as much as the war and Michelle messed you up. It's not something to talk about right now. Please just let me be alone for a while. I need to call in sick to work."

He snatched his t-shirt off the end of the bed, jerked it over his head, and stormed out of the room. Over his shoulder, he called back to her. "Fine, I have counseling anyway. Let yourself out when you're ready to go."

The slamming of his front door told her he had actually left. A moment later she heard his truck outside and knew she was completely alone. That's the way she always ended up: alone.

She touched the corner of her cheek then jerked her fingers away as pain arced through her head. She didn't think he'd broken anything, but she could feel swelling already. She found her jeans on the floor, slipped into them, and looked at her face in the mirror with a dresser. It looked like someone had put a plum under the skin of her left cheek.

"Great. Carol's going to have a field day with this."

But not today. She picked up her cell phone and dialed Carol's number. Her boss wouldn't be in yet, and sure enough the phone call went directly to voicemail, where she left a message saying she'd be out sick. She put the cell phone back down on the dresser, and shrugged herself into her t-shirt.

She was walking into the living room when Mike's doorbell rang.

"I guess you forgot your damn keys," she whispered. Bracing herself, she walked to the door.

*

Mike tried to relax in the hard wooden chair opposite Collins' desk, but in typical VA form the chair came from a 1950s school room. Its hard wooden slats gouged into his back, and the cold surface of the wood made his butt hurt. He shifted from hip to hip, but no matter what he did he couldn't get comfortable.

Behind the desk, Larry Collins listened, his hands folded across his chest and his eyes closed behind his wire-rimmed glasses. It gave him a serene look, one that Mike normally found comforting. Today it irritated him.

"When I woke up," Mike said, looking at his hands, "I took a swing. I didn't mean to, but I hit her. Right in the eye. I think she might have a concussion."

"And what happened after that?" Collins asked without opening his eyes.

"I apologized, but we had a fight anyway. It was over stupid stuff, and we both said things I don't think we meant. But I still left the apartment angry. And alone."

"What do you think made you hit her?"

"I was dreaming," Mike said. He didn't want to remember the dream, but he had to. "I was having this nightmare about Iraq."

"The same dream you were having before?" the counselor asked.

"Almost the same. Only this time in my dream I'm jumping up, trying to fight the gunman before he shoots. I never make it in time, but I'm jumping up. That didn't happen in the real world."

"And what do you think that means?"

"How the hell am I supposed to know? You're the shrink here, I'm just a patient."

Collins opened his eyes, pursed his lips, and leaned his elbows on the desk. Outside, cars passed by, their tires hissing on the leftover water from the rain the night before. Collins let out his breath in a similar hiss and leaned back again.

"I think it's a sign of healthiness," he said. "I think your subconscious wants you to fight back."

Mike thought about that. It kind of made sense, but something was missing.

"What am I supposed to fight back against?"

"What do you think?"

Mike sighed, irritated at the problem being put back on him. He needed answers, not more questions.

"So you think my subconscious wants me to fight for Annie." It was not a question.

Collins spread his fingers wide, shrugged, and locked his hands behind his head.

"I think your subconscious knows what's best for you."

"How can Annie be best for me?" Mike asked. This was something he'd debated with himself several times during the drive to the VA. "She's what they call a 'hot mess.' She's about to get fired, she's crazy enough to think there are ghosts flying around her house, and she has a crazy ex-boyfriend stalking her. If nothing else, I can't expose Maria to that."

"It sounds to me like she and Maria get along just fine."

Mike had no answer for that, because in short, the counselor was correct. Annie and Maria got along like long-lost sisters, like they were two pieces of the same puzzle that had just been fitted together.

"How has your PTSD been doing other than this morning?" Collins asked. He removed his glasses, set them on his desk, and rubbed his eyes.

Mike thought back over the last month. The nightmares had become less frequent, and he'd slept through the night more than he had in the two prior. He hadn't blown up at anybody until Annie this morning.

"It's been better," he said. "Fewer dreams, less anger. It hasn't gone away, but it's been better."

He told the counselor about the morning at Pitt's house, when Annie had calmed him, kept him from doing anything stupid. He even talked about how her touch seemed to soothe his frayed nerves.

"And yet you're walking away from a woman who is a positive influence on you. Why?"

"I punched her in the face."

"And how is that Annie's fault?"

"It's not really her fault, but I'm not sure she's such a positive influence on me after all. Let's face it: She's nuts."

Collins put his glasses back on and stared at Mike for a long time. He tried to see deeper into Mike with his gaze, to break through his defenses and read all was going on inside him. Mike kept his shields raised.

"Let me ask you something bluntly," Collins said. "Do you love Annie?"

That one caught Mike off-guard. He hadn't thought of it, intentionally ignoring the question in his own mind for fear of moving too quickly. Now, faced with having to decide, he found himself unable to speak the words. Instead he muttered his answer. "I don't know."

"I think you do," Collins said. "Are you afraid of loving her?"

"Maybe I should be."

Collins opened his mouth to reply, but Mike's cell phone rang, cutting them off. Collins shot Mike an irritated look. The man hated cell phones in his office, but Mike refused to turn his off. He never knew when Maria might need help. Especially with Pitt around.

Mike grabbed his phone and rolled his eyes. "Sorry, Larry," he said. "It's Michelle. This could be about Maria, so I have to take it."

Collins nodded, but the annoyed expression did not go away.

Mike answered, "Hi, Michelle."

"Mike, look, I don't know how to say this." Her voice sounded tenuous, as if she were fishing for words on the thinnest ice in the world. "I just came from your apartment..."

She let the sentence trail off as if Mike was supposed know what that meant.

"Yeah, and?"

"Mike, uhm, Annie was still there."

Mike's heart fell into his stomach. If Michelle had seen Annie's eye, she could easily get visitations supervised.

"You two didn't fight, did you?" he joked, hoping she hadn't seen Annie's eye.

"No, we actually had a civil discussion. But it looks like you two fought."

Mike sighed and ran his fingers through his hair. He stood, turned his back on Collins, and stalked to the window that looked out on the street.

"It was an accident," he explained. He struggled to keep the desperation out of his voice. "I was dreaming. About Fallujah. She tried to wake me up and it just happened."

He braced himself for a tongue lashing. This was just the sort of thing Michelle had been waiting for: a chance to take Maria away.

"That's what she told me," Michelle said, her voice calm. "Makes me feel better you told the same story. Mike, she doesn't know what to expect from you. She doesn't understand PTSD the way I did."

"I know," Mike said. "You were a military spouse, with training on PTSD, and you couldn't handle my disease. She's never been around the military before, so I can't expect her to do any better."

"You should take her to counseling with you, Mike. I never went, and I regret that now. It might have helped. We might not both be where we are."

Something had changed in her voice. There was more than just compassion there now, there was need. A hole that needed to be filled, something she couldn't fill herself.

"Michelle, what's wrong?"

"Nothing, really. Nothing you should worry about. I just wanted to tell you Annie will be okay."

Mike turned from the window, massaging the back of his neck with his own hand. He could feel the muscles in his neck tightening, firing a headache up into his skull.

"Michelle, come on," he said. "I've known you long enough to know when something's bothering you. If you don't tell me, I can't help."

She hesitated, and in the background Mike thought he heard the sound of traffic. She was out walking. She only did that when she was upset.

"Mike, Pitt cheated on me."

To his own surprise, his heart skipped a beat. He felt like pumping his fist in the air and screaming out, "Now you know I felt!"

Instead, he comforted her. "I'm sorry, Michelle. That must hurt."

"I don't know what to do, Mike. I don't think we have a chance now. Maria and I are still with Mom and Dad, but even with your child support and alimony, Maria won't be able to have many of the things she had. He even took her cell phone away when I left."

Mike's grip on his cell phone tightened. He forced himself not to crush it.

"I'll go out this afternoon to get her a new cell phone," he said. "Call it the birthday gift she should've gotten from me in the first place. Who did he cheat with?"

"Some client. She's in her twenties, single, and also going through a divorce. So I guess it's kind of ironic."

Mike shrugged, as if she could see his gesture. "Are you okay?"

"Define okay. If okay means smeared makeup, walking for miles, and feeling directionless, then I guess I'm okay."

Mike also knew when Michelle was trying to manipulate him. A certain tightness came into her voice, a tension that she wasn't aware of. This was important to her. Mike was at a loss for words, so he looked at Collins. The counselor raised his hand and mouthed, "I don't know."

"Is there anything I can do?" Mike asked her.

Again she hesitated, and a horn blew in the background. Not a car horn, but a train, loud and long.

"I just need someone to talk to," she said. "I know we're not married anymore, not even friends, but I can use an ear to chew on for a while."

Mike looked at the clock on the wall behind Collins. "Well, it's ten o'clock now. I'm done here in fifteen minutes, and then I have two jobs afterward. We could get together at the deli we used to go to. Talk over lunch, then go pick up Maria together. I think she'd like that."

This time the tension was gone from Michelle's voice. In its place was an almost musical happiness. She'd gotten her way and she knew it.

They hung up and Mike turned to find Collins staring at him, shaking his head.

"Am I making a mistake?" he asked the counselor.

"Only you can answer that. But consider this: your PTSD symptoms were getting better with Annie. Did that ever happen with Michelle?"

Mike shrugged.

"Have you reconsidered prolonged exposure therapy? This might be the right time to start it."

"I still don't have time," Mike said, knowing that was only half the truth. "Maybe this fall."

Collins put his glasses on the desk and studied Mike with his puppy-dog eyes, looking hurt.

"Avoidance isn't working, Mike. Facing things might."

Mike stood, determining the session was done. "Avoidance will have to do for now."

Chapter Twenty-Five

Mike sat in his truck, listening as the rain pounded on the roof like a thousand ballpeen hammers. He'd turned off his windshield wipers already, so the glass sheeted over. He sat in the driver's seat, hands locked on the steering wheel, breathing in slow, rhythmic measure. The rain turned Downing Street into a small river, as the water ran down either side of the road before disappearing into the storm drains.

Lunch with Michelle had not gone as he'd hoped. Things had started off positive enough, as Michelle opened up about the pain of finding out Pitt had cheated on her. As soon as Mike said he knew her pain, though, Michelle had slammed down her fork and stomped from the restaurant, sticking Mike with the bill.

That had been two days before, and Mike's mood still mirrored the weather: cold and gray.

He'd parked at the curb outside an apartment building, the site of his next job. In the midst of a rainstorm, a pipe had broken one of the upstairs apartments. Water was floating up from the basement and down from the other apartment. Mike's job was to fix the upstairs leak.

Yet as he sat wrapped in the hissing torrent of the rain, he found himself frozen, unable to move. He kept seeing Annie's face in his mind, her eye swollen shut, tears running from her good eye. She'd called him earlier that day, as he drove towards this job. Mike had ignored it. He wasn't ready to talk to her, wasn't ready to face the damage he'd done.

She hadn't left a message.

He still didn't know what to think of any of the things happening in her house. His logical, military side would not let him believe her mother haunted the house, but something was going on, something that frightened Annie enough that she couldn't sleep there very often. Mike suspected Frank had something to do with it, but the fact that Annie blamed it on ghosts made him skeptical about her own stability. Either she was playing some sort of weird game, messing with his head, or she truly believed there were ghosts in the house. Either way, combining that sort of mindset with his PTSD could be a deadly combination.

His cell phone rang again. He looked the caller ID: Annie. This time he hit the button to send it directly to voicemail. He waited a minute and no message notification appeared. Maybe she'd give up this time.

With a deep breath, he grabbed his tool bag off the passenger seat, opened the door, and stepped out into the pouring rain. As soon as his feet hit the sidewalk, a young man with an umbrella approached him, a manila envelope tucked under his arm.

"Are you Mr. Michael Tolbert?" the young man asked, extending his hand.

Mike shook his hand and nodded. "Yes, that's me."

The man handed Mike the manila envelope, then took two steps back.

"Congratulations Mr. Tolbert," he said. "You've just been served."

Rather than get back in his truck, Mike jogged to the open door of the apartment building and took shelter in the foyer, dropping his tool bag to the floor. Inside, the building smelled musty and moldy, as if it hadn't been cleaned in years. Upstairs a baby cried, and down the hall from him a small dog yipped and yapped, frantic that someone was in the hallway.

Mike jammed his thumb under the lip of the envelope and ripped it open. He'd heard of other contractors being sued by customers, but he'd avoided that fate until now. He couldn't think of which customer would be upset enough to do it, though. Taking a deep breath, he withdrew the small stack of papers from the envelope.

As he read them, the strength seemed to leave his legs and he leaned back against the wall for support. His suspicions had been wrong: It wasn't a disgruntled customer. Michelle was taking him back to court. The letter summarized her demands succinctly. She wanted Mike's visitations reduced to once a week, supervised, at a controlled location of the court's choosing. And she wanted his child support and alimony both increased by ten percent. It cited lack of responsibility in picking Maria up, potential for domestic violence, the bad influence of Annie's personality, and Mike's unsteady job situation as justification for reducing his time with his daughter.

Unsteady job situation his ass. At least he had a job, unlike Michelle, who'd grown used to leeching off her lawyer boyfriend. Another ten percent wouldn't cripple Mike, but it would make things even tighter than they already were.

He ran his fingers through his hair, as shock settled in like an old friend to sleep on his couch. Michelle's bullshit shouldn't have surprised him anymore, but it did. He'd thought they were getting along.

The reduction in visitation really bothered him. He looked forward to his Friday nights and Sundays with his daughter. He loved just watching a movie or going to the zoo with her. Those nights, even more than the nights with Annie, were free of his PTSD symptoms. That's when he felt the most complete.

Well, almost. When the three of them were together—him, Maria, and Annie—he felt the most complete. Not that it mattered now.

He rubbed his forehead, this time frozen not by an inability to move, but a lack of desire to move. He could feel his energy draining into the floor, seeping through the baseboards and into the flooded basement of the apartment building. For a moment—for one frozen, stunning, terrifying moment—he thought it would be easier to simply drown in the basement than keep fighting the battles his life threw at him.

He chased those thoughts away. Even supervised visits with Maria were better than nothing at all, or abandoning her to suicide. He'd had suicidal thoughts before. Most PTSD sufferers did, since depression went hand-in-hand with the disease. And every time, it been the thought of his daughter being left alone without her father that kept him alive.

His cell phone rang again and he almost ignored it. But this time the ringtone told him it was Michelle. He wound himself up to launch on her and pushed the talk button.

"Your process server just handed me the papers, Michelle," he snapped. "You really are an ice-cold bitch."

His words must have taken her aback, for her reply took a moment to come out.

"I can't allow you to continue to expose Maria to the negative influence of your life," she said. Her voice rang with sharp tension, like a piano wire strung across the throat. "I have to think of my daughter and her well-being."

"She's *our* daughter," Mike reminded her. "I don't see how denying her quality time with me is going to help her at all. Let's face it, it's all about the money for you. You lost your sugar daddy, so now you need to find a way to soak more money from me."

She hesitated again, like he'd thrown her off-guard.

"Look, Mike, you can avoid all this trouble. We don't have to go to court, you don't to reduce visitation, and you don't pay your money. In fact, you can see Maria anytime you want, and pay me absolutely nothing. As long as you meet my terms."

Every alarm in Mike's head rang loud and clear. He didn't doubt for a moment that he was stepping into a clever trap, designed to cut him off at the knees and force him into slavery. But the thought of unlimited time with Maria was enough to make him ask.

"What terms are those?"

Her voice took on an unexpected coolness, a business-like manner so completely unlike her that Mike wondered if his ex-wife was still on the other end of the line.

"It's simple, really. We've been going about this wrong all this time, Mike. Maria needs a family, a real family. One that's together with both a mom and dad for her. None of this bullshit about two mothers and two fathers. That's proven to not work."

"What are you getting at, Michelle?" In his heart he knew what she meant, but he wanted to hear her say it. Needed to hear her say it.

"I think we should get back together."

Emotions whirled in a confusing mix, and Mike knew he couldn't sort them out even if he tried. A normal family for Maria was a tempting thought, as was returning to a stable family where he was never alone. The only part of him that rebelled was the part that hated being blackmailed into doing something. He suppressed that part with more ease than he thought possible.

"It doesn't have to be intimate," she added. "We can just start by living in separate rooms in the same place. Maybe just spending weekends together at your place. You know, ease into things. I think that would do Maria a lot of good. She's pretty upset about Pitt leaving me."

Mike rolled his eyes. *Yeah, I'll bet she's crying her eyes out over that.* Still, to his own surprise, he found himself considering her proposal. It might be best for Maria, giving her some semblance of a normal family. And it would keep him out of court, allowing him to both see his daughter and keep what little money he had.

"And if I go along with this crazy plan," he said, "you have these papers rescinded? No more suing, no more courts?"

"There won't be any reason to do any of that. We'd be a family again."

Mike fought a battle with himself, a fight that raged as intensely as Fallujah. He knew he was being manipulated, knew that she would turn right back into the same negative influence she had been when they were married. But this was about Maria. A chance to see her every day, to not have to worry about losing her.

"Can I have a couple of days think about it?" he asked.

Her response was an irritated sigh. "If you really need it, I suppose. I'll give you until Monday. That's five days and ought to be more than enough."

Without waiting for anything else, she hung up.

Mike grabbed his tool bag, took a cleansing breath, and marched up the stairs. As he walked, he could almost feel the marionette strings pulling at his arms and legs.

Chapter Twenty-Six

Annie slouched at her desk, wearing her nerdy horn-rimmed glasses, hoping no one would see the bruise through her makeup. She even looked down at the keyboard while she typed, something she never did anymore, because she hoped it might hide her face from her coworkers.

She knew she'd have to face Carol eventually, as her boss would be upset about her sick day Thursday. She had the sick time saved up, and had thought about taking off today as well, but when she called Carol, the tone of her voice made it clear she was to come to work.

Now she had to find a way to explain the black eye to Carol without causing caustic remarks and possibly ridicule.

Not that it mattered, since Michelle had already seen her bruised face. Annie tried not to think about their encounter, how their dislike for one another had become muted by an awkward camaraderie that formed between them. Michelle had seemed genuinely shocked when she saw Annie's eye, but had also accepted Annie's explanation without question. Almost too easily, in fact. Annie would almost bet Mike had already heard from his ex as she tried to leverage his mistake against him.

Annie became so lost in thought that she didn't see Carol arrive. Veronica snapped her out of her memories by leaning on her cubicle wall.

"Carol wants to see you, Annie," she said. Annie didn't look up, and Veronica didn't try to get a closer look. Maybe the makeup was working. "She says it's urgent."

"Okay, tell her I'll be right there."

She kept her eyes on her keyboard while Veronica walked away. When her coworker was gone, Annie pulled a small compact mirror out of her purse and examined her eye. If she kept her right side turned toward Carol, her left side angled away, she might be able to pull this off.

She knocked on Carol's door, and her boss looked up from the desk before she had a chance to turn away. The look of surprise on Carol's face told Annie she'd seen her black eye.

"Annie, my God, what happened to your face?" Always the caring one.

Annie stepped inside, still angling herself to try and hide her bruise.

"My paintings fell over," she said. "Corner of the frame caught me right in the eye."

Carol stared at her, a dubious look on her face. Then she shook her head and wrote something on a piece of paper on her desk in front of her.

"You should get help," she said. "Or just stay away from men."

"Thanks for your concern." Annie didn't even try to keep the sarcasm from her voice. "You needed to see me about something?"

"Are you going to charge him for hitting you?"

"No. It was an accident while he was dreaming." She couldn't look Carol in the eye while she said it.

"Well, it's good to see you've developed the ability to forgive," Carol said. "Too bad you didn't have that a year ago."

"You know, Carol, I think I'm done with this conversation." Annie turned to go.

"You're done with a lot of things," Carol said. "One of them is employment here."

Annie wheeled on her, and her heart jumped into her throat. "You're firing me because someone hit me?"

"No, I'm firing you for everything else. You handle personal issues on company time. Take a large number of sick days. Your productivity has declined. And you have become a disruptive force among the other employees. No one wants to work with you anymore."

Annie leaned on the doorframe for support. She couldn't believe this was happening. "You can't fire me. You haven't documented a single performance problem."

Carol spread a stack of papers on the desk in front of her. "This is the Colorado work-at-will law," she said. "I can read it to you verbatim, but it says I can fire you for any reason I want. I can fire you for being ugly, smelling bad, or because I don't like your sister. I should've done this a year ago. You have thirty minutes to pack your things from your desk, but I want you out of this building."

A uniformed security guard appeared behind Annie in the doorway, arms crossed over his chest.

"Clarence here will escort you out."

"Well," Annie said, "since I have nothing else to lose, I might as well get this off my chest now. You're a fucking bitch."

She whirled, shoved past Clarence, and stomped away. She fought down the flush she felt creeping to her cheeks. Her coworkers stared, some with mouths open, as she strode to her desk. She drew on her mother then, going for a look of frost that would wilt flowers. It seemed to work, as most of her coworkers dropped back into their seats, minding their own business. As she arrived at her cubicle, two IT techs were removing her computer, both giving her apologetic looks as they left.

Looking at the things scattered on her desk, Annie decided she didn't really need any of them. She grabbed her purse and stormed out of the building, leaving Clarence behind.

*

Annie stood, hands on hips, glaring at the portrait of her mother where it leaned against the wall in her studio. Mike had returned the paintings the day after her art show closed, putting them all back the way he found them, including the one of her mother. He'd covered it with another painting so that Annie couldn't see it.

Annie had other ideas, though, and uncovered it specifically so she could glare at it. So there she stood, firing lasers from her eyes and trying to burn a hole in her mother's painting.

She stood that way for several minutes, gathering her thoughts about how to proceed with the rest of her evening. When she looked inside herself, all she found was fire. Fire in her gut, fire in her heart, even her mind felt like it was burning.

She was angry at Mike. She was angry at her mother. Hell, she was even angry at Frank, Carol, and Daniel. Most of all, Annie was angry at herself. Angry because once again, she'd allowed other people to determine her happiness. Or in this case her misery.

"Well, Mom, I guess you were right!" she snapped at the painting. "Mike turned out to be nothing but trouble. I should've known better than to get involved with a guy who has PTSD. What was I thinking? Certified mental illness?"

She stomped closer, standing just a foot from her mother's portrait. She wanted the painting to come alive, like it had the day she'd moved in, or the other times when her mother had haunted her. But the eyes remained flat, nothing more than paint on canvas. No life, no fire.

"This is just like you," she said. "I'm ready to give you a tongue lashing, you run and hide. Well the first thing I'll tell you is that Mike is out of my life. In fact, I think I'm done with men all total. All they cause is heartache and pain. I suppose you tried to tell me that, but I didn't listen. I was too caught up in his blue eyes, and his six-pack abs, and his overly empathetic personality. Well I'm done needing men. I hope you're happy, because you sure worked hard to make this happen.

"I'm done with art too," she said, packing up her brushes and dropping them into a zippered plastic bag. Some would need cleaning, but she could take care of that later. "No matter what I paint, it somehow comes out looking like you. Unless it looks like Mike, of course. Doesn't matter that I sold paintings that way. Painting was supposed to be about me, but it ended up being about you. Just like everything, it's always about you."

She felt her anger rising in her like a volcano. She stood and paced, trying to calm herself but it did no good. Her rage kept boiling upward and upward and before she could stop it, it exploded.

She lashed out with her foot, catching her mother's portrait smack in the face. She didn't break through the canvas, but some of the paint chipped off and fell to the floor. She pulled back her foot to kick again, but fought back the urge. Instead, she picked up the portrait, turned it around, and leaned it against the others, facing away from her. She picked up a smaller portrait of her mother that sat on an easel against the back wall. This one had only taken her a couple of hours, so she had no issue raising it above her head, then smashing it down on the pointed top of the easel. The wood tore through the canvas with ease, shredding her mother's face diagonally from her left eye across her nose and down the corner of her jaw. Annie raised the painting again and this time smashed the frame across her knee. She threw the shredded remains into a corner and stomped from the room, slamming the door behind her.

"There you go, Mom!" she yelled. "You see, I'm done with art, and I'm done with you. I'm done with men, art, and my smother."

She marched down the hallway, proud that she'd finally stood up to her mother, despite the fact that her mother been dead for over a year. She just reached the bottom of the stairs when the phone rang.

She grabbed it without checking caller ID, and answered. "Hello?"

"All right Annie, I'm giving you one more chance." Daniel's voice held the same contemptuous sneering sound it always did when he talked down to his sister. Annie rolled her eyes, but held her tongue. "I'm giving you one more chance to join with me, sell that old house, and split the profits. You know in your heart this is the best thing to do. Don't make us do something you'll regret."

"What do you mean by that?" Annie said. She put her hand on her hip as if her half-brother could see her through the phone. She even considered doing a video call so he could see the expression on her face. "Is that some kind of a threat, dear brother?"

"It's a plea, Annie. We've been at each other's throats for over a year now, and I'm tired of it. Let's settle this and sell the house. You take half, I take half. It would be more than enough for deposit on a nice place downtown for you. It's an easy settlement we both can live with."

Annie took her phone to the dining room table, pulled out a chair, and sat down, suddenly unable to stand. This fight exhausted her, drained every remaining ounce of her energy. She'd hoped it was done when the court made a decision, but stubborn Daniel disagreed.

"Daniel, this has already *been* settled. The judge ruled, I won. Move on."

"Come on, Annie," he said. His voice took on a mocking kind of playfulness. "We both know you can't afford to make the repairs anymore, much less pay for utilities."

He left the statement hanging there, waiting for Annie to figure out what it meant. She wasn't interested in his game.

"What makes you think I can't afford those things?"

"Well, I mean, being without a job now…"

"How the hell do you know I'm out of work?" She didn't want to play his game anymore. "Who the hell told you that?"

"Let's just say a little birdie tweeted in my ear. So you got fired, you no longer have an income, which means you can't make the repairs the Historical Society requires. And you managed to ruin things with your hunky handyman. Sounds like you got this all under control, Annie."

"Up yours, Daniel," she said. Her momentum carried her, even though she knew letting him under her skin was never a good thing. He almost always used it against her. "Most of the repairs were already done, and I'll have a new job before the next utility bill comes due. Don't worry about me."

She couldn't sit still any longer and vaulted herself out of the chair, almost knocking it over. She stalked into the kitchen, looking for a box of wine Jason had left there.

"But I am worried about you, little sister. We're family. We're supposed to take care of each other."

"I suppose that's why you sued me."

She found the box of wine and plucked a red plastic cup from a package on the counter. Filling the cup, she held her cellphone between her shoulder and ear while Daniel rambled on.

"We don't need to fight like this," he said. She could tell he was hiding the spite from his voice. "I'll even make this offer sweeter. If you agree to sell the house, I'll put you up in an apartment downtown until you get a new job and pay your own rent. How's that for an offer?"

If the rest of the conversation hadn't been so confrontational, Annie might actually have considered it a good offer. Living downtown offered better access to restaurants, nightlife, and entertainment than living here in an old Victorian neighborhood. But her hackles were already up, her teeth were already bared, and no amount of yanking on her chain was going to pull her back from this fight.

"I got an even better deal for you, Daniel." She made her voice sound as much like her mother as she possibly could. It worked so well she scared herself a little bit. "Why don't you go to hell? That's my deal for you. Go to hell and leave me alone or I will take you to court for harassment, stalking, and collusion. And you can tell your mystery partner the same thing."

She hung up on him.

Back in the dining room, Annie plopped into the same chair, not caring that her wine sloshed over the edge of her glass on the table. She took a sip, winced at how sour the cheap wine tasted, and put the cup down. Her mind was spinning, and not from the wine. Somehow, Daniel had figured out she'd been fired. And he was working with someone to get the house. Her gut instinct told her Carol was the most likely culprit. She hated Annie, had no morals, and had access to the information. But Carol was smart, too smart to get involved with Daniel. As far as Annie knew, the two did not know one another. And Carol had no interest in the house.

So who was Daniel's mysterious partner? And what were they planning to do if Annie didn't cooperate?

"Well, Mom?" she said, her voice dripping with sarcasm. "Where are you when I need you?"

Her mother, if she heard, did not answer.

Annie looked out the dining room window and noticed that Mike had fixed the shutters when he'd been there last. His hammer still lay on the floor inside the window. A box of nails and a hammer sat on the table a few feet away, and a denim jacket of his hung on the back of a chair.

"Well, so far tonight I yelled at my mother and stood up to my brother. I guess it's time I stand up to Mike, too."

Chapter Twenty-Seven

A shimmering, brown drop of something that once been water dangled on the rim of the drainpipe directly over Mike's face. With no space to maneuver under Kathy Mainwaring's bathroom sink, Mike could only hope that the tiny drop didn't fall. Because if it did, it would land in one of his eyes.

Even worse, he could feel Kathy's eyes crawling all over him. Long past her prime, Kathy had seen her husband walk out on her two years earlier. Since then, she'd developed an unusually high number of issues with her three-year-old house. And every time she had an issue, she called Mike.

The scent that wafted from the drainpipe's lower half smelled like it'd been in the pipe for at least a year. Mold and scum and a brownish-green pudding substance had fallen out as soon as he disconnected the drainpipe from the drain. As far as he could tell, the mix amounted to cream of hair/toenails/fingernails/soap, and if left to dry would probably cure harder than titanium. Whatever was in the lower part of the drainpipe was probably just as bad.

"Where do you buy your jeans?" she asked. "I'd like to get into them."

Mike rolled his eyes, knowing she couldn't see. In fact, the only part of him she could see was covered by denim. She sat in the bedroom, watching through the bathroom door while he struggled under the sink.

"Don't worry about me," Kathy called, adding a sultry tone to her voice. "I'm just here enjoying the view."

Yep, this day was turning out great.

He resigned himself to the droplet falling on him. It would pretty much wrap up an already crappy week with the perfect crappy ending.

His shoulders ached as he held a wrench over his face, trying to twist the drain. In the back of his mind, he wished he could get a beer. He'd had a lot of beers of late, drinking almost nonstop since Annie and he split up. There was even a six-pack in a cooler in his work truck, something he'd never done before, even though it was quite common in his industry.

His guilt nagged at him for drinking so much, but he felt like he had good reason. He missed Annie more than he'd expected. In her place, Michelle had been at his apartment so much, she'd started leaving an overnight bag there. Some nights, she and Maria slept in his bed while Mike crashed on the couch, so his sleep cycle was disrupted. As much as he loved having Maria around, he and Michelle were starting to grate on each other's nerves again.

She nagged him for never being around, but when he turned down jobs to be at home, she complained about him not having money. It was almost as bad as being married again, but this time he was willing to suffer it for Maria's sake.

As he turned the plumber's wrench to remove the drain from the sink, the drop of disgusting brown water stretched, wavered on the rim, and fell. Mike snapped his eyes closed just in time. Whatever the substance was hit his left eyelid and ran down into his lashes.

He couldn't exactly let go of the wrench or the drain cap, so he tried wiping his eye on the shoulder of his t-shirt. He was in the middle of doing that when his cell phone rang.

He'd assigned a new ring tone to Annie's number, a recording he'd secretly made of her over-loud laugh. This time it startled him so much he sat up suddenly, smacking his forehead on the drain. Stars danced in front of his eyes, and he launched himself out from under the sink.

He ignored the towel hanging by the sink, not wanting to dirty his customer's linens, and clawed frantically for toilet paper. When he had a sufficient wad in his hand, he wiped his eye, then pressed it to the wound on his forehead and held it tight, fairly certain he was bleeding. His phone rang again, Annie's laugh barking out through the bathroom. Even in pain and still angry at her, he chuckled at the sound.

He opened his eyes, glad the bathroom had stopped spinning, and answered the phone.

"I'm on a jobsite right now," he said. He kept his voice cool and distant. "Can this wait until later?"

"There is no later for us," she said. Her voice carried a harshness he hadn't heard before. "So no, this needs to happen now. Fortunately, it won't take long."

"Fine, Annie. Spit it out."

"You left a bunch of your stuff here in my house. A hammer, a jacket, and a bunch of other crap. I'm going to stack it in the middle of my dining room. I'd like you to come and get it."

Mike sighed. He'd known this was coming, but he'd hoped to put it off another week or so.

"Okay, I'll come get it after work."

"Just leave your key on the counter," she said. "I'll leave yours there as well, so you can grab it."

"Fantastic," he snapped back. "I need to get a copy to Michelle anyway."

That shot hit the target. On the other end of the line, Annie fell silent for a moment and Mike could hear her breath escaping from her mouth in one giant puff. It was as if he'd stomped on her chest and deflated her.

"So, uhm, what time will you be over?" she asked. "I'll make sure I'm not around."

"Worried I might hit you again?" This time he regretted the snarky tone, as he heard her suck breath back in. That one had hurt her.

She gathered herself quickly though, and when she spoke her voice was cold and hard as tempered steel. "Just tell me what time."

Mike pulled the tissue off his head and looked at it. Sure enough, a bloodstain marred the white paper. Great. God only knew what kind of infection he'd get.

"I don't know, a couple jobs after this. Will eight o'clock work?"

"That's fine."

And she hung up.

Cursing, Mike forced himself to return his cell phone to his pocket gently to avoid breaking it. In the next room, Kathy rose from the couch and walked towards him.

"What was that all about?" she asked. She wore an old sweatshirt, cut like something out of an eighties movie, with one side of the collar down off her right shoulder. "Sounds like you and the girlfriend were having a bit of a tiff."

She lowered her chin to the side where her shoulder showed. It made his skin crawl.

Probably not the effect she wants, Mike thought.

"She's not my girlfriend," he said. "Not anymore anyway. But that's not important. Let me get your sink finished so you can use your bathroom again."

A look of disappointment flashed across Kathy's lined face, but she got the hint and left the room. A moment later, just as Mike was going back under the sink, rock music blared in the living room, the base rattling the items on the counter above him.

He flinched. His fists came up in defense and he closed his eyes, squeezing them tight. For an instant, as panic twisted his gut, he saw in his mind a desert. Tan and gray rocks everywhere, men with guns. One of them pointed a gun at him.

He shook himself. He hadn't had an attack like that during his time with Annie, but now that they were apart, the flashbacks had returned with a vengeance. He'd almost forgotten how completely terrifying they were, how they froze his insides and made him want to curl up in the fetal position until the images went away.

"Damn you, Annie," he cursed. "I was just starting to get better, and you had to go make it worse. Thanks for nothing, babe."

He hauled himself back under the sink, lifting his wrench back to the drain. The sooner he got this job done, the sooner he could open a beer.

Chapter Twenty-Eight

Annie always felt safe at Jason's apartment. With its cool, all-white decor, postmodern furniture, and high-end electronics, his place had an almost antiseptic feel to it. Kind of like a doctor's office, only without the sick people. There was nothing to get attached to, except Jason himself course, and absolutely nothing frightening about his pad. Other than the temperature—he kept his apartment as cold as a refrigerator—his apartment felt safe. Neutral.

Curled up on the couch, her feet tucked under a blanket to keep them warm, Annie pretended to watch The Sound of Music, one of Jason's all-time favorite movies. Instead, her gaze drifted to the window beside the TV, studying the intricate patterns the rivulets of water formed as the drizzle ran down the pane of glass.

"If there was such a thing as a water spider," Annie said, "I think that's the web it would weave."

Jason tore his attention from Julie Andrews long enough to give her a puzzled look. Then he shook his head and went back to the movie. "Honey, I don't know where you are, but it ain't here with me."

"I know, and I'm sorry. I just have a lot on my mind right now."

Aiming the remote at the TV, Jason paused the movie. He turned his body on the couch, so his knees were facing her, and he sighed. "Most of those things on your mind, you put there. You create your own problems, Annie Brown. As if it's not enough for trouble to stand on your front porch and knock on the door, you have to go to the back door and call in even more. When you going to stop getting in your own way?"

His words hit close enough to home that Annie shifted on the couch, averting her gaze and wishing he'd turn the movie back on.

After a moment she met his gaze, trying not to flinch in the golden stare that so often stripped away her defenses.

"I know. But what was I supposed to do? He punched me in the eye, Jason. And then he sat there and argued with me about it. He got mad at me!"

"So what do you do now?"

"I think I may have to sell the house," she said. "Sell it, give half to Daniel so he'll leave me alone, and then maybe move someplace far away. Maybe California."

"What the hell is there for you in California?" Jason said. "I mean, you might find a job up there. Hell, you might even find a man up there, though I think that's not on your to-do list right now. But everything else about your life is here. Your best friend is here. You grew up here. Your home is here. And like it or not, Mike is here."

"Mike being here is why I need to go. If I stay here without a job, there's no way I'll get this house fixed up before the Historical Society takes me to court. Especially without Mike's help."

"So you're just gonna pack up and run away? Funny, I never saw you as a quitter. I mean, you stayed with that jackass Frank longer than you did Mike."

"That jackass didn't punch me," Annie said.

"No, he only tried to rape you. He only manipulated you, used you, ignored you, and belittled you."

"Seriously, Jason? You're going to use Frank against me? Frank didn't have PTSD, a custody battle, or a crazy ex-wife. Mike has all of those things."

"That's true," Jason said. "He has all of those things. He also has one thing Frank never did: class. Annie, I've never seen you as happy as you were when you were with Mike. Are you really going to throw it all away over one mistake?"

She realized he was right. Her weeks with Mike had been the happiest of her adult life, almost a fairytale world where she'd found a knight in shining armor. In the weeks they'd been apart, her world of color changed to one of grayscale, a world devoid of beauty. Had she tried to paint, she had no doubt she would have needed only black and white mixed to make various shades of gray.

"I don't want to talk about this anymore," she said. "Just watch the movie."

Jason shrugged and turned Julie Andrews back on. Annie tried to snuggle down into the couch, pulling the blanket up over her shoulders, but she couldn't get comfortable. Something Jason had said had struck a nerve, making her antsy, jittery. Her legs longed to get up and move, and sitting on the couch seemed restricting and limiting.

A few minutes later, she threw the blanket off, put her shoes back on, and stood up. She looked at the clock on Jason's wall. Eight fifteen. If she hurried, she could still catch Mike.

She looked at Jason and her friend smiled.

"About time you figured it out," he said. He winked as Annie turned and strode from the room.

Chapter Twenty-Nine

Mike didn't believe in ghosts, trolls, bogeymen, zombies, or other things going bump in the night. But he had to admit, with lightning flashing and rain pounding its roof, Annie's house looked like something out of an Alfred Hitchcock movie. It hunched under the storm, as if rolling its shoulders up to its ears and hunkering down to ride out the thunder, lightning, and rain. And as it sat hunched like that, he had the distinct feeling it watched him.

He sat in his truck at the curb, searching the house for any signs of life. One light was on—he thought it was in the kitchen—but nothing and no one moved. His mind told him the house was empty, but his heart told him it was watching him nonetheless.

He shook himself and braced for stepping out in the rain. Annie's Fiesta was not sitting in the driveway or garage. And that was good. He didn't think he could stand another confrontation with her.

He reached in the pocket to the short jacket he wore and pulled out Annie's key. He'd taken it off his keychain in anticipation of this moment. Now that the moment had arrived, he didn't want to do it after all. He would miss this old house, with its creaks and groans and broken things. And Annie.

A car sloshed past on the street, splashing his passenger-side window. The driver craned his neck backwards as he drove away, obviously thinking Mike looked suspicious. And he did. One man in a truck outside an empty house on a stormy night. Nothing suspicious about that at all.

He killed the engine, tossed the keys in his pocket, and put on a baseball cap to keep his hair somewhat dry. Then, taking a deep breath, he opened the door and sprinted for the porch.

He hadn't gotten around to redoing the concrete sidewalk yet, and water had pooled in all the uneven spots, splashing and soaking into his pant legs as he ran. The smell of loam reached his nose, stirred up from its underground grave by the fury of the storm.

He'd gone five yards when lightning flashed, and for fragment of a second, he saw someone. They stood in the master bedroom window, little more than black silhouetted against black, but he could've sworn their eyes blazed blue. Mike took his eyes off the way ahead, tripped on an uneven section of sidewalk, and stepped with a splash in a puddle of mud. When he looked up, the lighting had ended and the window looked dark and empty again.

His jacket didn't last long, the rain soaking through it into his t-shirt by the time he reached the porch. He took it off and used it to do the best job he could wiping mud from his pants. As mad as he was at Annie, he didn't want to track mud into her house. They were broken up, not at war.

A crash sounded to his right and Mike spun, his hands coming up, fists clenched. He thought he saw a shadow move, but when the lightning flashed again, a shutter banged against the house, followed by an explosion of thunder. Mike laughed, tossed his jacket on her porch rocker, and unlocked Annie's front door.

The interior was only somewhat brighter than the night outside. He flipped on the hallway light with a switch beside the door and could see right into the dining room. As promised, Annie had stacked his things on or around the dining room table.

He passed the living room and paused, reliving in his mind the night he'd fixed her bathroom outlet and came down to find Annie and Maria curled up together on the couch. Before he could stop it, a smile spread across his face. Warmth spread through his chest despite his soaked t-shirt.

"For a haunted old house, you sure do have some good memories."

In the dining room, he pulled out a chair and sat. He took out his cell phone, placed it on the table in front of him, and closed his eyes. Something wasn't right about this. He'd broken up with women before, and every time it felt like the end. Even with Michelle. But this time it felt...unfinished.

"Maybe I shouldn't be doing this," he said. "Maybe Collins is right. Annie and I might just belong together."

In his mind, he pictured their kiss, the one where he'd seen fireworks, and to his surprise his stomach tied itself in a knot again. Just like it had that night, the memory of the kiss was enough to make him weak in the knees.

Thunder cracked again outside, rattling the windows and shaking the floor, jarring him from his reverie.

Mike knew what he needed to do. Opening his eyes, he reached for his cell phone, but as he picked it up, something cold and clammy crawled across the skin of his neck. It didn't feel like a draft, at least not a normal draft. It had substance, matter. As it slithered down across his back, Mike couldn't stop a shiver from running through his body.

He vaulted to his feet, and the feeling disappeared.

He took a deep breath, raised his phone, and started to dial Annie's number. He'd only gotten through the first three digits when the battery symbol drained and the phone shut itself off.

His stomach knotted again, only this time not the pleasant, tickling kind of knot, but the over-tightened sort that made him feel like he wanted to retch. Maybe there was something to what Annie said about this house. His every instinct, every fiber of his being, told him to run. To not even worry about his tools, just to run.

But Mike had never been much of a runner.

He took a deep breath again and shoved his cell phone into his pocket. Annie didn't have a landline, so he'd have to call her from the truck, where the charger was still plugged in. In the meantime, he figured he might as well take his tools out to the truck since he'd need them in the morning.

He bent and picked up his tool bag, lifting a box with the other arm, and stood back up.

That's when he saw her out the corner of his eye: Annie's mother. He froze.

She stood in the kitchen doorway, cloaked in the same dark blue velvet dress from the painting, her gray-streaked hair piled high in a bun on the top of her head. He could see through her, at least through parts of her. An arm, her hip, the side of her head. Nothing of her was really solid, and she wavered like heat waves coming off the pavement. Only her eyes, blazing azure from across the room, seemed real.

Real, and mad. Very mad.

She crossed her arms and glared at him, her mouth turned down in her perpetual frown.

Mike felt his heart thumping like a bass drum in his chest. He actually put his right hand over his heart, as if pressing on his chest would slow his heartbeat. He looked at her and she disappeared. As soon as he turned away, she appeared in his peripheral vision again.

Mike had hallucinated before. Plenty of his medications caused hallucinations as a side effect. This looked different, however. Hallucinations always seems surreal, either bigger than life or warped almost beyond recognition, and the fear they caused was unreasonable. The fear of the familiar being destroyed.

The fear he felt at her mother's appearance came from a deeper place, down below his heart, down in his gut where primal instinct fired up his fight or flight responses. It came from the same place his fear had come from in Fallujah and a dozen other battlegrounds he'd seen in Iraq. The place that said, "Run or you'll die!"

But Mike hadn't run in Iraq, he hadn't run in Afghanistan, and he sure as hell wasn't going to run in Denver. So he straightened, squared his shoulders, and hefted the box under his right arm. Without making eye contact, he trudged down the hallway and out onto the porch. When he turned around, the figure had disappeared.

Shaking his head, he took the supplies to his truck. He fought with the door as it blew in the wind, trying to slam on his hands as he held it open. Thunder rolled all around him, as if avalanches careened down on him from every side. But he got the box and the tool bag in the truck, and slammed the door.

Back inside the hallway, Mike left the door open. His next load would be an armful, so he wouldn't be able to open the door and carry it. He propped the door open with a shoe and went back to the dining room.

He bent to pick up a stack of scrap wood, and as he stood back up the front door slammed. Lightning flashed, and thunder split open the sky outside, making him drop the bundle of wood. He picked up his hammer from the table and held it in front of him as he walked back down the hallway to open the door.

He twisted the doorknob, but nothing happened. The latch had jammed.

He swallowed the knot that had risen in his throat and went back to the dining room to see what tools he had. Most of what he'd use to fix a lock was now inside his truck, so getting this door open would be a problem. He felt the cold clammy slither across his skin again, and this time it came with the smell of rotting meat, as if a grave had opened up beneath his feet and let both rise to the surface from hell.

He shivered, but braced himself and tried to ignore it. His mind was playing tricks on him.

He also ignored the foggy shape of a woman that appeared in his peripheral vision. If he ignored her, she'd go away. Or so he hoped.

A full minute later, she hadn't gone away. In fact, she moved closer, floating a few inches above the floor and gliding toward him. Mike started to wonder if this really was his imagination.

He turned, hammer in hand, and faced her.

The ghost disappeared.

Fear clawed its way up from his gut again, and his knees wobbled. His mind whispered that none of this was possible, that he was only seeing things. But every other part of his being screamed out that he needed to run.

Someone jiggled the doorknob. The hammer came up again, and Mike worked his way in silence down the hallway. As he neared, he heard the sound of a key sliding into the lock. He stopped, pressed himself against the wall behind the door, and waited.

The doorknob turned, creaking like a casket lid, and the door eased open. Mike held the hammer above his right shoulder, ready to strike.

"Mike?" Annie's voice echoed down the hallway. "Mike, are you here? Well, that's a stupid question since I saw your truck out front, but—"

Mike stepped from behind the door, making Annie jump and spin around. They wound up face-to-face, chest to chest, so close he could feel her breath on his chin.

Annie cleared her throat and stepped back. She eyed the hammer, which Mike lowered slowly, and put up her hands in self-defense. "Hey, I know we broke up, but isn't that a little extreme?"

Mike chuckled and set the hammer on the table by the doorway. "Sorry, it's been a little strange here tonight."

He felt himself blushing, his cheeks turning warm. Annie reached around him and pushed the front door closed with bang.

"So now you believe me?" she asked.

Mike looked at the floor. "Right now, I don't know what I believe. But I know I want to get my stuff and get out of here."

Annie stepped back against the wall, motioning toward the dining room. "I won't stop you," she said. "But I'd like it if we could talk a little."

Mike eyed her, a little warning bell ringing in his head. Any time a woman wanted to talk, a man was probably going to be trapped for at least two hours. He wanted to get home go to bed, but he couldn't bring himself to say no. "We can talk," he said. "Nothing ever got worse from people talking."

Annie tilted her head to the left and wrinkled her nose. "Pretty sure our relationship got worse the last time we talked."

"Well the good news," Mike said, "is that I don't think it can get any worse than it already is. So we have nothing to lose by talking."

"Good point. Let's sit in the living room."

Mike nodded and followed her to the couch.

Chapter Thirty

Annie had been wrong. After an hour of talking, things *had* gotten worse. They'd been sitting in the dark, talking the entire time. Well, arguing was a better word for it. And they'd gotten nowhere.

They'd danced around the eight-hundred-pound gorilla in the room, both of them avoiding the black eye he'd given her. Instead, they stuck to the one subject even harder to agree on: her mother's ghost.

Mike had told her the things he'd seen that night, but somehow remained convinced it was his mind playing tricks on him. He refused to believe that her mother's ghost inhabited the house with them. It was as if his years of military conditioning made it impossible for his mind to accept something he couldn't physically touch or shoot.

Which, in turn, meant he did not give any credibility to Annie's version of what had happened to her in the house. He still thought everything she'd seen and heard came from inside her head, figments of her imagination and constructs of her shattered childhood. That frustrated her so much she felt a tightening in her chest, as if all of her muscles recoiled in on themselves and were waiting to lash out again.

Outside, the first line of storms had moved on, turning to a distant rumble to the east, fading memories of violence. But a second set of storms had sprung up to the southwest, and peals of thunder rolled slowly over the city, rallying to the cry of the departed storms. For the moment, the rain had stopped, but the brisk smell of it remained on the air and Annie knew more was coming; she opened the windows to let in fresh air while she had a chance.

"Seriously?" she said. "You seriously believe, even after you saw things tonight, that we're both imagining the same things in the same house?"

Mike pushed himself up off the couch and paced in front of her TV. "What else can we attribute it to? That your mother's ghost is still here?"

Annie threw up her hands and let them drop into her lap. "When the overwhelming amount of evidence supports that, yes. I've come to accept it, why can't you?"

"Because there's no such thing as ghosts. If there were, why don't I see…"

Now Annie could see the primary roadblock in Mike's thinking on this matter. If ghosts existed, why didn't he see Kyle, the soldier killed in Fallujah. If she could have her mother back, even against her will, why couldn't all of Mike's wanting bring Kyle back at least for a while?

"I don't know," she said. "I don't know how these things work anymore than you do, but I know we both saw the same things in the same house on separate occasions, which seems highly unlikely."

Mike opened his mouth to respond, but a sound outside interrupted him. It came from behind them, outside the dining room window perhaps, a low grunt or groan. They both froze, not even breathing, and Mike even tilted his head to one side like a dog trying to understand its master's words. For a moment, nothing happened. Then a second grunt came again, this time louder.

Annie and Mike exchanged worried glances, and Annie rose from the couch, trying to stay quiet. When the sound happened a third time, Mike took a cautious step toward the dining room.

Together they crept toward the dining room picture window, moving as quietly as they could across the creaky old wood floors. Annie caught a glimpse of something, a shadow perhaps, moving outside the picture window. Mike saw it too, for he stopped and motioned for them both to kneel. Annie did so without question.

On hands and knees, they crawled right up to the underside of the window. Mike rose on his knees, and peered outside.

"Someone's out there," he whispered. "They're moving toward the front door."

Annie's stomach tried to give back the dinner she'd eaten at Jason's, but she fought back the retching and made herself peek outside. Sure enough, the shadow of a man peered out from behind the giant oak tree, studying the area where her front porch wrapped around this side of the house. While she watched, the shadow slipped from behind the tree and sprinted toward the house, disappearing behind a corner.

Just before he disappeared, a flash of distant lightning gave just enough light for Annie to make out his face.

"Frank," she growled.

"Are you sure?" Mike asked

She nodded.

Mike stood, flexing his right arm and rolling the shoulder in its socket as if it was sore. "I'll take care of this, then," he said. "I've about had it with this asshole."

Annie put her hand on his elbow. He turned and looked at her, and the rage she'd seen in his eyes the morning he hit her had returned. But this time it wasn't directed at her.

"Are you sure?" she asked. "Maybe we should let the police handle this."

Mike shook his head and gently pulled his arm from her grasp. "If you want to call the police, that's fine. They can clean up the mess when they get here."

And with that, he started softly down the hallway toward the door.

*

Mike paused in front of the door, one hand lingering near the knob, the other paused near the light switch on the wall. Footsteps sounded on the porch outside, heavy and hollow, like someone chopping an old, decayed tree. A key clicked into the lock, and Mike knew what he had to do.

He yanked the door open, flipping the light on at the same time. Blinded, Frank lifted his hands to block the light from his eyes, a blade flashing in his right hand. Mike moved like lightning.

He grabbed the hand that held the knife, slugging Frank in the nose with his free hand, crunching bone and cartilage. Frank's head snapped back and he grunted, but Mike wasn't about to let him fall backwards off the porch and possibly run away. He yanked the wrist holding the knife, stuck out his foot, and tripped Frank in through the front door.

Frank fell forward, landing facedown, his forehead striking the wooden stand on the way down. Mike let go of his wrist as he fell and the knife flew from his hand, skidding across the floor and coming to a stop at Annie's feet. She started to reach for it.

"No!" Mike yelled. "Don't touch it. We don't want fingerprints on it."

Wiping his bloody nose on his sleeve, Frank rolled over and started to rise. Mike stepped up, straddling the man's chest, and punched him hard in the mouth. Pain lanced up Mike's hand into the wrist, but the punch did the trick. Frank fell back to the floor and didn't move.

Mike looked at Annie. "Now you can call 911."

Annie nodded and pulled her phone out of her pocket. Before she could dial, a second cell phone chimed somewhere in the hallway. She and Mike looked at each other, neither one knowing where the sound was coming from. Mike listened, but it didn't chime again.

"It must be Frank's," Mike said, kneeling beside the unconscious man.

He frisked Frank's figure, finding a smart phone in the man's front pants pocket. He pulled it out, touched the screen, and saw a text message preview there. What he read made him suck in his breath.

According to the message preview, the text had come from someone named Carol. It read, simply, "Is it done yet?"

"What is it?" Annie asked, moving closer. Mike held up the cell phone so she could read for herself. Her hand flew to her mouth. "Oh my God! Can you open the phone? Frank never used to use a PIN."

Mike swiped his finger across the screen and sure enough, the phone opened. Annie snatched it out of his hand before he could react. She tapped the screen a few times, then cursed under her breath.

"Yup, it's Carol. The number matches hers."

"Okay, we need to call the police now," Mike said. He stood, backing away from Frank's body. As he did, Annie's eyes went wide and her mouth opened to scream.

Out of the corner of his eye Mike saw movement, but he reacted too slow. Pain exploded in the back of his head, white light flashing before his eyes. He was falling and managed to put his hands out in front to catch himself. He landed on top of Frank, but rolled off and brought his hands up even while lying on his back. His vision blurred, and stars still danced in front of his eyes, but he could make out the fuzzy shape of a man standing over him, pointing a pistol at his head. He held something red in his free hand. As Mike's eyes focused, he realized it was a gas can.

"Daniel, what the hell?" came Annie's cry. "What are you doing?"

"I can't let you keep this house." The voice sounded pinched, nasally. "By rights it should be half mine, and I should be a hundred thousand dollars richer and the bullshit that happens here should be someone else's problem. It's the only way to get her out of our lives forever. But you're too damn stubborn to sell, so I figure I'll collect the insurance money. And since you are going to be trapped inside the house, it looks like I'll get it all."

Mike's vision had cleared now, and he could see Daniel clearly. He bore little resemblance to his younger sister, having only the jet-black hair of their mother. His face sagged, his eyes bugging out like a Chihuahua, and his teeth were crooked and smoke-stained. His clothes—ratty jeans, a gray t-shirt, and a short jacket—hung from his rail-thin frame as if set out to dry on a post.

The only things intimidating about Daniel Brown were the .22 caliber pistol in his right hand, and the gas can in his left. Looking down the barrel of the gun brought back an instant memory, a memory of a desert, of sun beating down, of men screaming. Mike felt his bowels turn to water and had to fight the urge to curl up in a fetal position. He fought off the urge, pushed the images away, and gritted his teeth. He didn't know if he could move fast enough to surprise the other man, but he knew he had to try.

Daniel turned, pointing the gun at his sister as a cold, maniacal grin spread like blood across his face.

Mike vaulted to his feet and jumped between Annie and the pistol. The gun cracked and Mike's left shoulder snapped back, stopping him cold. The gun cracked again, and this time the bullet whizzed past Mike's left ear as he fell to the floor.

"Mike!" Annie cried. She started to reach for him, but Daniel stopped her with a look.

Mike hit the floor and pain exploded in his shoulder, making him wince and almost lose consciousness. He knew he had to move, knew he had to save Annie. He couldn't let her die like Kyle. But he couldn't move, couldn't even lift his head much less climb to his feet. He felt his blood pooling under the back of his shoulder and knew he wouldn't last very much longer at this rate. He'd pass out soon.

He gathered as much strength as he could find, letting it build up inside his chest, hoping it would be enough to do what he needed to do. He coiled himself inwardly, preparing to launch his body between Annie and the gun.

But he didn't have it in him. His strength failed, and he collapsed back on the floor. He rolled his head to one side, met Annie's eyes with his, and mouthed the words, "I'm sorry."

To his surprise, she smiled as tears formed in her eyes.

Chapter Thirty-One

Annie had never stared down the barrel of a gun before, and she didn't like the feeling now that she saw it firsthand. She raised her hands defensively in front of her body and took a step back. Her half-brother lifted the pistol and pointed it at her head.

"Just stay right there!" he snapped. "I don't want to shoot you, Annie. I'd prefer you died in the fire."

They stood in the hallway outside the dining room, where Daniel had dragged Frank's body and Mike had managed to scoot himself on the floor. Mike, who had just taken a bullet for her, the single most heroic thing she'd ever seen. She didn't deserve it, not with the way she'd treated him, but he'd done it anyway. It took every ounce of her willpower not to run to his side and hold him in her arms.

Outside, lightning flashed, followed immediately by a blast of thunder that shook the windows and rattled the shelves. Rain began a torrential downpour, and hail clattered on the roof and pinged off the window panes.

"Daniel, please," Annie pleaded. "We can work this out. We can sell the house. I'll give you half, just like you asked."

Daniel threw his head back and laughter rolled from his mouth like thunder from the sky. Annie saw something in her brother then that she hadn't seen before. She'd always thought their mother's treatment had never affected Daniel, that his own internal strength had kept him from the emotional damage Annie had suffered. Now she saw that was not true. Daniel had simply kept his emotional troubles bottled up inside him, until her mother died and they came spilling out like blood on white sheets.

Her anger at him turned to pity.

"Do you think I'm that stupid?" Daniel asked. "I shot one person already, and I threatened you. I know you well, Annie, you would never let me get away with that. Now take a seat in the chair, and don't move. Even if I shoot you, the authorities are going to assume your crazy ex-boyfriend there did it. Just like they'll assume he shot Mike in a fit of jealousy."

Annie did as she was told, sitting in the dining room chair with her hands on her knees. Her mind raced, her stomach tightened. Her half-brother moved around the dining room, pouring gasoline from the can on the table, floor, carpet, curtains, and even a little bit on her shoes and pants. He poured the last little bit on Frank and Mike where they lay. When the can was empty, he tossed it in a corner and pulled out a box of matches.

Annie started plotting ways she could get out of the house once the fire started. Dousing the curtains by the picture window made it impossible to go out there, and he'd made puddles of gas near the entrance to the kitchen, dining room, and living room, essentially trapping her where she was. And even if she could get out, she couldn't leave Mike to die in the fire. She would have no way to get him out. She wasn't that strong, but he'd jumped in front of a bullet for her. She owed him.

"Daniel, please, if you love me, don't do this."

He stopped and looked at Annie. He tapped his temple with the barrel of the pistol, then shook his head. "I'm smarter than you think," he said. "You never loved me anymore than Mom did. I'm your half-brother, not your real brother. She never loved my dad, she never loved me. All she ever cared about was precious little Annie, her little Angel with the tattoos and the crazy piercings. Annie this and Annie that, Annie gets the house, but Daniel gets nothing. That all ends tonight, just like Mom's interference in our lives."

He pulled a zippered plastic bag out of his pocket, but Annie couldn't tell what was inside. She heard him open the bag, and he removed something. Lightning flashed and she saw he held a cloth that dripped fluid onto the floor.

"Chloroform," he taunted. "Believe it or not, it's pretty easy to buy. I slipped a couple of bucks to one of my clients in the medical business, and they brought me a whole bottle. Cops will probably never even do a toxicology report on you. They'll assume you died of fire-related injuries.

"And when you're gone, I collect the insurance settlement, put a couple hundred thousand dollars in my account, and forget that old bat ever lived. With the house destroyed, she'll finally leave us alone."

As he rambled, something shifted in the shadows behind him. An inky cloud formed in midair, and a cold breeze slithered across Annie's skin like a serpent.

"You did see her!" Annie exclaimed. "Daniel, why didn't you—"

Her mother materialized directly behind Daniel, dressed as she always was in blue velvet, her ethereal hair piled high on her head. As Annie watched sidelong, lightning flashed, showing her mother more clearly and lighting up her blue eyes as if they were electric themselves. Annie had seen the look on her face before, had felt the terror and the pain that glare could deliver to her system. Except the anger wasn't aimed at her now. Her mother glared at Daniel's back.

"So this is the end, little half-sister," Daniel said with a sneer. He reached for Annie, the chloroform-soaked cloth getting close enough that she could smell its antiseptic fumes. Dizziness swirled inside her head, and she felt herself going black. "Goodbye, you little bitch."

*

Mary saw her daughter's fear now—stark white and frigid—as Daniel aimed the gun at her head. She watched the color drain from Annie's pretty face, leaving her pallid as she trembled, but she saw something else, too. She noticed where her daughter's eyes darted once. Twice. Three times.

Mike didn't stir, his head on the floor, eyes closed. Faced with her own impending death, staring down the barrel of a gun pointed at her head, Annie was frightened not for herself, but for Mike. For the man who sought to steal her from her mother, to make her his own and see that she never needed her mother again. But also the man who had risked his life for her.

And Mary knew what she should have known all along, what her heart told her but her mind had ignored: Annie loved him. She loved him, and he loved her in return.

Perhaps, Mary thought, she'd been wrong about Mike. Maybe her daughter chose well.

She moved closer to Daniel, so close she could hear his heart pounding in his chest. She smelled the copper of Mike's blood, heard the subtle chattering of Annie's teeth as she waited for her half-brother to pull the trigger.

Mary knew what she had to do, what rule she needed to break, but her hand would not move. They were her children, both of them, and choosing between them was her worst nightmare, a moment that would drag itself out throughout eternity, no matter what she did.

She fought back the pain and blocked off the sorrow rising in her chest, for she knew now her purpose, understood that she'd known it all along. She was there to protect Annie, but not from herself or from Mike. She was there—held back from rest for so, so long—so she could save her daughter's life. Everything she'd ever been, in life or after, came down to that moment, that instant. That second.

She had no choice to make.

Steeling herself, she drew back her hand and shoved it forward, into Daniel's back. His warmth was foreign to her, it'd been so long since she touched a human being, and for a moment it gave her pause. But Daniel tensed, straightened, sucking in a breath and turning his attention from Annie.

Mary pushed her hand as far in as she could, until she felt the thud of his heart, the warm rush of his blood coursing through her being. She noticed then the flutter, the tiny weakness he'd had all his life. The thing that would undo him.

Screaming, Mary grabbed his heart and squeezed with all her might.

*

Annie watched as Daniel stiffened, his eyes going wide as baseballs, his mouth open in a silent, agonized scream. Behind him, her mother stood, fist extended, ghostly tears streaming down her cheeks. Daniel looked over his shoulder, his eyes widening even more. He tried to speak, to say something to their mother as she squeezed the life from his body, but all that came out was a strangled gasp.

An instant later, he toppled to the floor, motionless.

Annie tore her eyes from her mother's face and knelt by her half-brother. She put her fingers to his carotid artery and felt no pulse. Mike lay unconscious beside him, but she could hear his breathing laboring in and out, so she knew he lived. She turned and faced her mother, but the ghost was gone.

It took every ounce of strength she had, but Annie dragged both Mike and Frank to the front porch, away from where a fire might actually start. Once there, she dialed 911 and knelt with Mike's head in her lap.

As the 911 operator talked her through applying first-aid to Mike's shoulder, Annie realized how close she had come to losing the best thing that had happened to her in years. Holding pressure on his shoulder with one hand, she stroked his hair lightly with the other. He didn't stir, but she leaned down, planted a kiss on his forehead, and let her tears drip on his skin.

"I was wrong, and stupid," she whispered. "You've got to live, Mike. I need you. I love you."

In the distance, sirens blared, echoing through the city. Thunder still rolled, but in the distance now, off to the east where it could no longer hurt her.

In her pocket, Frank's cell phone buzzed again. She pulled it out and looked at another message from Carol. It read simply, "Well?"

Annie placed the cell phone on one of her porch chairs, out of the drizzling rain. The police would need it for evidence.

No, she wouldn't let Mike go after all. She was done letting other people determine her happiness. And she was done letting other people make her sad. Including her mother.

Chapter Thirty-Two

Mike woke in a hospital room, staring up at the textured surface of the white tile ceiling. At first his vision seemed fuzzy and out of focus, but it worked its way clear. On the wall at the foot of his bed, a mounted TV showed a silent news broadcast. Judging from the date and time shown in the corner, it was the morning after he'd been shot. He tried to lift his left hand, but when pain arced down his arm from his shoulder, he gave up on the motion.

He turned his head to the left and found only a green hospital curtain. He presumed another person lay in bed on the other side of the curtain, but he couldn't see to be sure. His left shoulder was wrapped in bandages, a tiny bloodstain showing through the top layer.

Slowly, memories trickled back. They'd been in Annie's house. Frank and Daniel had shown up. Mike had been shot.

Annie! Daniel had been about to shoot Annie when Mike blacked out. He snapped his head to the right and breathed a sigh of relief.

Annie slept in a chair, her knees pulled up to her chest, her head tilted back against the window behind her. Sunlight streamed in around her, forming an almost halo effect around her head.

Annie stretched, yawned, and then her eyes settled on Mike. Her face lit up, a smile breaking across her lips, her own green eyes seeming to come alive. Sleep fell away and she practically jumped from the chair, rushed to Mike's side, and put her arms around his neck. He winced as pain shot down his arm again.

"Hey, there, go easy on me. Little bit sore over there."

"You scared me half to death!" Annie said, not loosening her grip at all. She buried her face in the nape of his neck, and he thought he felt tears on his skin. "Don't ever do that again!"

With his right hand, Mike rubbed the back of Annie's neck, burying his own face in her hair. He didn't care about the pain in his shoulder anymore, this was healing the pain in his heart. For a time, he thought he'd never hold Annie like this again. Now he knew he'd never let her go.

"What would you have me not do?" he asked, easing her back from him now. "Punch out your crazy ex-boyfriend, or get shot?"

She gave him a playful slug on his good shoulder and smiled as tears dripped onto the sheets across his chest.

"Don't get shot, smart-aleck," she said. "And you won't need to worry about punching Frank out anytime soon. He's sitting in jail right now, getting to know his new girlfriends."

She helped Mike sit up a little bit, propping a pillow behind his shoulders and head. Then she sat on the edge of his bed, her hand on his.

"How was your house?" Mike asked. "Is it still standing?"

Annie laughed. "Yes, it's still standing, and you're still going to have work to do on it. Daniel had a heart attack before he was able light the match."

"Heart attack?" Mike asked. "That was fortuitous timing."

Annie shrugged. "Someone may have influenced his heart's ability to function properly. I suppose anybody's heart would stop with her ice cold hand wrapped around it."

Another memory came back too, one that happened just before he passed out. He remembered seeing Annie's mother materialize behind Daniel. She'd looked pissed.

"I'm sorry I didn't believe you," he said. "But I do now."

"Did you see something?"

This time, Mike shrugged. "I don't know what I saw, but I know I'm not willing to rule anything out. I hope it's enough."

Annie's smile held something back.

"What is it?" he asked.

She looked at the floor, then took a deep breath and met his gaze.

"Mike, I need you to promise me one thing if we're going to make this work."

"Never again." He didn't even need to ask what she meant—it had been bothering him for weeks. "I will never raise a hand to you again."

She shook her head. "No, not that. That was an accident, and I know it'll never happen again. Just never push me away when I need you to pull me closer. When you blew up at me, I started thinking it was my fault. Don't ever let me go again."

Mike smile as relief rushed through him like a flood of warmth. “Deal.”

“And therapy. Do what Collins wants you to do, so we can live without this someday.”

Mike nodded. “I’ll need your help. I can’t face it on my own.”

“I’m not going anywhere,” she said. “We’ll face those demons together.”

He nodded. “Then you have my word. I think, with you by my side, I can actually beat this.”

Her smile glowed. “How do you feel?”

“All things considered, not too bad. My shoulder hurts like hell, but otherwise I’ll be all right. I’m hungry though.”

Annie checked her watch. “I’ll tell the nurse on my way out.”

“You have to leave?”

Annie nodded. “I’m going to confront Carol. It’s part of a police plan to get her to admit her involvement. They don’t have quite enough evidence with just the text messages, since they’re not specific. They’re hoping she’ll talk while I’m wearing a wire.”

Mike remembered the text messages. “So Carol was behind it?”

“It looks like it,” Annie answered. “Looks like she was trying to get revenge on me for getting Frank fired, so she worked with both Frank and Daniel to come after me. I don’t think it went down the way she wanted it to. But Daniel’s dead, and Frank’s not talking. So the police need a little more proof.”

Mike tried to get out of bed, but the pain in his shoulder made him fall back against the pillow.

"What do you think you're doing?" Annie asked.

"I'm trying to come help you," he answered.

"If there's one thing I learned last night, it's that I can do just about anything, even without help. Second, I won't be alone, I'll have the police with me. I don't think they'll let you go along anyway. You stay here and get better."

She rose, grabbing her jacket off the back of the chair, but before she could go, the door opened. Maria burst through the door, arms in the air as she ran to her daddy.

"Daddy! You're okay, you're okay!"

She practically dove on him, and Mike was thankful she chose his right side. He wrapped his arm around her, squeezed his little girl tight, and gave her a kiss on the top of the head.

"Oh my Princess, it's so good to see you. Daddy's fine, don't worry."

A moment later, Michelle stalked into the room carrying a bouquet of flowers with a balloon. She took one look at Annie and winced. The dislike and contempt on her face reminded him of spoiled milk.

"I suppose you're the one who told the hospital to call me?" she said to Annie.

Annie nodded.

Michelle sniffed, as if she was surprised Annie had thought of it. "Well, I suppose I should thank you, but if it weren't for you Mike wouldn't be in the hospital anyway. I think you should leave now, before some other crazy ex of yours hurts him even more."

Annie drew herself up, fists clenching at her sides. She took a step towards Michelle, but Mike cut her off.

"Michelle, shut the hell up," he snapped. "It's not her fault, and she's not the only one with a crazy ex."

Michelle pivoted her head, locking her smoldering eyes on Mike. He could see her drawing up to fire back, but wasn't about to let her get up a head of steam.

"No, Michelle! That's enough. Thank you for bringing Maria, but I think you need to leave."

Michelle looked like she'd been slapped, and felt more indignation about it than pain. She straightened her backbone and sucked in her breath. "Maria, let's go," she said. "We're obviously not welcome here."

Maria squeezed Mike tighter and shook her head.

"Maria can stay," he said. "You can come pick her up later. Right now I want to see my little girl, and I do believe it's my visitation day anyway."

Michelle gave Annie one last contemptuous glare, then pivoted on her heel.

Mike stopped her with the ice in his voice. "Oh, and I'll bring your things by from my apartment. You won't need them there anymore. I'd rather face you in court than put up with your manipulation any day."

Michelle's eyes burned as she spun to go. "See you in court, Mike."

She stomped out of the room. Her heels seemed to click on the floor forever as she retreated, until she passed out of earshot and all three of them in the room relaxed. Maria crawled up in the bed with her daddy, snuggling her head down into his shoulder.

"Yuck, the news? Can we watch something else?"

They all laughed, and Annie started toward the door. She stopped at his bedside, squeezing his hand and giving Maria a hug.

"You take care of your father, okay?" she said. "Don't let him get shot while I'm gone."

Maria nodded.

As Annie slipped out of the room, Mike looked out the window. The rain had stopped, and the clouds were breaking up. Sunlight slanted in through the window, which dripped with condensation.

Mike snuggled into Maria's hair.

*

As police officers held Clarence outside, Annie strode into the cubicle farm, Frank's cell phone clutched in her left hand. She marched past her own desk, then past Veronica's as well, ignoring the ditzy brunette as she stood up to say hello. Her eyes were fixed firmly on Carol's door, an oak barrier that stood between her and the satisfaction of finally getting this bitch everything she deserved. By the time she reached the door, most of the employees in the cubicle farm had popped their heads up, gossiping little gophers looking for the next juicy tidbit to talk about.

Annie turned and looked them all in the eye, one by one. It was like that arcade game, where you use a mallet to whack a mole on the head and knock it into its hole. Every person she made eye contact with dropped back down into their chair, uncertain what to expect but knowing they didn't want to be on the receiving end of it.

Annie chuckled. Some of them probably thought she was a workplace shooter, come to take out her revenge for being fired. She didn't really give a shit.

Making sure the tiny microphone in her shirt wasn't visible, she knocked on Carol's door so loud the thin, artificial wall shook. Something clattered to the floor inside and Carol cursed. An instant later the door swung open and a fuming Carol faced her, finger up, ready to point.

Annie cut her off by holding up the cell phone. "Recognize this, Carol?"

The color drained from her ex-boss's face, and her lower lip actually quivered. Her eyes darted around the room to see if anybody was looking, then she stepped aside and motioned Annie inside. As soon as Annie stepped in, she closed the door.

"What do you want?"

"I want to know what I did that was awful enough to make you hate me. What was it, Carol? You sent Frank to burn down my house. What did I do to earn your hate?"

Carol plopped down in her office chair, her hands trembling on her oak desk. She looked down at her lap and rubbed her temples with the tips of her fingers.

"What did you do? It's not *what* you did, but *who* you did. Before you came along, Frank and I were in love. We went out every night, to seedy little bars where nobody from work could possibly see us. We rented out cheap, flea-infested hotel rooms so no one would see us coming and going from our apartments together. It sucked, but it was adventure. The most alive I've felt in decades.

"Then along came cute little Annie, with her tattoos and her big green eyes. You just swept in here and stole him from me. You took away the only exciting part of my life, then you had the gall to throw it away. You made up your ridiculous story about him, got him in so much trouble, and then got him fired.

"He was more than just my lover, he was my understudy, as well. I groomed him to replace me, and thanks to you all that work was for nothing."

Annie couldn't believe it had been that easy. She wondered how long Carol had kept all this bottled up inside, dying to scream it at Annie but unable to do so. She almost felt sorry for the woman. Then she remembered the gas can, the gun, and the bullet in Mike's shoulder. Her pity turned to anger.

"And all of that was worth killing me? An affair with a coworker?"

Carol sighed and leaned back in her chair. "I don't think I should say anything else."

Annie put her hands on the desk and leaned over until her face was just an inch from Carol's. She lowered her voice to barely more than a growl. "You can tell me, or I can give the cell phone to the police. Do I need to stand here and read you the text messages that came in that night?"

Carol paled again, and she shook her head.

"You weren't supposed to be there. No one was supposed to get hurt. Frank was just supposed to burn the house down, so you'd be forced to move. We didn't know you'd come home."

"So Daniel decided to do the killing on his own?"

"Daniel? Who's Daniel?"

Annie stood and turned her back on Carol. She needed to gather her thoughts. Carol had sent Frank, but didn't seem to know anything about Daniel's presence there that night. That must've been Frank's doing. He had taken it on himself to contact Daniel and the two had come up with a plan.

She turned around and fired a laser glare at Carol. "Well Frank saw fit to team up with my half-brother," she snapped. "My half-brother brought a gun, which is why Mike's now in the hospital with a bullet in his shoulder. And I'm lucky to be alive."

Carol's mouth fell open, and her eyes looked as big as light bulbs.

Annie kept going. "What made you think a psycho like Frank would stick to just property damage? He's been stalking me for months, breaking into my house. He threatened me!"

"Oh my God, Annie," she said. Her words stumbled over one another coming out. "I had no idea. I didn't know he'd take it that far."

"Bullshit, Carol. I think he was reporting back to you on everything he did. And I think if we check your old text messages, we'll find that you knew about everything he was doing to me."

"We? Who's we?" Carol asked.

As if in answer, the door opened and two uniformed police officers stepped inside. They motioned for Annie to stand outside the door, so she left. She stood there, arms crossed over her chest, as the officers led Carol out of her office.

This time, when the gossip gophers stuck their heads up over the cubicle walls, Annie let them stare. When Carol and the police were finally gone, she turned to all her coworkers, hands on hips.

"This company will be seeing me again," she said. "I'll be filing a wrongful termination lawsuit, along with harassment and assault charges against the company itself. Since all of you like to talk so much, make sure that gets up the chain to the CEO."

And with that, she strode from her office for the first time in years feeling like she'd had a good day at work.

Chapter Thirty-Three

Mike sat in a wooden chair, alone at a long wooden table, facing the judge's wooden bench. He couldn't afford an attorney, and didn't even have any papers spread out in front of him. He'd worn his best button-down shirt, and a tie that came from the nineties, and even put on the only pair of non-jeans he had, a pair of khaki pants also from 1995. But with his arm in a sling, the tie hung crooked and the shirt had wrinkled.

At least he'd shaved.

Michelle, on the other hand, wore the same outfit she'd worn on the day they got divorced. A simple black skirt, pinstriped, with a white blouse and conservative heels. It was the perfect outfit to make her look innocent, but formal. As if she respected the court and the judge's decision.

They may have broken up, but Pitt still represented her, as he sat in a chair beside her, stroking his goatee. He wore one of the many very similar gray suits he always wore in the courtroom. Mike couldn't tell if it was the same one he worn for their divorce or if he just had so many they all looked the same.

It made Mike feel little better that Pitt looked uncomfortable, shifting in the hard wooden chair and fidgeting with his tie as if it was a fraction too tight. Mike wondered how Michelle had talked him into being there, and wondered if the judge would think it was a conflict of interest. He decided not to bring it up.

The judge looked up from the papers spread out before her and regarded Mike and Michelle each over the tops of her bifocals. Her hair reminded Mike of a conservative grandmother. Graying and styled, it didn't shift a bit when she moved her head. It was almost sculpted in its perfection, as if she were some Greek goddess on display with the columns out front. She picked up a pen, tapped it on the papers in front of her, then chewed on the tip.

"So if I'm to understand your motion correctly," the judge said, "you wish to reduce your ex-husband's visitations with your daughter Maria to supervised only. You presented me with statements by you, your attorney, and two neighbors, saying that Mr. Tolbert verbally assaulted you at your attorney's residence. You've also presented a photograph of a woman you allege Mr. Tolbert struck in the face, as well as documented lapses in judgment as a father. Do I have the thrust of your case essentially correct?"

"Yes, Your Honor," Pitt said, rising from his chair. His movements were stiff, like he'd had a rough night sleeping. Mike could guess how Michelle had retained his services. "While Mr. Tolbert is taking steps to remedy his PTSD, we feel it poses a threat to those around him, especially his daughter, who would be unable to protect herself should he have one of his episodes while she's around. Until he gets a grip on his emotions, we would like Mr. Tolbert to have only supervised visitation with his daughter."

The judge turned her attention on Mike, and he felt like his grandmother was staring him down.

"Mr. Tolbert, you presented me a written testimony by your therapist, Mr. Larry Collins, at the Veterans Administration. While he says his opinion is that you're not dangerous, in the same testimonial he admits you do suffer from PTSD and have had violent incidents as a result of it. You also admit to having lost your temper and spoken harshly to your ex-wife and her attorney at his residence, as laid out in their affidavit."

Mike's heart sank into his gut. He thought he'd made a good case, but when she laid it out that way it sounded bad for him.

"Yes Your Honor, but—"

She cut him off. "You also admit that you do consume alcohol, sometimes to excess, and you admit to having punched your former girlfriend, Miss Annie Brown, in the eye during an episode of PTSD."

Mike looked at his hands in front of him, finding he could not meet the judge's stare.

"Yes, Your Honor."

The judge made a sour face, but then looked at Mike with something akin to pity in her eyes. Mike wondered if she had her own children, possibly grandchildren, and had seen someone go through the pain he was going through now. He didn't envy her the job she had to do.

"Then I'm afraid, Mr. Tolbert, I have no choice but—"

The doors to the courtroom crashed open, and a crowd of people poured in. First through the door came Jason, dressed impeccably, followed by Larry Collins, Christine Stanley, and Kathy Mainwaring. Striding in behind them, head held high, came Annie. She smiled and winked at Mike, while the others took seats behind him. Annie stopped beside Mike and looked the judge square in the eye.

"Your Honor, we would like to testify on behalf of Mr. Tolbert, if it pleases the court."

Across the aisle, Pitt and Michelle exchanged confused glances. The judge removed her glasses and stared down her nose at Annie. A small, almost imperceptible smile crept across her lips.

"What's your name?" she asked.

"Annie Brown, Your Honor. Mr. Tolbert's girlfriend."

The judge stared a moment longer, then nodded. "Bailiff, swear in the next witness."

Forty-five minutes later, everyone but Annie had testified on Mike's behalf. Now she stood, her hand on the Bible, swearing to tell the whole truth and nothing but the truth. She opted out of saying, "So help me God." Mike smiled.

"Now, Miss Brown," the judge began, "is it true that Mr. Tolbert punched you in the eye during a PTSD episode?"

"He was sleeping, Your Honor. Having a nightmare about the war. But I tried to wake him up and startled him enough that yes, he punched me."

"So you're saying it was an accident?"

"Completely, Your Honor. In fact, Mike has never been anything but a gentleman to me. He's never raised a hand to anyone when he's awake. He's my hero."

"Why would you say that?" the judge asked. "Asleep or not, the man gave you a black eye."

Annie looked at Mike, smiling like he hadn't seen her smile in weeks. "Your Honor, during a recent break-in at my house, Mike subdued one intruder and took a bullet in the shoulder trying to stop the other from killing me. He saved my life. And as far as being a danger or bad influence to his daughter, Maria, I testify that that is complete crap. From what I've seen, Mike is a wonderful father. He's attentive, encouraging, and has a good, solid friendship with his daughter.

"And since Mike and I have been together for several months now, he has a stable relationship in his life, which is a positive influence on Maria. In my opinion, Your Honor, it would be a travesty to deny him any kind of visitation. If anything, his ex-wife's attorney should be denied any kind of contact with her."

Judge raised her eyebrows and leaned forward. "Would you care to explain that comment, Miss Brown?"

Annie made eye contact with Pitt, then Michelle, before looking back at the judge. "Well, that incident at the attorney's residence? That happened because Mike felt that Maria was in danger from her mother's attorney. I'll let them give you the details, should you choose to pursue it."

Pitt looked like he wanted to sink into the cushions of his chair, while Michelle fired angry laser beams at Annie.

The judge leaned back in her chair and studied Mike for almost a full minute. Then she sat forward, scribbled something on a piece of paper, and cleared her throat.

"The court finds in favor of the defendant. Mr. Tolbert can keep his regular visitations with his daughter, and I see no need or justification to increase child support or alimony payments since the plaintiff has a relationship with a good-earning attorney.

"Further, the court would admonish the plaintiff for wasting the court's time with a frivolous suit. Should you waste this court's time again, Ms. Tolbert, I will find you in contempt and issue the appropriate punishment. This court is not a place for you to exact your own personal revenge on the father of your daughter. Now get out of my courtroom."

The smack of her gavel on the bench made Mike's heart soar as he watched Michelle storm out, Pitt groveling at her heels.

He wheeled around in time for Annie to fly into his arms. He hid his tears in her hair.

Chapter Thirty-Four

Annie accepted the glass of champagne from the tuxedo-clad waiter, then moved off into the crowd of well-dressed people. Around her, the sounds of soft conversation mingled with the clinking of glasses, all carried on a soft pathway of piano music filtering from a baby grand at the back of the gallery.

She wore her finest dress, one she and Jason had bought just two days earlier, when she got word her art would be featured here, at a more upscale gallery. It swept low in the front and even lower in the back, highlighting her pale skin against the blue velvet material. As soon as they'd seen it on the rack, they both knew it was right for her. She remembered looking in the mirror while trying it on, and seeing how the green in her eyes looked almost blue above the dark navy dress.

Her mother would be proud.

She hadn't seen her mother since the clash at her house. Still, Annie knew she was around, watching and waiting for Annie to make her next mistake. Now, though, she didn't mind having her around.

"Holy crap, you look amazing!" Mike approached from a crowd of people to the right, his eyes as big around as an artist's pallet. His grin threatened to tear the skin on his face, but as he leaned in to kiss her on the cheek, she also noticed he'd shaved.

She took a step back, pushing him out to arm's length. His tuxedo fit perfectly, and he'd selected a tie with cream and navy stripes that went perfectly with her dress. He'd stopped wearing his arm in a sling right after the court date, but still carried the arm as if it were fragile, the only visible reminder of their ordeal that night.

"You shouldn't say crap in an art gallery," she laughed. "Somebody will think you're talking about my paintings."

"That is highly unlikely. Have you heard any of these people talking?"

Annie took a sip of the champagne and sighed as the alcohol washed down her throat. "No, I just got here. I haven't overheard anything yet."

Someone touched her left elbow and Annie turned. Jason grinned at her, his pearly whites outshining even the gallery's halogen lighting, his gold eyes glittering. He too wore a black tux, but his shirt underneath was pink, and his bowtie white.

"Well, you need to listen," he said. "This gallery is positively buzzing with talk of your talent."

"Not to mention the price tags they put on your paintings," Mike added. "If you sell even one of these, you'll probably make more than I make in a month."

Annie took both of their elbows, Jason on the left and Mike on the right. She'd seen Mike every day since he got out of the hospital, as he worked to get her house back into code. Most nights, they spent there together, wrapped around each other in the master bed.

"I got the settlement check," she whispered to both of them. "Exactly what we asked for. Two years' salary, severance, and medical coverage until I find my own. And of course, a written apology."

"If you keep painting like this," Jason said, "you won't have to go back to the corporate environment ever again."

Annie looked around. Her paintings hung everywhere, many of them new works that she'd done since the incident in the house. She'd had plenty of time, and with her mind free of distraction, she'd been able to paint like a madwoman. Of course, the large portrait of her mother in the velvet blue dress still took up the majority of one wall, her private tribute to her mother and how she'd saved them.

One painting stood on an easel, covered with a canvas cloth. Mike saw her looking at it.

"Curious about that one?" he asked.

"I don't recognize it," she answered. "I don't recall painting anything that size, at least not in portrait orientation."

Mike led her toward it, and she noticed Jason grinning on her other arm.

"What are you two up to?"

They stopped in front of the painting. Mike separated from her arm and took her champagne glass. He climbed up on a small platform near the easel, held up her glass, and tapped it with his pen until everyone was looking at him. He handed her glass back to her, then faced the crowd.

"I hope everyone's enjoying Annie's show," he said. His voice made him a natural public speaker, ringing out clear and strong across the room so people yards away could hear what he was saying. "You probably noticed this covered painting to my right and are likely wondering what is. Well, the time has come to unveil it. Jason, would you come up and help me?"

Jason stood on the other side of the painting, holding one corner of the canvas delicately, as if it might bite him. Mike smiled at Annie and put his hand in his pants pocket.

"All right, Jason. Show her what's underneath."

Jason slid the canvas tarp off the painting, and the crowd gasped. Annie had never seen the painting before, and surely hadn't done it. It was awful. Mismatched colors and randomly slathered paints formed a background against which a circle had been painted in silver. Atop the circle, a crudely painted diamond sat, complete with a rivulet of silver paint that had run down the canvas. Annie studied the painting, and realization crept up on her like fog. When she realized what it was her hands flew to her mouth, and she looked at Mike.

He knelt before her, holding a tiny ring box inside which a diamond glittered atop a silver ring.

"Annie, with everything we've been through, I feel like we're already kind of married. And you'd think with my history it would scare me, but instead the thought makes me deliriously happy. The thought of spending the rest my life with you gives me butterflies in my stomach and makes me smile like a fool. I've loved you since the moment I saw you, even though neither of us would admit it at the time, and I can't imagine my life without you. Or, surprisingly, without that house that we've come to make our own.

"So, Annie Brown, will you marry me?"

Annie couldn't even see the ring, her eyes were so full of tears. But she could see Mike kneeling before her, and even more clearly she could see her future by his side for all of time. Covering her mouth with her hands, she nodded until she made herself dizzy.

"Yes, Mike, of course."

He rose, slipped the ring on her finger, and pulled her in for a long kiss.

Again, fireworks went off, their concussions thudding in time with her heart. It took her a moment, but she realized they were actual fireworks this time. She looked at Mike, worried about his PTSD, but he smiled.

"Rockies game must be over," he said. "We should go outside and watch the fireworks."

She sold three paintings that night and earned enough money to finish fixing her house. As the show drew to a close, Mrs. Mudge appeared and strode up to Annie, a wrapped painting under one arm, face looking carved from granite. She produced a paper and extended it toward Annie.

"What's this?" Annie asked, not taking the paper. She'd been served before.

"It's a declaration from the Historical Society," she said. "Since your house remains below code, you left us no choice—"

"Seriously? You come here to my art show, and do this to me? After what I've been through?"

Mike moved protectively beside her, his arm around her shoulders. "I assure you Mrs. Mudge," he said, "the repairs will be done within a month. I was working on them before I was hospitalized."

Mrs. Mudge adjusted her glasses, cleared her throat, and tilted her nose up slightly. "The Society is aware of your recent difficulties, Ms. Brown. That's why we issued a declaration granting you a thirty-day extension."

She pushed the paper into Annie's hand, spun on her heel, and started for the door.

"Wait!" Annie shouted. Several people nearby turned and looked at her, but Mrs. Mudge simply stopped and stared straight ahead.

Annie walked around to stand in front of her. She looked her in the eye, put her arms around her waist, and gave her a hug. "Thank you, Mrs. Mudge. It means a lot to me."

Mrs. Mudge sniffed and patted Annie lightly on the back, then separated herself from the uncomfortable hug.

"Just make sure you meet the deadline this time." She patted the small eight-by-ten frame under her arm. "You're quite good. If you make the house look half as good as your art, we'll get along well."

And she walked out.

Mike put his arm around Annie, kissed the nape of her neck, and whispered in her ear, "Your mom would be proud."

Annie thought for a moment, then smiled. "You're right. I think she would."

Epilogue

Mary watched again from the upstairs window, knowing her time was short, wanting to catch one last glimpse as her daughter came home to stay. She put her hand on the tempered glass, feeling its warmth from the setting summer sun. It was the only warmth she felt, but it was enough to sustain her for a few more minutes.

The truck came to a stop at the curb, idled for a moment, then shut down. The little girl crawled out of the back and made a dash for the front porch swing. Mike got out next from the driver's side and walked around to open the passenger side door.

Mary no longer hated him. He was good for Annie, fought for her. Risked his life for her. He would take care of her.

Annie stepped out, her raven hair billowing on the light breeze, skin gleaming alabaster in the light of the setting sun. Even from the window she could see Annie's eyes, as crystal jade as ever.

She started to fade, and wished she had more time, so she could watch the man and the daughter and the girl build a life. She knew they would. They'd build a life filled with happiness and joy, a life that she herself never knew.

She could see the light now, beckoning to her, tugging on her very being, as if it had tied a chain to her and slowly, inexorably, wheeled her toward itself. Fighting it was useless. She'd served her purpose. She would cross now, and finally rest.

She laughed at her actions in those early days, when she'd thought her purpose was to keep the daughter safe from all men. That had been a lie she told herself to give her more time with Annie, more time to mother her. More time to make up for not doing a good job when she lived. So she told herself her purpose was to bodyguard the heart of the daughter. To build a wall around it and keep men out. All men.

But in doing so, she had actually given the daughter exactly what she needed, for the girl was so much like the mother that when told she couldn't have something, she wanted it all the more. She'd been that way as a child, and she remained that way as a woman. Mary should have remembered that. It would have made things easier.

No, she'd served her purpose that night, in the dark of the storm, as the cold rain pounded the yard outside and the lightning shredded the sky. She'd found her reason for being in the house, and as much as it had broken her heart, she'd done what was needed. She'd protected Annie.

The light grew more intense, closer and warmer, its tug irresistible. She gripped the wall on either side of the window and pulled herself toward the glass for one last look.

There, in the lush green carpet of grass, Annie lay in her man's arms. The child ran around them in circles, her giggles a kind of music not heard there in a very long time.

Maybe Annie had grown up after all. Maybe she made better decisions than Mary ever had. Maybe she'd find a way to be happy.

As if on cue, Annie sat up, turned her head, and looked at the window where her mother watched. She stared for a long time, Mike looking too. Then Mike rose and made his way into the house. He clomped up the stairs, eased open the door to the master bedroom, and smiled at Mary. She stared back, taking in the kindness in his eyes.

Take care of her, she mouthed, hoping he would understand.

"I will," he replied. "I promise."

Yes, Annie had chosen well.

Mary smiled and let go of the window frame, allowing herself to be pulled toward the light. She hadn't been a very good mother during life, but she thought she'd redeemed herself in death, setting right some of the things she'd done wrong. Now she could rest.

Her mothering days were done.

THE END

Acknowledgments

This book would not have come into being without Russell, Michaela, Candace, JS, and the other mentors who taught me that a story's a story, if you tell it right, so who cares about the label someone puts on it? And to the Master Fiction Assassins – you know who you are – who pushed, encouraged, scolded, and hugged me, often at the same time. And finally, to the Winlock folks who loved the story enough to give it legs.

* * *

Visit B.T. Clearwater here:
Blog: www.btclearwater.blogspot.com
Facebook: www.facebook.com/authorbtclearwater
Twitter: @clearwaterbt

About The Author

B.T. Clearwater started writing at the age of fourteen, and completed a first novel by seventeen. B.T. edited the literary magazine of Lake George Central High School in upstate New York, and was awarded Literary Student of the Year in 1984. Following high school, B.T. earned a Bachelor's degree in English from the University of Nebraska at Omaha, and went on to earn a Masters of Fine Arts in Creative Writing from Western State Colorado University, specializing in popular genre fiction. B.T. has traveled the world, from Europe to Asia and all over North America, studying both cultures and languages. Having studied German, Korean, and Japanese gives B.T. a unique outlook on the power of language, and the differences in storytelling around the world. B.T. has published stories under various pen names in the genres of fantasy, science fiction, horror, western, and paranormal romance. B.T. Clearwater currently lives in Colorado.

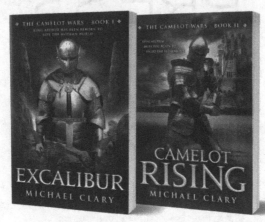